Fresh Blood 3

edited by Mike Ripley
& Maxim Jakubowski

BLOODLINES

A paperback original.

First Published in Great Britain in 1999 by
The Do-Not Press Ltd
16 The Woodlands
London SE13 6TY
www.thedonotpress.co.uk
email: thedonotpress@zoo.co.uk

ISBN 1 899344 52 7

British Library Cataloguing in Publication Data. A catalogue
record for this book is available from the British Library.

b d f h g e c a

Printed and bound in Great Britain by
The Guernsey Press Co Ltd.

Fresh Blood 3: Contents

Mike Ripley
Foreword

This book needs no introduction, because Ian Rankin (Gold Dagger winner and contributor to the original *Fresh Blood*) has done it for us.

Writing in *The Independent* in January 1999, Ian analysed the move 'away from Marple' and towards a more realistic portrayal of crime and its consequences in British mystery writing over the last forty years. One facet of this, as he rightly pointed out, was a tendency towards using policemen rather than 'the gifted amateur' as the detective hero.

So far, so good, but there is a 'but' and it is worth quoting Rankin in full as he puts his finger just to check for signs of life – on the pulse of what the *Fresh Blood* anthologies are all about.

'But Britain's "new wave" writers feel constrained by this, and many have begun writing from the criminal's perspective, or from the point of view of a new breed of private eye. Quite a few even choose to set their books in the United States either in homage to writers they admire, or because they have one eye on an American sales market. Or maybe just to show that they can.'

This 'new wave' in British crime writing dates from around 1988/89 and was undoubtedly influenced by the emergence of a revitalised American hardboiled crime scene (Elmore Leonard, James Ellroy, James Lee Burke, Sarah Paretsky, James Crumley et al) and a revival of interest in some of the past masters of the genre such as Charles Williams, Charles Willeford and David Goodis. Indeed, when eleven British authors were asked by *The Guardian* to name 'the crime writer's crime writer' in August 1998, six plumped for Americans including Leonard, Ellroy, Ed McBain, Patricia Cornwell and Carl Hiassen.

And so, not surprisingly, if a hardboiled realism is your chosen medium, America is the logical place to look and it is a mark of growing confidence that, as the new wave comes of age, British writers can set their novels and stories in America, the home of the hardboiled, and be believed. One of the last constraints on British crime writing is being overcome.

Not that the 'new wave' is obsessed with aping the American greats. That is merely one example of the new attitude among writers towards crime fiction, it gives them a new canvas on which to work, a new set of social problems and conventions on which to turn their analytical eye.

Perhaps the real trick is to adapt that hardboiled view to Britain as it is today, and not the time-locked rural vision of a Britain (particularly England) where a lukewarm evil lurks behind the net curtains, policemen always get their man and the working class still know their place. This vision, once the dominant aspect of domestic crime writing is still, cosily, with us both in print and on television. In book form, it could be argued that the traditional 'whodunnit' is in fact retreating in time given the continued output of historical mysteries set in just about every period from the Seventh to the Seventeenth centuries, when life was well-ordered and blissfully free of faxes, mobile phones, closed-circuit TV and DNA testing. On television too, the 'cosy' survives. For every *Prime Suspect, Cops* or *Cracker,* there is a *Hetty Wainthropp,* a *Midsommer Murder* or a *Jonathan Creek* waiting in the ratings.

In the past ten years a new school of (mostly young) British writers have set out to upset the conventions of genteel mayhem and the *Fresh Blood* anthologies are proud, in the words of that distinguished critic Philip Oakes of *Literary Review:* 'to fly the black flag of new crime fiction'.

But the British 'new wave' is not the homogeneous group its description may imply. There are clearly differences in approach between the sexes, on political grounds, on the perspective of crime (be it an individual assault or a corporate crime) or on its moral solution, as well as in technique.

There is one common factor, identified by Stella Duffy in *A Career In Crime* (Ed. by Helen Windrath, Women's Press, 1999):

'What most of us do have in common, though, is that our baddies matter. They are often as interesting (if not more so) than the hero. We may not even write a hero. And these "new wave" villains regularly get away with it. The cops don't rush in at the end of our books and cart the bad guys off to jail, leaving society the better for their removal. Not only that, but the protagonist the reader is supposed to identify with is often as unpleasant as the obvious bad guy. There is a blurring of the lines between good and bad, between goodie and baddie. Kind of like real life.'

So the new wave does agree on something.

Actually, it agrees on something far more fundamental.

The majority of contributors to this volume, and previous ones, are writers with one or two, possibly three at the most, books behind them. In many cases, this is the first short story they have ever done (or admitted to).

What they *have* all done on embarking on a writing career is choose crime fiction as a vehicle for their talents.

The great thing is that crime fiction is a broad church and a genre big-hearted enough to embrace them all.

Fresh Blood 3 contains stories of victims, of killers, of innocent and not-so-innocent bystanders, drifters, grifters, policemen – even a crime writer! The first contributor, however, may not seem to sit comfortably in a line-up of new talent.

The multi-award winning **Minette Walters** burst on to the international crime scene in 1992 and has come to dominate the 'psychological mystery' in a style she has made her own, once described by Nicholas Blincoe as 'Southern (England) Gothic'. No one has ever described her as 'hardboiled' but there is certainly a hard realism in her portrayals of characters and situations on the blurred border between good and evil. A great supporter of the British 'new wave', Minette's first short story is a little nugget of unease.

Martyn Waites has reintroduced the hardboiled crime novel to *Get Carter* country up on Tyneside, with a series featuring a journalist hero, Stephen Larkin. When not writing he is also an actor and consequently, his story is sub-titled 'a short piece of luvvy noir'. One hopes for the sake of his agent, that it is fiction.

In a very impressive début novel, *Mortal*, **Andrea Badenoch** put an ungainly, Geordie heroine in jeopardy on the mean streets of London. In *Jimmy's Story*, she returns to the equally mean terraced streets of Newcastle's West End.

The music business probably has a higher body count than the CID have to deal with, so after a career in it, **Paul Charles** turned logically to crime writing. His series heroes – Christy Kennedy and ann rea (always lower case, like kd lang) – abandon their Camden beat for once and unwittingly play the voyeur on a crime waiting to happen.

HR (Helen) McGregor's début novel *Schrodinger's Baby* was a heady brew of drugs, alcohol, sex and quantum physics. In other words: life as a student. Her story here, *The Confession*, is a cautionary tale which illustrates one of the unwritten laws of crime writing (new or old wave) – always be kind to cats.

Humour, especially black, is an element in most crime writing, although few new entrants to the genre go the whole hog and opt for comedy crime. **Peter Guttridge** is one who did, with his three (to date) adventures of the accident-prone and self-depreciating journalist Nick Madrid. His story here though, *The Postman Only Rings When He Can Be Bothered*, is more restrained and set in a rural idyll which looks suspiciously like Mayhem Parva. At first.

Denise Mina and **Paul Johnson** are two of the three winners of the John Creasey Award for best first crime novel in this collection (Minette Walters being the third). Denise's début novel *Garnethill* had the critics drooling. Her short story here – a new take on the traditional country house mystery – draws on her own medical career and from which the lesson can be drawn: Don't Get Old, Get Even. Paul Johnson has set his novels in an Edinburgh City State not that far in the future (and getting nearer!), neatly folding social satire into a yeasty thriller mix. His story *Crime Fest* is, however, closer to the present and disturbingly close to home – if you are a crime writer.

Rob Ryan's début, *Underdogs,* is a stunning chase thriller set in the underground ruins of the old city of Seattle, raising the ghosts of Vietnam which are still embedded in the American psyche. *Shit Happens* is a pistol crack of a story and the first of three set in America but written by Brits in this collection.

Manda Scott has made her reputation as a feminist writer with more than a working knowledge of veterinary medicine, surgery and pathology. In *99%*, there is plenty of evidence of her concern for animals and her medical know-how, but also, spookily, much more.

Phil Andrews' first novel, *Own Goals*, appeared in mid-1999, set in a football-obsessed northern city and whilst it is by no means the first football-based thriller, it is certainly the funniest. Its hero is a would-be private eye whose qualifications begin and end with a knowledge of American *noir* cinema, a strong influence in his story here.

Adam Lloyd Baker's first novel, *New York Graphic*, brought a new eye and a new voice to a New York underworld the like of which had not been examined since the dark, revolutionary work of Andrew Vachss. In that, and his story here, there are traces of Jim Thompson at his claustrophobic best.

In three novels set in America, **Lee Child** has created an all-American hero in the shape of Jack Reacher : drop-out, drifter and ex-Military Policeman, but at heart a knight in only slightly tarnished armour. Reacher makes a guest appearance in *James Penney's New Identity*, a story with resonances of the late, great, Charles Williams.

Finally, the editors – three words welcomed by any crime writer. **Maxim Jakubowski** provides, as usual, a tongue-in-cheek tale, albeit with his customary erotic charge: *The Day I Killed Tony Blair.*

For myself, a bit of self-indulgence and the chance to look at a series hero through different eyes.

Mike Ripley, October 1999.

Minette Walters
Notes

Why Crime?
Several years ago, I heard David Lean being interviewed on the radio. Among other things, he was asked
why he chose to make the sort of films he did. At the time I
thought it a ridiculous question. As opposed to what? I wondered. 'Blue' movies? 'Carry on...' movies? Disney cartoons?
There was a short pause before Lean answered, as if he were
trying to work out which category the interviewer thought
Lawrence of Arabia fell into.

'They're the kind of films I like to watch,' he said simply.

I chose crime for the same reason.

English Autumn – Summer Fall

by Minette Walters

I remember thinking that Mrs Newberg's problem was not so much her husband's chronic addiction to alcohol as her dreary pretence that he was a man of moderation. They were a handsome couple, tall and slender with sweeps of snow-white hair, always expensively dressed in cashmere and tweeds. In fairness to her, he didn't look like a drunk, or indeed behave like one, but I cannot recall a single occasion in the two weeks I knew them when he was sober. His wife excused him with clichés. She hinted at insomnia, a death in the family, even a gammy leg – a legacy of war, naturally – which made walking difficult. Once in a while an amused smile would cross his face as if something she'd said had tickled his sense of humour, but most of the time he sat staring at a fixed point in front of him afraid of losing his precarious equilibrium.

I guessed they were in their late seventies, and I wondered what had brought them so far from home in the middle of a cold English autumn. Mrs Newberg was evasive. Just a little holiday, she trilled in her birdlike voice with its hint of Northern Europe in the hard edge she gave to her consonants. She cast nervous glances towards her husband as she spoke as if daring him to disagree. It may have been true but an empty seaside hotel in a blustery Lincolnshire resort in October seemed an unlikely choice for two elderly Americans. She knew I didn't believe her, but she was too canny to explain further. Perhaps she understood that my willingness to talk to her depended on a lingering curiosity.

'It was Mr Newberg who wanted to come,' she said *sotto voce*, as if that settled the matter.

It was an unfashionable resort out of season and Mrs Newberg was clearly lonely. Who wouldn't be with only an uncommunicative drunk for company? On odd evenings a rep would put in a brief appearance in the dining-room in order to fuel his stomach in silence before retiring to bed, but for the most part conversations with me were her single source of entertainment. In a desultory fashion, we became friends. Of course, she wanted to know why I was there, but I, too, could be evasive. Looking for somewhere to live, I told her.

'How nice,' she said, not meaning it. 'But do you want to be so far from London?' It was a reproach. For her, as for so many, capital cities were synonymous with life.

'I don't like noise,' I confessed.

She looked towards the window where rain was pounding furiously against the panes. 'Perhaps it's people you don't like,' she suggested.

I demurred out of politeness. 'I don't have a problem with individuals,' I said, casting a thoughtful glance in Mr Newberg's direction, 'just humanity *en masse*.'

'Yes,' she agreed vaguely. 'I think I prefer animals as well.'

She had a habit of using non-sequiturs, and I did wonder once or twice if she wasn't quite 'with it'. But if that were the case, I thought, how on earth had they found their way to this remote place when Mr Newberg had trouble negotiating the tables in the bar? The answer was straightforward enough. The hotel had sent a car to collect them from the airport.

'Wasn't that very expensive?' I asked.

'It was free,' said Mrs Newberg with dignity. 'A courtesy. The manager came himself.' She tut-tutted at my look of astonishment. 'It's what we expect when we pay full rate for a room.'

'I'm paying full rate,' I said.

'I doubt it,' she said, her bosom rising on a sigh. 'Americans get stung wherever they go.'

During the first week of their stay, I saw them only once outside the confines of the hotel. I came across them on the beach, wrapped up in heavy coats and woollen scarves and sitting in deckchairs staring out over a turbulent sea which laboured beneath the whip of a bitter east wind from Siberia. I expressed surprise to see them, and Mrs Newberg, who assumed for some reason that my surprise was centred on the deckchairs, said the hotel would supply anything for a small sum.

'Do you come here every morning?' I asked her.

She nodded. 'It reminds us of home.'

'I thought you lived in Florida.'

'Yes,' she said cautiously, as if trying to remember how much she'd already divulged.

Mr Newberg and I exchanged conspiratorial smiles. He spoke rarely but when he did it was always with irony. 'Florida is famous for its hurricanes,' he told me before turning his face to the freezing wind.

After that I avoided the beach for fear of becoming even more entangled with them. It's not that I disliked them. As a matter of fact I quite enjoyed their company. They were the least inquisitive couple I had ever met, and there was never any problem with the long silences that developed between us. But I had no wish to spend the daylight hours being sociable with strangers.

Mrs Newberg remarked on it one evening. 'I wonder you didn't go to Scotland,' she said. 'I'm told you can walk for miles in Scotland without ever seeing a soul.'

'I couldn't live in Scotland,' I said.

'Ah, yes. I'd forgotten.' Was she being snide or was I imagining it? 'You're looking for a house.'

'Somewhere to live,' I corrected her.

'An apartment then. Does it matter?'

'I think so.'

Mr Newberg stared into his whisky glass. ' "*Das Gehimniss, um die grosste Fruchtbarkeit und den grossten Genuss vom Dasein einzuernten, heisst: gefahrlich leben*",' he murmured in fluent German. 'The secret of reaping the greatest fruitfulness and the greatest enjoyment from life is to live dangerously. Friedrich Nietzsche.'

'Does it work?' I asked.

I watched him smile secretly to himself. 'Only if you shed blood.'

'I'm sorry?'

But his eyes were awash with alcohol and he didn't answer. 'He's tired,' said his wife. 'He's had a long day.'

We lapsed into silence and I watched Mrs Newberg's face smooth from sharp anxiety to its more natural expression of resigned acceptance of the cards fate had dealt her. It was a good five minutes before she offered an explanation.

'He enjoyed the war,' she told me in an undertone. 'So many men did.'

'It's the camaraderie,' I agreed, remembering how my mother had always talked fondly about the war years. 'Adversity brings out the best in people.'

'Or the worst,' she said, watching Mr Newberg top up his glass from the litre bottle of whisky which was replaced, new, every evening on their table. 'I guess it depends which side you're on.'

'You mean it's better to win?'

'I expect it helps,' she said absentmindedly.

The next day Mrs Newberg appeared at breakfast with a black eye. She claimed she had fallen out of bed and knocked her face on the bedside cabinet. There was no reason to doubt her except that her husband kept massaging the knuckles of his right hand. She looked wan and depressed, and I invited her to come walking with me.

'I'm sure Mr Newberg can amuse himself for an hour or two,' I said, looking at him disapprovingly.

We wandered down the esplanade, watching seagulls whirl across the sky like wind-blown fabric. Mrs Newberg insisted on wearing dark glasses which gave her the look of a blind woman. She walked slowly, pausing regularly to catch her breath, so I offered her my arm and she leaned on it heavily. For the first time I thought of her as old.

'You shouldn't let your husband hit you,' I said.

She gave a small laugh but said nothing.

'You should report him.'

'To whom?'

'The police.'

She drew away to lean on the railings above the beach. 'And then what? A prosecution? Prison?'

I leant beside her. 'More likely a court would order him to address his behaviour.'

'You can't teach an old dog new tricks.'

'He might have a different perspective on things if he were sober.'

'He drinks to forget,' she said, looking across the sea towards the far off shores of Northern Europe.

I turned a cold shoulder towards Mr Newberg from then on. I don't approve of men who knock their wives about. It made little difference to our relationship. If anything, sympathy for Mrs Newberg strengthened the bonds between the three of us. I took to escorting them to their room of an evening and pointing out in no uncertain terms that I took a personal interest in Mrs Newberg's well-being. Mr Newberg seemed to find my solicitude amusing. 'She has no conscience to trouble her,' he said on one occasion. And on another: 'I have more to fear than she has.'

During the second week he tripped at the top of the stairs on his way to breakfast and was dead by the time he reached the bottom. There were no witnesses to the accident, although a waitress, hearing the crash of the falling body, rushed out of the dining-room to find the handsome old man sprawled on his back at the foot of the stairs with his eyes wide open and a smile on his face. No one was particularly surprised although, as the manager said, it was odd that it should happen in the morning when he was at his most sober. Some hours later a policeman came to ask questions, not because there was any suggestion of foul play but because Mr Newberg was a foreign national and reports needed to be written.

I sat with Mrs Newberg in her bedroom while she dabbed gently at her tears and explained to the officer that she had been sitting at her dressing table and putting the finishing touches to her make-up when Mr Newberg left the room to go downstairs. 'He always went first,' she said. 'He liked his coffee fresh.'

The policeman nodded as if her remark made sense, then inquired tactfully about her husband's drinking habits. A sample of Mr Newberg's blood had shown a high concentration of alcohol, he told her. She smiled faintly and said she couldn't believe Mr Newberg's moderate consumption of whisky had anything to do with his fall. There was no elevator in the hotel, she pointed out, and he had had a bad leg for years. 'Americans aren't used to stairs,' she said, as if that were explanation enough.

He gave up and turned to me instead. He understood I was a friend of the couple. Was there anything I could add that might throw some light on the accident? I avoided looking at Mrs Newberg who had skilfully obscured the faded bruise around her eye with foundation. 'Not really,' I said, wondering why I'd never noticed the scar above her cheek that looked as if it might have been made by the sharp corner of a bedside cabinet. 'He told me once that the secret of fulfilment is to live dangerously so perhaps he didn't take as much care of himself as he should have done.'

He flicked an embarrassed glance in Mrs Newberg's direction. 'Meaning he drank too much?'

I gave a small shrug which he took for agreement. I might have pointed out that Mr Newberg's carelessness lay in his failure to look over his shoulder, but I couldn't see what it would achieve. No one doubted his wife had been in their room at the time.

She bowed graciously as the officer took his leave. 'Are English policemen always so charming?' she asked, moving to the dressing table to dust her lovely face with powder.

'Always,' I assured her, 'as long as they have no reason to suspect you of anything.'

Her reflection looked at me for a moment. 'What's to suspect?' she asked.

Mike Ripley

Notes

Why crime? Why not?
I wish I had a pound for every début crime writer who has said: 'Of course I didn't know I was writing "crime" when I started my first novel.'

Well, *I* did. Or at least I knew I was writing a novel about, and containing, a lot of criminals. even though it was very far from a 'whodunnit' or a 'detective story' in the accepted sense. I had no aspirations to opening windows on the soul or putting society to rights; I was just a would-be comedian who couldn't do stand-up and couldn't face writing a sit-com for TV.

Crime fiction was the mechanism I chose as a base for telling jokes and the great strength of the genre is that it can accommodate me along with the genuine mystery writers. Crime fiction no longer has to have a moral conclusion, a detective, a set circle of suspects, fair 'clues' for the reader, nor even a puzzle. Nor does the crime have to be murder. When we had hanging, perhaps it had to be, but life is a paler shade of grey than it once was. Crime fiction is also one of the last refuges of the series hero and, because it is such a flexible and forgiving genre, it allows – on occasions such as this – to view a first-person series hero through someone else's eyes.

That's what I've done to my hero, Angel.

It's just a pity that the other eyes had to belong to Veronica Blugden. The lad really did deserve better.

Angel Eyes

by Mike Ripley

Because I just *knew* he would give me trouble, I recorded the phone call on our answerphone and typed it up later to put on file so that Estelle could read it. Not that she spends much time going through the filing cabinet because of her nails. Perhaps I'll email it to her.

VB: Hello? Is that Angel?

ANGEL *(in a silly voice)*: Pronto!Pronto!

VB: Angel? That is the right number isn't it?

A: *Che?*

VH: I know this is the right number. Can I speak to Angel please?

A: *Ich bin ein Auslander, ich spreche keine Englisch...*

VB: That *is* you, Angel, stop messing about. This is Veronica. Veronica Blugden.

A: *(Unintelligible possibly Japanese)*

VB: Hello, Angel What's that noise? *(Beeping sound)*

A: ...or you can send a fax right now.

VB: Angel, *will* you behave? This is Veronica from Rudgard and Bludgen Investigations.

A: ...at the third stroke it will be ten fifty-three precisely. Bip! Bip! Bip! Ten fifty three. Wow! Time travel!

VB: I'm not going to let you put me off, Angel. I know you, you know.

A: *(Funny voice,)* Earth to Major Tom, Earth to Major Tom...

VB: Are you drunk, Angel? Or just messing about? You've no right to mess me about. I'm ringing to offer you a job.

A: *(In a very bad Scottish accent)* Ah, to be sure, darlin', yer man will be off for a wet of his morning pint o' stout and you'll not be wantin' to make him late for Mass, will yer?

VB: It's an undercover job and you'll get paid.

A: *(Persisting with his stupid Scottish character)* Ah, whisht, woman, yer know yer man doesn't agree with work. He'll work like the vurry divil to avoid it.

VB: It involves working in a bar A girlie revue bar, I think they call them. *(12 seconds silence)*

A: Give me that phone! Get back to the attic! Sorry about that, Veronica. My mad cousin Dorian *(check spelling?)* got to the phone before me. What was that about a revue bar?

VB: So, suddenly I have your attention, do I?

A: Absolutely, hanging on your every.

VB: I thought I might. You know, this hard-to-get act you put on really is rather tiring. The one thing they stress on my Interpersonal Communication Skills course is that you never—

A: Get to the point. Can we do that? Preferably while I'm still in my thirties?

VB: There's no need to take that tone. it might be better if you came to the office for a briefing with the client. When are you free?

A: Hang on, I'll consult my diary. *(Sound of faint whistling)* Now's free.

VB: Pardon?

A: I'm free now. Today. All day, actually.

VB: I think I can get the client to come it about two-thirty this afternoon.

A: Sounds good, see you then. Oh, Veronica?

VB: What?

A: Will Stella be around?

VB: No, Estelle is giving a talk at Hendon Police College today. *(Silence)* Hello? Angel, are you still there? Is that you laughing?

I was never too sure exactly what Angel's relationship with Estelle was, other than he insists on calling her 'Stella' like the so-called friends she goes drinking with do. But since we started up the agency he has always checked to make sure she was out if he ever came to the office.

Estelle, of course, comes from a good family. Her father is Sir Drummond Rudgard, who used to run a Classic Car museum out at Sandpit Lodge, the family home in the country. There was some sort of incident there and a lot of the cars got damaged and had to be sold off, though the auction was in all the papers. I always suspected that Angel had something to do with the trouble there but neither he nor Estelle have ever talked about it.

I suppose I was responsible for introducing them in the first place, though I've heard Angel say it was him who brought me and Estelle together – the very idea!

I was actually 'tailing' (as we say) Estelle for Albert Block. my old boss who used to run the agency. It was, I suppose, my first 'case' and Estelle had run away from her father and was living with a religious cult down near Sloane Square. I had to get her out of their clutches and organise her 'deprogramming'. It's something we've been consulted on quite a few times since we started the agency together and it's involved some of sons and daughters of really quite well-known people, although Estelle prefers to handle that side of the business herself.

All Angel had to do with it was that he just happened to be there in that taxi of his, pretending to be a taxi-driver like he always does. I thought he was a genuine cab. A lot of people do. He relies on it.

But at least through him I got to meet Lisabeth and Fenella (he sub-lets a room in their house in Hackney) and they helped me a lot with that first case. I don't think Angel ever really liked that. And I just know he resented the way his cat used to make a beeline for me, looking for affection.

After Estelle and I started the business, *R&B Investigations* (which Angel always thought funny for some reason), we did try to put the odd bit of work his way whenever we needed someone to go in the places where women on their own ought to be able to go but don't feel comfortable doing so.

When we heard he'd got involved with that Amy May woman – the one who designs clothes – they're in all the shops now, I thought he'd have other things on his mind. Estelle (who had laughed a lot when she'd heard the news) said that we ought to 'give him six months' and then he would 'be up for it' – whatever that means.

Mrs Delacourt had taken the initial call from the brewery telling us how worried they were about their new girlie bar down near Piccadilly Circus and she was the one who arranged for me to see their District Manager.

Even as she gave me the message she couldn't help smirking, 'This is one for your friend Angel, sounds right up his street.'

One of these days I'm going to have to remind Mrs Delacourt that despite her age and all those certificates she has now for computing, not to mention the law degree she's studying for, she is in fact the junior of the office.

I was, naturally, delighted to see that the brewery's District Manager was a woman, but I certainly hadn't expected one so young.

Her name was Deborah Tracy Rex according to her business card but she told me straight away to call her Debbie, so I did. I had never heard of the company she worked for and while we were waiting for Angel to be late (as usual), I got Mrs Delacourt to make her a coffee and tried to put her at her ease, because visiting a detective can be rather stressful.

'I suppose you have to drink a lot of beer in your job?' I said.

'Christ, no,' she said rather abruptly. 'I can't afford to lose my office and anyway it would go straight on my hips and they're like Zeppelins as it is.'

Quite honestly I don't know what she was complaining about as she had a perfectly trim figure, verging on the skinny. She wore a blue blazer with a gold salamander brooch on the lapel, black trousers which used to be called flares but are now bootlegs for some reason and, of all things, a white TAL top – the blouse which made Amy May's name as a designer. (Though before she met Angel.)

'Lose your office?' I asked her.

The card she had given me just had phone numbers on it – four of them – but no address. I hadn't noticed before. I mean, it's not the sort of thing you do notice.

'My car is my office,' she said. 'I have a mobile, a car phone and voice mail, and I hot desk it when I have to do paperwork. Car parks cost less than office space in London – and you can have a cigarette when you want one.'

'Interesting,' I said. 'I suppose that means you can get round your pubs more easily.'

'That's the theory,' she said, 'but it's an impossible task. I'm responsible for over three hundred RLOs within the M25. Take out holidays, sales conferences and marketing presentations, not to mention licensing appeals, new product launches and staff recruitment, I'm lucky if I get round half of them once a year.'

'What exactly is an RLO?' I asked.

'Retail Leisure Outlet. We don't call them pubs any more.'

'Don't you? I didn't know that.' It was true, I didn't. 'But it must be fun mixing with all those customers. You must get to meet all sorts.'

'Customers? Sh—!' she said, just like that, out loud. Then without asking she lit up a cigarette and used her saucer as an ashtray. 'Don't get time to talk to them. We have to *count* them of course. The success of an RLO depends on its RVFBs.'

I wondered whether I should be taking notes and she saw my concern.

'Repeat Visits for Food and/or Beverage,' she said, 'but don't worry about it. The punters aren't the problem this time, I'm pretty sure it's an inside job.'

For once I was rather glad to see Angel arrive, even though Mrs Delacourt buzzed him straight up without asking him to identify himself and there was a lot of silly banter in the outer office about who was 'looking well-handsome' and 'tasty yourself', all of which we could hear quite clearly.

'Do come in and join us when you have a minute, Angel,' I said as loudly as I could. Giving an impression of the command structure in an organisation is very important and one of the modules on my Interpersonal Skills course.

'Yo, boss,' he said as he sauntered in, not hurrying himself. 'My, Vonnie, but you're looking good. You've lost weight and you've been pumping iron, I see.'

I knew it was just his way of trying to disarm me but I took it as his best attempt at an apology for being late.

'Can I introduce Deborah Rex. from the brewery,' I said, but Angel was already grasping her hand.

He seemed very interested in the TAL top she was wearing, and its plunging V-shaped neckline. No doubt he would be reporting back to Amy May on another successful sale, as I had seen him do this before and he had called it 'market research'.

Ms Rex handed him one of her cards when she managed to break his grip.

'Great T-shirt,' she said to him as he read it.

I didn't see what was so great about it. It was just a white T-shirt with some printing on which read: MY OTHER T-SHIRT'S A PAUL SMITH. Though I might have known he wouldn't bother to wear a tie or anything, just his leather jacket, a pair of black jeans and some Reebok trainers which, frankly, had seen better days. With all Amy May's money you'd have thought he could have afforded a suit.

'Thanks,' he said. smiling, showing his teeth. 'You must be 27 and your father was a Marc Bolan fan.'

'Spot on,' she laughed, showing *her* teeth. It was like they were snarling at each other. 'You're quite a detective.'

'You don't have to be Sherlock,' he said, laying it on a bit thick. 'Deborah the song, Tracy gives you the initials for T Rex. I was guessing at the date of birth. Bit of a glam rocker, was he?'

'Still is. Sad case.'

'I know a few.'

'Could we get on?' I said, re-establishing control of the situation. 'Ms Rex is very busy and her time is valuable.'

'Sorry, I forgot the meter was running,' he said, pulling up a chair and placing it very close to Ms Rex's knees.

I really wanted to tell her not to encourage him, but he seemed to have put her at her ease and that's always important with first-time clients.

While she spoke he at least pretended to be attentive, sitting there at hanging on every word almost, leaning forward with his forearms on his knees and his head on one side. I had never really noticed his profile before, but it is quite impressive if you like that sort of thing. The short, curly hair makes him look a lot younger than he is, or course, but even so he does have the air of a young Roman emperor like you would see on a coin. Estelle once said she thought he had the touch of the gypsy or a Heathcliff about him, but I think that's going too far. He's softer than that and he does have a nice smile – everybody says that. In fact, Mrs Delacourt says that his smile 'starts in his eyes and works its way down'.

'The pub was originally called the Disraeli,' Ms Rex was saying, 'but the name was changed to the Greasy Pole about ten years ago.'

'Fair enough,' Angel said as if that made sense.

'So it seemed the ideal place to introduce our new TLC – sorry, Themed Leisure Concept – especially as the site is so central, just off Piccadilly.'

'I know it,' he said. 'I went the week it opened.'

'Like it?' she asked with an odd smile and, I think, a hint of colour in her cheeks.

'It's well done and will be popular with a certain clientele. It's not that far from the House of Commons, is it? Not for me, though. Don't like the House Rule.'

'You mean, "Look But Don't Touch"?'

'That's the one.'

They grinned stupidly at each other and I began to wonder just how Ms Rex had got on in her job.

'So what happens in this Greasy Pole pub?' I asked, my notebook open and my pencil poised.

'Pole-dancing,' they both said together, looking at me as if I was slow or something.

Estelle staggered back to the office at about six o clock, claiming that her speaking engagement at Hendon had turned into a 'late lunch' and she had been driven back in a police car.

'You missed your old friend Angel,' Mrs Delacourt told her as they both slumped into the chairs in my office.

'How was he?' Estelle asked her, perking up.

'Fit as a butcher's dog!' said Mrs Delacourt coarsely. 'He had this Ungaro jacket which was soft as a baby's bottom... and talking of bottoms, that guy has buns you could take bites out of. If only he was twenty years more desperate.'

'What was he doing here?'

'Your partner here has him working undercover in that new girlie bar near Piccadilly – you know, the one with the pole-dancing at the tables.'

'What, the Greasy Pole? You've got Angel a job there?'

'Must've thought it was his birthday,' said Mrs Delacourt. breaking into a fit of giggles, which Estelle soon joined in.

When I finally managed to get a word in, I explained the situation.

The Greasy Pole did indeed have scantily-clad young girls (mostly American, I was assured) dancing suggestively around poles which ran through the middle of tables. It was an American idea and the brewery was hoping it would catch on so they could franchise the formula to other Retail Leisure Outlets.

They employed six girls to do the dancing and all had been thoroughly vetted, so Deborah Rex had said. (At this point, Estelle had made rather a crude remark about Angel 'going to the vet' if he had to work there.) But the dancing girls as such were not the problem. ('They will be,' Mrs Delacourt had interrupted.)

'The brewery had received complaints from a sister company which installed AWPs in the pub. (I thought at first Deborah had said 'OAPs' but then she'd explained that she was talking about Amusement-With-Prizes machines, the slot machine things which used to be called One-Arm-Bandits.) Apparently. the pub had twenty of these machines and all were losing money at the rate of twenty to thirty pounds a week and the machine company couldn't work out how it was being done.

Apart from the money being lost, the brewery was concerned because the Greasy Pole 'concept' as they called it. was being investigated by the licensing authorities and if they didn't get a full bill of health they would have trouble franchising the idea elsewhere, So they wanted this business cleared up ASAP and they were convinced it was an inside job.

'How do they empty the machines?' Estelle asked.

I was ready for her, with my notes.

'One electronic key opens the back of all the machines. It's just a little thing like an earring on a chain, but the machine company keeps them for when they have to empty the machines. The pub doesn't have one.'

'That they know of,' said Mrs Delacourt.

'But the machine company reps do,' Estelle observed rather airily, 'and I'll bet the guys who come to empty them could be sorely tempted by half-a-dozen pole-dancing bits of totty.'

'That was my initial observation.' I said, stretching the truth a little, 'but Ms Rex assures me that the licensee, who's a woman, keeps the girls well away from the customers. She's very strict, that's why she got the job. So it must be one of the bar staff who has got hold of one of these keys somehow. That's why Angel starts tonight as a relief barman, to keep an eye on things.'

'Does the landlady know who he is?' Mrs Delacourt had a lot of questions considering she wouldn't actually be involved in any executive decisions.

'No she doesn't. She asked the brewery for a stand-in while one of the staff goes back to Ireland for a funeral.'

'And what do we know about her?' Estelle asked me, just as Angel had asked Deborah Rex, funnily enough.

'She's called Opal Smith and sounds a bit brassy. She's been a licensee for ten years, divorced twice, has a good track record with the brewery, but is rather – eccentric – with a private business in aromatherapy massage.'

'Why does that make her "brassy"?' Estelle asked in a sarcastic tone she really shouldn't use in front of the staff.

'She wears a lot of jewellery it seems, a bit like a trade mark. All opals, because of her name. Earrings, necklaces, rings. Ms Rex said she never goes abroad on holiday because she'd set off all the metal detectors at the airport.'

Estelle and Mrs Delacourt looked at each other and then started giggling again.

'So you've put Angel in a pub with six pole-dancers and a tarty landlady with a sideline in ungents and massage for – how long?'

'Five nights.' I said. 'The pub only does the pole-dancing in the evening.'

'Boy'll be able to sleep during the day,' burst out Mrs Delacourt. 'Get his strength back!'

'Bit like Dracula with the keys to the Blood Bank!' shrieked Estelle, and that set them off again.

I call it childish.

In fact, Angel only needed three nights and then there was a fax waiting for me as I got to the office. From the top of the first of the two sheets I could see it had been sent at 04.32 that morning and it was hand written. It said:

TO: VERONICA BLUGDEN AT R&B

1. Opal Smith DOES have a spare key to the AWP machines. Don't know how she got it but suggest that Debbie checks back on recent employees of the machine suppliers who might have taken up an interest in aromatherapy.

2. She keeps it attached to her pierced navel ring, something not as rare as you might think in women of her age. This is not obvious, except on close examination.

3. Tell Debbie to arrange a visit to the pub TODAY with someone from the AWP company, Get them to empty the machine nearest to the door to the Ladies lavatory, the one called '5 Card Stud'. You'll find one of Opal's opal rings in the cash box inside at the back, that should be proof enough.

4. Opal is offering a £25 reward for anyone finding her lost ring. It's mine.

5. Expenses to follow.

6. Going to sleep for two days.

Angel.

I rang Deborah, getting her on her mobile and told her what Angel had written and she had said that was great and she would act on it and, sure enough, she rang me back after lunch to say that Opal Smith, once confronted with her ring where it most certainly should not have been, had admitted everything.

Deborah said she was pleased with our work and I offered to pass on her thanks to our operative, but she mumbled something about doing that herself and all I had to do was send her the bill, including Angel's expenses.

I was glad she raised that point as I was a bit dubious about the expenses he had listed on the second sheet of the fax.

That afternoon I told Estelle and Mrs Delacourt about the successful outcome of the case, but quite honestly, they did not seem able to take it seriously.

'How'd he slip her ring?' Mrs Delacourt said, wiping a tear from her eye.

'And how did he get the key?' Estelle shrieked as if she was in a playground.

'How did he find it?'

They looked at each other and then collapsed into each other's arms, their shoulders heaving with laughter.

I thought showing them Angel's expenses claim would bring them down to earth.

Instead, it just made them roar even louder.

'Well, I don't think it funny,' I said. 'How do we explain to the client this claim for a £147.50 bar bill? I mean, there aren't even any receipts!'

Estelle took the fax I had thrust at her and Mrs Delacourt read it over her shoulder. 'That's how!' they blurted out together and collapsed in hysterics.

'What do you mean?' I think I was shouting now. I was angry enough.

'Not the drinks,' gasped Estelle, trying to draw breath. 'The other items.'

I looked at the fax again.

Expenses:
To:

Bar bill	*£147.50*
Bottle of Johnson & Johnson Baby Oil	*£1.35*
Use of microwave oven (estimate)	*£0.10*

'Oh, I see,' I said. But I didn't.

Martyn Waites

Notes

This is supposed to be an introduction to my short story, in which I bang my self-important drum, settle the argument once and for all as to why British crime writers are crap (apart from me) and American ones are great and explain My Struggle To Create Art. That sort of thing. But instead I'm going to talk about one of the most formative influences on my work. It's a play called *Comedians* by Trevor Griffiths.

It's set in a night school for aspiring comedians in a working class area of Manchester. They get the chance of instant, fleeting fame, but it means sacrificing their beliefs.

'A joke,' Griffiths says during the play, 'should do more than release tension. It should change the situation.' 'What's wrong with wanting to be famous?' one character asks. 'Nothing,' goes the reply, 'But be good first. Because you'll never be good later.'

The sell-outs take the easy route. They change their acts, making them crude, racially offensive, sexist and shallow. They confirm and luxuriate in ignorance and prejudice. They don't ask questions. They don't challenge. Consequently, they go on to become famous. The others retain their principles. They ask difficult questions. They avoid easy resolutions. They look for, and tell, the truth. They don't become instantly famous. But they are good and they are working. And, more importantly, what they're doing feels right.

I suppose if you substitute 'joke' for 'crime writing' and 'comedian' for 'crime writer' and work out for yourself which side of the argument I'm on, then you'll have the key to my writing. Simple.

Comedians is a brilliant piece. But don't take my word for it, go and read it for yourself.

Just remember to read my stuff first.

Lucky Bastard

(a short piece of luvvie noir)

by Martyn Waites

The call came through on Friday night, twenty past five. Ten minutes before I could pack up and haul my arse out of that boring mind-fuck of a place. My head was down, my phone was out of group and the weekend couldn't come quick enough. It was an internal call.

Chris? said Angie. She was my boss, this officious, matronly type. All offices have them, apparently.

I said *Yeah.*

Your agent for you, she said and put the call through, sounding pissed off because I've got a life outside of this place and she hasn't.

Chris? said a voice. *Hi, it's Derek here.*

I said *Hello.* Here we go, I thought. He's camp as Christmas but because I'm northern and heterosexual he tries to sound all matey, like a bloke I'd meet in the pub. Not the kind of pub he goes to, though.

How you doing, mate? he said next, then, *Listen, I've got an audition for you.*

I was immediately interested.

Listen to this, he said. *It's on Tuesday afternoon, rehearsal rooms at the back of the Fortune Theatre. Just off Drury Lane. D'you know it?*

Course I fucking knew it. I asked him what it was for and he started slipping back into campness. He'd be talking palare next. *You've to meet Campbell Menzies, that's Sir Campbell Menzies, and his director Simon Prine, he said. They want to see you for – are you ready for this? The lead part in Sondheim's Sweeney Todd! How d'you feel about that?*

I tried to be cool about it, but I was glad I was sitting down because my legs went. *Fuckin' great!* I shouted.

Angie gave me a disapproving look and said, *We're still trying to work here. Callers don't want to hear you swearing.*

Fuck off, Angie, I thought in reply, I'm going to be out of here soon enough. I didn't say it, though, just turned away from her, containing the buzz of anger that coursed through me.

I thought you would, said Derek. *Well, don't get too excited because it's not West End. It's coming out and going on National Tour. Number one theatres, though, love, and he's interested in you taking over. Good, isn't it?*

It was good. Fucking good. Derek and I talked a bit more, told me I needed an acting piece and a song – I could do one from the show, that was fine – and I'd turn up on Tuesday.

I walked out of there feeling like the dog's bollocks. This was going to work. I knew this was going to work. I was going to get this and it was going to make me. I had all weekend to work on it and I was going to be so fucking good by Tuesday that Campbell would have to give me it. No two ways about it, I was going to be out of that miserable telemarketing hole faster than it would take to throw my headset on the floor.

I had all weekend to work on the audition, true, but not tonight. Tonight was Friday and that meant out with the boys.

I phoned Jeanie before I left. She's my wife, an actress I'd met in rep a few years ago. She didn't do much acting now, though, because she was at home with the three kids. The twins Robert and Steve (after DeNiro and McQueen) and their younger sister Isobel (after some relative or other of Jeanie's). She still looked all right, but she'd let herself go recently. They say women do after they've had kids. When she answered the phone I could hear the kids whingeing and screaming in the background. Anyone would think she wasn't looking after them properly. I told her the news and she sounded pleased at first, then she started with the fucking Inquisition.

Where's it going to be? she asks.

National tour.

How long for?

Dunno. 'Bout a year.

And then she was off on one. The twins would be going to school in September, how could she come with me, I wouldn't be home all that time… on and fucking on. Her, her, her. So I told her straight.

Listen, I said, trying to hold it down, *this could be the best thing to happen to me. To us as a family. If I get this I'll be fucking made. So what's the matter with you?*

Then she asked me to get some milk on the way home. I told her it was Friday, I was going to meet the boys.

She said, *So I'll have to put the kids to bed by myself? Again?*

I said, *I've been at work all day, I'm entitled to let off steam.*

She put the phone down on me. The kids were still screaming. I was seething. I tell you, if I wasn't against hitting women, I'd have gone home and given her a fucking good hiding. Never marry an actress. Never. They're all fucking maniacs, like wolves in heat. I saw that on this wildlife programme once. The female wolf goes all out to get the bloke wolf, sticking her arse out, giving it the full pricktease, the lot, until he eventually shags her. Then once he's done, she clamps her fanny muscles round his cock and won't let him out. Walks round, leading him by his dick. Honest. And actresses are just the same. Maybe all women, I don't know, but especially actresses. Quick enough to open their legs for you, but once they've got you there, they never let go. Squeeze the fucking life out of you. And they hate it if you have any success and they don't. Hate it.

I walked round for a bit, angry as fuck, imaginary conversations going through my head about what I'd say to her, how I'd tell her the facts of life, keep her in line. I must have been muttering to myself because even though the pavement was crowded, people still gave me plenty of room.

It's been said before that I've got a bit of a temper on me. Which is true. It's also been said that I'm too volatile. Which I'm not. I know exactly when to use it and when to lose it. Exactly. It was the child psychologist at school who tried to explain my temper. She said it was understandable because of my troubled upbringing.

Because of my father, she had said pointedly.

She was a right smug tosser, had an answer for everything. But she was the one who started me off acting. It was therapy at first, a way of working out my emotions, she said. Then I realised I was good at it and since there were fuck all other options where I grew up that didn't involve factory work, McDonald's or the dole, I decided to make a living out of it. And here I am. Working in a call centre with a whole load of talentless, unemployed and unemployable drama queens, married with kids because actresses are too fucking thick to know how to use contraception.

By the time I met the boys, though, my anger had worked itself out and I was in a Friday night mood. No problems.

We went to The Spice Of Life in Soho, where everybody meets. They're a good bunch of lads, known them for years. All actors, we get together about once every couple of weeks to get pissed and trade war stories. We're all in the same boat, really. None of us have made it, all of us think we should. But it hasn't happened yet, and we all know how miserable it gets, waiting, but we never let on to each other. Instead we tell each other how well we're doing. It's all shite, we know that. Inside I know that they're just as pissed off and depressed as me, *I know that*, but I know they won't let on. Just like I won't. Because it's all front. The whole thing. Front.

That's the thing about acting, you see, the great lie. Everybody on the outside, the hordes, *the audience*, think it's so glamorous. Is it bollocks. Yeah, you get the premieres, the awards ceremonies, but they're the exceptions not the rules. It's a life of constant rejection, always being told you're shit. Imagine how you feel when you don't get a job interview that you think you're perfect for. Now imagine that happening to you six or seven times a week and you're never told why. You try not to let it get to you, the show must go on and all that crap, but it does something to your head, I tell you. You lose a bit of yourself every time. So you try to look strong and respond with front. And you can't crack, can't let it show, can't let on to your mates, even if you feel like shite. The business is built around bullshit, you tell yourself, so who cares?

We got the beers in and Jeff started. He's going to be with the RSC for the next year. He tried to pretend they were just piss poor parts but we knew they weren't. We were all jealous as fuck, but we didn't let on. We fronted. Mind, he's the opposite of front, he is. Doesn't talk it up, tries to play it down. He works hard at that. Ambitious as fuck, but pretends he's not.

Tony's got a couple of ads coming up and a casting for a tv series. Some pilot for an ITV comedy so it'll be shite anyway. He knows that. We told him so. Frank's doing all right, though, he's in a Channel Five soap, on every weekday. Shame no fucker watches it. And Trev... well, Trev's thinking of knocking it on the head. He turned up in his suit. He's working for some firm of accountants in the City. Can't hack the acting anymore. Wants to do the suit thing. Have a mortgage, a wife and kids. I told him I had all that. Apart from the mortgage. Told him you didn't have to sacrifice it all. He didn't say anything. None of them did, they just went silent.

I don't tell them about the telemarketing company, even though we all do something similar to make ends meet. We never mention things like that, but we know we all do it. But I told them about the audition.

Lucky bastard, Chris.

You jammy fucker. You'll get that.

Fuckin' walk it. Lucky bastard.

It was my turn to play it down, look nervous, say I didn't know. Use the opposite of front. But I knew. They were right. I'd fucking walk it.

The night ended with us all snogging and groping some birds we pulled at The Borderline. I didn't want to, but you know, you do these things. To keep up with the lads. Front. Student nurses, I think they were. Can't even remember what mine looked like. She was a laugh, though. Better than that miserable bitch at home.

On Saturday, once I'd got shot of my hangover, I started working on the pieces. The kids tried to interrupt, wanted me to play and stuff, but I told them I was working. *Go and see Mummy.*

Jeanie just gave me daggers. Don't know what I'm supposed to have done now.

Daddy's far too busy to spend time with us, she said sarcastically to the kids. Anyone would think she didn't want me to be a success.

I asked her to sit in a chair, be the Judge while I practised as Sweeney. Give me a neck to aim for with the blade when I'm doing it on Tuesday. The story is, you see, the Judge raped Sweeney's wife and had him deported to Australia on trumped up charges. He then comes back and tries to get revenge on the Judge, blaming him for all the shit he's had in his life, and goes mad in the process. I stood there, moving, acting, singing my fucking heart out, imagining the music in my head, looking like I was going to cut her throat at the beginning of each line, pulling the blade away just in time, working at getting the timing just right. Jeanie, the bitch, just sat there looking bored shitless, while I tried my damnedest. She even fucking yawned a couple of times.

Anger boiled up in me again and I could have slapped her. Slapped her fucking senseless. What the hell was she playing at? I'm trying to work here. I had to put the knife I was using down in the end. It was too much of a temptation.

Can I stop now? she said. *Are you finished?*

No, I said, *One more time.*

She huffed and sighed, trying to put me off, but I just started from the beginning again. I worked through the song, timing it just right this time. The bladework at the end of each line was perfection. I was fucking good, I thought. When I reached the end though, started to scale the big climax, instead of pulling the blade away, I kept it on. Pressed right up close to her neck, digging in. I grabbed her hair, pulled her head back, singing all the while.

You should have seen her, she went fucking mental. She struggled and screamed, but I just sang louder and held on. I kept her there right until I'd finished, until the song had crashed out on a huge crescendo, the blade millimetres from breaking skin, then let her go. She fell on to the floor in a heap, and crawled away from me, scuttling quickly like a crab. She looked up at me. There was fear in her eyes. Fear and something else that I couldn't read. Respect? Fucking should be.

Are you finished with me? she asked in a quiet voice.

I told her I was.

I have to go and feed the kids, she said, and slunk out of the room.

I air punched my way round the room when she was gone. Not only was the piece now in a perfect state to be seen, but I'd put her in her place and it felt great. Then I made a decision. When this tour starts, I am not coming back. That's the end. I've had enough of her whingeing, dreary face, nothing I ever do or say is right, and those bastard kids screaming all the time, snot all over their noses. That's that. After Tuesday, you won't see me for fucking dust.

Of course, I still had Monday to go through first, but the thought of Tuesday was enough to keep me going. While I was on the tube that morning, Paul Harrison came into my head. I don't know why, I've got better things to do than think about him. He was a director that I'd had at drama school and he hated me. He was a really bitter, vindictive old queen, a total failure in the acting business, and rather than blame his lack of success on a complete absence of talent like he should have done, he blamed everyone and everything else instead. Including me. He picked out all the pretty boys as his favourites, gave them the best parts, and the talented heterosexuals like me had to make do with what was left. He tried to make my life a misery, giving me crap parts, dance routines when he knew I couldn't dance, humiliating me at every opportunity. One day I'd had enough. I got his home address from the college records, went there, and waited round the corner for him. He came home and went out later, in the dark, all dolled up for a night out. I followed him as he cut through a park. He slowed down and sat on a park bench. Cottaging bastard. I was wearing a balaclava, pushed up to look like a woolly hat, which I unrolled over my face. He sat there alone, clocked me coming towards him, expecting sex, but I, the sockful of pound coins in my pocket and my size eleven DMs, gave him more than he bargained for. He was away from college for a month and a half and when he returned he was a changed man. Broken. Maybe that'll teach you to treat heterosexuals with more respect now, I said to him one day. You should have seen the look in his eyes. He never asked if I was the one who'd done it but he looked on me with, if not respect, fear. And that was good enough for me. He left soon after that.

There had been others, people who'd got in my face when they shouldn't have, said the wrong thing about me in front of the wrong people, but he was the one I felt best about. Thinking about him and the audition kept me going all morning. I went for lunch at the Filipino café I always go to – crap food, but cheap – and came back to my desk, counting off the hours until I could leave.

Angie was waiting for me. The smile on the cocky bitch's face should have told me something was up.

Your agent called, she said.

Yeah? I replied.

He said the audition's off tomorrow. She couldn't keep the triumph out of her voice.

I felt like I had suddenly been transported down the wrong end of a telescopic lens then pushed back again. The world tunnelled in and out of focus. *What d'you mean?* I asked.

He said that Campbell, she really sneered on the word, *had bumped into someone, an old friend of his on Saturday and given it to him instead. So they said they were sorry to mess you around, better luck next time.*

I sat down, head spinning. I was straight on the phone to Derek. *What the fuck's going on? I* shouted.

He told me. That was what happened. Some fucking faggot gay mafia fucking boyfriend of Campbell's had been given the part. *My* part. Derek made some placating noises but I hung up.

So, said Angie, *you'll be coming in to work tomorrow now.*

My head was spinning, pounding. Everything was red, like a filter had been put over my mind's eye. All the people who'd ever done me down, ever made me feel worthless, ever stopped me doing what I wanted to do in my life came back before me now. My father, the teachers at school, Paul Harrison, Jeanie, every fucking casting director who'd looked me over for someone else, all those public school directors and ad agency staff who wouldn't know talent if it kneed them in the balls. All of them. And they all stood in front of me laughing, telling me once again how talentless and worthless I was.

I said, said a voice through the red fog, *you won't be having tomorrow off now.* It was Angie.

I just sat there and thought, this is it. This is all there is. This is your sad, miserable, fucking life. Sitting on a phone being polite to arseholes forever. Saying the same things over and over again. Asking complete strangers how I could help them, thanking them for picking up the phone and calling me. I could have cried, just broken down and cried. But I didn't. Because just then, something snapped inside me. All those years of being told I was worthless. Home, school, drama school, the business. Well I wasn't. I was good. Fucking good. I'd had enough of taking shit and I was going to do something about it. I was going to let people know how good I am.

Yes I will have tomorrow off, Angie, I said. I will. *I've booked it off and I've still got something to do.*

She bustled off to annoy someone else, pissed off because I hadn't collapsed in front of her. Because I wouldn't give her the satisfaction of letting her think that she, like all the others, had won.

But inside my head a plan was taking shape. Tomorrow. Yeah, I thought, I had something to do all right. I'll show them.

I didn't let on to Jeanie about the audition. I didn't let on to anyone. As far as she and everybody else was concerned, it was still on. I spent the night planning, rehearsing for the big day.

By Tuesday morning I had it all worked out. I left the flat with my bag of props at the same time as I would have to go to the audition and rode into town on a motorbike I'd borrowed from Jeff. I went to the rooms where the auditions were supposed to be at. This was the only risky part of what I had in mind because I didn't know if the other parts had been cast. Fortunately they hadn't. I sat in a café opposite and watched them all come and go. It was pathetic, really. Grown men and women going in to be subjected to scrutiny, so insecure they had to humiliate themselves in order to gain love, acceptance and employment from some overweight queen and his mincing public school sidekick. They went in all full of hope and neuroses and came out just full of neuroses.

I watched them all day, first in the café until I started getting looks from the café owners, then in a bar next door. That was better. I could stay in the bar as long as I liked, as long as I had a drink in front of me. Safe in the anonymity of alcohol. I watched the doors.

At five twenty, the decision makers themselves came out. Simon Prine, a talentless Oxbridge graduate came first. He wore rumpled linen and had floppy hair. Looked vague as fuck. He shook hands with Sir Campbell and they both went their separate ways, Campbell getting into a black cab. I got on the bike and, at a discreet distance, followed.

I was in luck. He was going home. I knew from trawling through files at Spotlight and from asking around that he had a huge house in Holland Park. The kind you see in *Hello!*. Up close it wasn't that impressive. It was big, yes, but not hugely so, and it needed a bit of work doing to it. Campbell got out and paid the cab fare. I parked up the bike away down the street and walked back to the house. He probably had all sorts of security systems but I'd have to worry about them later. I had a job to do first.

I walked to the front door and rang the bell. After what seemed like ages, it was answered. Sir Campbell himself stood there. He took a moment then the penny dropped.

Chris McCann, he said, surprise all over his well-fed face. *What are you doing here?*

Can I come in? I asked. *I've got something to show you.*

He started to look worried then and tried to close the door. The way he glanced round towards the street told me he was alone.

I'm really sorry about the part but I don't think this is a good time, he said, swinging the door shut, *call my office in the morning. We'll try and sort something out for then.*

I caught the door as he tried to shut it and held it. The red filter came over my vision again and I pushed the back hard, hitting him in the face, knocking him on to the floor. I stepped in to the house.

Get out! Or I'm calling the police! he wailed.

I gave him a quick kick in the balls to shut him up. He curled up foetally and I bent down to him.

Just do what you're going to do, he sobbed, *then leave.*

Now listen, I said, *I've come a long way for this, and the least you can do is see me. It won't take long.*

He saw something in my eyes and slowly hauled himself off the floor. He walked down the hall, all faux-Regency and beige, and led me into the front room. It was the same, except instead of paintings he had pictures of himself all over the walls. Himself with other stars. Himself with politicians. And just himself.

Sit down, I said. He sat. I stood right in front of him, towering. *Now what you did to me wasn't very nice, was it? Getting someone else in to do my part.*

Call my office, he pleaded again. *I promise we'll work something out, get something else for you. I promise.*

Too late for that, Campbell, I said. *I've spent all weekend – all my fucking life! – working on this, and you're going to see it. Whether you want to or not.*

I pulled an expensively brocaded straight-backed chair to the centre of the room and stood behind it. I took the bag off my shoulder, unzipped it, and put it on the floor. I stood as if I was ready to start.

Wait a moment, I said. *This isn't going to work. You see, I've been practising with someone, a real person, and I need that to help me get this piece right. Would you be so kind as to sit here, please, Campbell?*

He looked rooted to the spot. *Please,* I said to him, *it would help me enormously. The quicker I do this, the quicker I'm gone.*

Slowly, he got up and made his way to the chair. As soon as he was seated I took a length of rope out of the bag and secured his wrists. He started to struggle, but I just pulled all the harder. Knots tied, I wrapped the rest of the rope around his fat body. That was when he started screaming.

I quickly dived into the bag and pulled out a roll of gaffer tape, pulled a strip off and secured it over his mouth.

I doubt the neighbours round here would do anything, I said, *but just in case. Besides, you won't be able to hear me with all that wailing.*

I'm going to do a piece from Sweeney, I said. *And you're going to hear how it* should *sound. Lucky you. Don't worry about accompaniment, the music's in my head.* I took the knife out of the bag, and that was when he pissed himself.

I laughed. *When was the last time a piece of theatre moved you that much, Campbell? Not one of your productions, I'll bet. Was that chair worth something, by the way? Because it's not now.* His eyes were pleading with me. I ignored them.

This is the scene where Sweeney has the Judge in the barber's chair and since he blames him for all the fuck ups in his life, all the chances he should have had, the happiness that's been denied him, he's about to kill him. I bent down to his sweating face. *But something stops him, doesn't it? I spat. D'you think it will now?*

Underneath the tape, he began to cry.

Shut up, or you won't hear it!

I began singing, knife in hand. The whimpering in the background continued. I ignored it.

At the end of the first verse I placed the knife against his neck. He went beserk. Struggled and squirmed against the rope, making the knots tighter, trying to shout through the tape. I kept singing. I pulled the knife away. He calmed down a little.

You enjoying this, Campbell? I asked, bending down to look at his face. *What's it like to be on the other side for once, eh? To be powerless, to have no say in the matter? To have your future decided by someone else? You don't like it, do you? This is what it feels like,* I said, flashing the knife in front of his face. *This is what it feels like at auditions. This is how people like you make people like me feel!*

I straightened up, started on the second verse. *Keep listening,* I shouted to him halfway though. *Don't get bored now.* I built up to the end of that verse and brought the knife close to his neck again. This time I pressed harder, drew it along. It broke the skin.

I held the final note of the verse then bent over him again. *You'd better not have AIDS, you fat faggot, or I'll kill you!* I laughed at my own joke. He didn't. Suddenly, an awful smell started up in the room.

Have you shit yourself, Campbell? He had. *Not surprised. Your arse isn't as tight as normal people's, is it?*

I started the final verse. As I reached the crescendo, the song lyrics spilling out hatred and revenge, the red filter in front of my eyes deepened. My head began to pound even harder, my vision swam. It was an effort to keep singing, but I did. Because I'm a trouper. A pro. Then suddenly, they were back. All the people who'd ever done me down, ever got in my face, ever upset me. My father, the teachers at school, Paul Harrison and the rest of the drama school wankers. They never liked me, they only let me in because I could get a grant and they knew the money would be guaranteed. Then after that came the directors, casting directors, producers, all the ones who'd turned me down, talked through my auditions, laughed and smirked when I was performing. All of them were there and I could see their faces perfectly. Jeanie. She was there too. For once, thankfully, her mouth was shut and I didn't have to hear that whingeing fucking whine of a voice telling me how miserable her life was. Angie from the office. You might be the lifer, darling, but you're not taking me with you. They were all there, all in front of me, watching me perform. And none of them was laughing now. No, that was the best thing about it, the awe in their faces. They were all watching me, seeing how talented I really was, realising for the first time that they were wrong and I, as I had always known, was right.

The song built to its climax. My voice was at full throttle, I was in the part, of the part, I was giving the performance of my life. It was beautiful. Fucking beautiful. I stepped up to the final long note and drew the knife along the Judge's neck. The blood came arcing out, spraying against the far wall, turning beige to deep red.

As I held the final note, I watched the blood run down the walls. It began to thicken, mingle with the red filter in my head until the whole wall was one huge, red velvet curtain. The curtain parted, lifting at either side to reveal a huge, ornate auditorium. The kind of theatre you dream about playing. Gold plasterwork, polished bronze balcony rails, seats in luxurious crushed velvet. Sitting in those seats were the people, all of them, the ones who'd done me down, and they were on their feet, clapping, whistling, cheering. There were tears in their eyes, I had moved them so much. The noise of their applause and adulation was deafening.

I walked to the front of the stage and the applause grew louder. They loved me. Absolutely, fucking loved me. There were tears in my eyes as I took my bow. Real tears. I looked around the audience again and raised my bloody hands to wave. They were my people, all of them. They had come to see me, to acknowledge me, to praise me. I loved them. And they loved me. It was a moment so beautiful, so true that I could do nothing else but just stand there, drink in the acceptance, lap up the love.

I knew then that was what I would do with the rest of my life. I didn't care about anyone or anything else. I was going to stand there forever. And be loved.

Andrea Badenoch

Notes

I am very observant in a way that at one time was unproductive. Whilst hopeless at directions and other similar life skills, I can nevertheless remember the colour of people's eyebrows, what brand of toothpaste is on their washbasins, the particular smell inside their cars. This apparently meaningless attention to detail only became helpful to me once I'd started to write. It was then I discovered I had a talent for conveying the surface minutiae of people's lives in a way that could create both setting and character. Subsequently, when I began to describe gestures, habits. possessions, rooms, I found that the accumulation of these impressions started to suggest mood, motivation and then finally, plot. I realised that what I was amassing was *evidence*.

A preoccupation with evidence seemed to lead naturally to the *whodunit* or *whydunit* style of fiction. It became clear that the inclination of my main protagonists towards the interpretation of signals and signifiers fitted perfectly the conventions of the detective novel. The heroines in my imagination seemed to embody qualities which insisted upon persistence, deduction, quest.

In short – the way that I construct stories in my mind seems to fit the crime genre better than any other. My once apparently futile powers of observation have found an outlet at last.

Jimmy's Story

by Andrea Badenoch

He comes in at the same time every evening, five thirty. He's not the first of the night-time regulars, but he's early. He's always alone and he sits on the same bar stool, the one next to the cigarette machine. He's called Jimmy Jacobs. I'm told he's been coming here for years.

His daytime face, before his first drink, is sad, greyish and unhealthy, with an oily sheen. He walks in with a kind of shuffle. He's not old, but he acts old. He has a round-shouldered stoop and climbs on to the stool, slowly, as if it's an effort. He orders his first double whisky and it's the same every day. His routine never varies. He downs it in one, orders another and says, pointlessly: 'It's years since I've been to the coast. Seen the sea. Focking years.'

In the beginning I kept telling him he ought to go. It's only twenty minutes on the Metro, I said. It's only half an hour on the bus, its only ten miles. He never listened. Now I don't bother to reply. I just nod and serve him, get him a clean ashtray, wipe the bar in front of his elbows and say nothing. I don't know what to say to him. Not anymore.

He knocks back the first few glasses in minutes. His downcast expression changes to one of relief as the whisky warms, blurs and lifts his spirits. His head starts nodding in time to the juke box, his hand jerks as he tries to light one cigarette from another, his eyes water a little in the corners. He mutters to himself.

'The sea,' he sometimes says, 'the focking sands.' He coughs into a soiled handkerchief.

Jimmy's just a lonely old drunk. No one bothers with him. He's got no job except delivering leaflets. He never married and his clothes stink. He probably lives in a grubby flat with a black and white television and a stained armchair, the curtains always closed. There's one like him in every bar in Newcastle. Or so I thought.

Once Jimmy told me his big secret. I wish he hadn't. It's a secret so terrible that it's made him what he is. It's affected me too, but in ways that I can't understand or explain. All I can do is go over his story in my head. I remember it, examine it again and again, but somehow never get to the bottom of how it's changed me or why I'm stuck here, in this pub, in a town that's not my own, pouring him double after double, every night.

When Jimmy Jacobs was a boy, about ten years old, he lived at the top of a hill in the West End, where the terrace sloped steeply down, a slit of sky at the end and a grey glimpse of river. The street was cobbled and narrow, the houses divided into rooms which were damp, overcrowded. Beyond it, to the east, where similar ranked terraces had stepped down for a hundred years towards the Tyne, there was now an army of heavy bulldozers attacking and collapsing dwellings. The whole area was scheduled for demolition. This was the brave new world of slum clearance, of shifting people to high rise. It was modernisation. Each new morning heard the roar of engines, shouts and the crash of falling masonry. Clouds of plaster and brick dust blotted out the sun. There was a permanent smell of burning.

As the corporation men gradually came nearer and nearer. Children ran shrieking from their bonfires, their giant shovels, their boulders swinging on lengths of chain. Then in the evenings, when it was peaceful, they played in the ruins which were open to the sky. They set light to pathetic leftovers and to furniture, too bulky to move. They clambered over the sleeping machines.

Jimmy did all this. He played with Mickey Hutt who'd once had polio and with a ginger, skinny lad called Billy Bishkip who couldn't go home because his mother was on the game. They often played until the sun had sunk below the skyline and their limbs were grey with dust, but sometimes Jimmy went off on his own, to a private place where he never took his friends.

Lower down the hill, near the Scotswood Road, close to Vickers Armstrong, was an old house. A few such buildings had been left stranded and lonely amongst the rubble because permission wasn't available to knock them down. The house was large, stone built, with rotting gables, a patchwork roof, grimy windows, an overgrown garden. It stood isolated, its back to the river. Jimmy knew that a man lived there, a stranger, who came out every afternoon, looking smart, with a hat and rolled umbrella, got into an old car and drove away. He was never back before dark. He wasn't a doctor, like the generations of men who'd lived there before him. No one knew him, or understood what he did, but he was referred to locally, for some reason, as 'that bloody nancy boy'.

Jimmy broke into the house a few times when the man was out. There was a ground floor window with a broken sash. After a while he got brave and started going in there every day. It became a habit, a compulsion. Inside, it was old fashioned, dilapidated, but full of nice things. He liked going there because of the paintings, the ticking clocks and the smell of wintergreen. At first he only stared, wandered about, sat on the leather sofas, but after a while he began taking things. He liked the house so much he wanted to possess some of it, make it more his own. He pocketed some sugar tongs and hid them under his mattress. He took a bottle of sherry and drank it with his friends. He removed a tea caddy with a picture of the Queen and gave it to his mother. He stole a box of carved chessmen. Soon he was familiar with the whole place – the bedrooms, the indoor lavatory, the attics.

One hot evening, about six, he entered the house and drank a glass of whisky from the decanter on the sideboard. He ate some biscuits from a tin and tried to smoke a cigar. He'd been there so often, he felt he belonged. It was more comfortable than his mother's rented rooms in the short-life street at the top of the hill. He sat in a brocade wing backed chair and watched the television. He smiled to himself because he didn't have a television set at home.

Later, after drinking another glass of whisky, he washed and replaced his glass, disposed of the half smoked cigar and decided to look in the garage. This was a wooden lean-to and the only place he'd never explored. It could be accessed directly from the house through a side door which was always locked. He rummaged in a kitchen drawer and found three keys which didn't fit. He found the right one hanging on a hook in the pantry.

The garage was dark, airless and smelled of oil. He turned on the overhead light. There was a black patch on the ground where the car stood but otherwise nothing of interest. He noticed an old mangle, a rusty lawnmower, tea chests full of yellowing magazines. Then, in the far corner he saw a bicycle. It was half covered in tarpaulin. He decided to take a look. He didn't have one of his own and thought it might be worth stealing. In front of it was a pile of old rags. He pulled at these but something heavy was concealed inside. He felt the bundle. It was warm. He started to unwrap it.

Suddenly there was a small, animal-like moan. It sounded loud in the silence, in the warm, oily air. He jumped back, afraid. He thought it was a dog, but then he saw a grazed knee on the floor, a small hand. His heart started bouncing like a ball, hitting against the wall of his chest. His mouth went dry, his knees weak. He bent down and pulled aside the wrappings. It was a small boy, asleep and wearing no clothes. The side of his head was caved in and there was stickiness on the surrounding cloth, on his hair. Jimmy knew who it was. This was Mickey Hutt's kid brother. Timmy. No, not Timmy. Tommy. It was little Tommy Hutt. He was sleeping but he moaned again and a bubble of blood burst upon his lips. His eyes stayed closed, and Jimmy noticed that their lids were pale violet like a baby's, their lashes long and silky. His hair, where there was no sticky wetness, was curly.

Jimmy touched him, then roughly covered him up. He backed away holding his hands in front of him as if fending off an attack. Never, he remembered saying aloud. No. Never.

In the kitchen he turned on the cold tap and vomited in the sink. He washed this down the plughole, locked the door to the garage and hung the key back on the hook. He left the house by his usual route and ran back up the hill. It was getting late and Mr and Mrs Hutt were both calling for Tommy. After a while, other parents came out with their older children and they all started searching the half demolished houses, the smouldering fires, the piles of rubble, the empty buildings from which people had recently been moved. It got dark and they shone lights into corners, poked in holes, shouted endlessly: 'Tommy! Where are you? Tommy!'

Jimmy perched on a wall then afterwards sat, head in hands, on his step. His mother was out with the search party and he hadn't had his tea. He thought about the small boy under the rags in the garage of the big house near the river. He was certain something very bad had happened to him, but he said nothing. He couldn't tell anyone, or show them the place. He was afraid, it was his secret and he didn't want them all to go there with their torches and sticks.

The next day the police arrived. A group of children, including Jimmy and his friends, but not Mickey Hutt, were assembled outside the Methodist Church. The Reverend said he was going to take them to the seaside to get them out of the way. The scout leader came and a lady from the Welfare. They got a bus into town, then an electric train from the Central Station to Tynemouth. It was a cloudless day and they played on the sands, paddled, ate ice cream and searched the shoreline for crabs. Some of them talked a little about the mysterious disappearance but Jimmy didn't join in. He built a sandcastle and when the Reverend bought him a windmill, he stuck it in the top like a flag.

When they all got back, it was dark with a red streaky sky. Everywhere was strangely quiet. Each child slipped behind a front door which was immediately closed. Upstairs in their back kitchen, Jimmy's mother was crying. She said that little Tommy Hutt had been found in the water. He'd been drowned. The police thought he'd wandered down there by accident, fallen,hit his head, then slipped into the dirty river. She didn't mention his missing clothes. It was in the paper the next day. Jimmy saw the headlines: *'Infant Drowns in Tyne'*, but avoided reading any further. He was too numb, too scared and the whole thing made him sick to his stomach.

He never went to the big house again. After a while the man must have gone because the corporation got permission to pull the place down and it was flattened. Jimmy and his mother were moved to the fourteenth floor of a new block half a mile away. The whole hillside above the river was smoothed over and carpeted with useless grass broken only by spindly, weak-looking trees.

Jimmy Jacobs told me this story, near closing time one night, a few months ago. He was very drunk, but lucid. He told me everything, got off his bar stool, coughed into his handkerchief, drained the dregs of his whisky and staggered out. The next night he said nothing except the usual: 'It's years since I've been to the coast. Seen the sea. Focking years.'

I don't think he remembers telling me his secret. He just drinks every night and this somehow both reminds him of and consoles him in a way that offers no solution.

Each afternoon I cycle listlessly up the Scotswood Road on my way to work and stare at the green hillside, where houses once stood and at the tower blocks in the distance. The sun glints off these glass columns changing their windows into closed eyes. I never look at the river. I make plans to return home but can't act upon them. I pour drinks for Jimmy every night but I don't talk to him. I feel connected to him in some way, but I don't know what to say. I don't know what to do.

Paul Charles

Notes

I got into crime novels quite late. Yes, I'd read Christie, Doyle, Francis and the classic *Anatomy of a Murder* by Robert Traver and my favourite true crime book, *The Executioner's Song* by Norman Mailer. But these were all mixed up amongst other books on various subjects, including about two hundred concerning the Beatles. Then came Morse.

I can remember, very vividly, watching an early TV episode. Morse and Lewis were on their way back to Oxford when they stopped to collect their thoughts on the case. Both had their backs to the camera, they were standing looking out on to a yellow cornfield, the background was a beautiful blue sky, with green trees on the horizon and the red Jaguar over on the right hand side of the screen. It was a classic shot and the camera stayed with them for what seemed three minutes; absolutely no dialogue, just breath-taking visuals and emotive music. And we, the viewers, were being encouraged to recap on the facts of the case thus far, just as the two characters on screen were. I considered it brave television, and I found myself wondering who was responsible for that scene. The director, the writer of the screenplay, or, Colin Dexter, author of the original book?

The following day I rushed out and bought a copy of Dexter's *The Secret of Annex 3*. From that moment on I was hooked, loved each and everyone of his books. I still do. I ventured further, into the novels of Ruth Rendell, PD James, Ian Rankin, John Dickson Carr, Martin Edwards and RD Wingfield. Somewhere in the middle of these new weird and wonderful worlds I found a framework for stories which had been floating around my brain for the previous few years. All were to feature Detective Inspector Christy Kennedy and he (and I) found a publishing home in Jim Driver's fiercely independent The Do-Not Press.

Fast forward several years to Philadelphia and last autumn's annual Bouchercon crime writing convention. For me, the enduring memory of the conference – apart from Ian Rankin heading off into the cold Philly night, dressed only in a kilt – was to overhear two crime writers, one British (male), one American (female), discussing some AGA (after gig activity). As a fan of crime writers, and a collector of their work, I was intrigued to see two of them step centre stage, potentially, in a drama of their own.

I'm continuously intrigued by all that's going on around us. All seemingly innocent. You sit in a public place, like a hotel lobby or bar (as in the case with *Frankie And Johnny were Lovers?*) and you just might see two people meet up by chance, perhaps for the first time, and anything is possible. I just love the fact that anything is possible! Especially when it's you who's controlling the story…

Frankie And Johnny Were Lovers?

by Paul Charles

He had nobody he could call at home, all those miles away. So, when his friends and colleagues went up to their room to 'check in with the missus' and freshen up before dinner he remained alone at the bar. Not that I'm saying being alone meant he felt morose. No, in fact, he was quite happy, his third glass of Sancerre was guaranteeing that. No, it was more that it was a sad state of affairs, as I'm sure you'll agree.

However, had he gone to his room he might never have met her – met the woman who was to change his life.

Got your attention? It certainly got his. He wasn't to know that the biggest change she would bring to his life would be to end it. End it as he knew it.

Don't you see? It's all there for us. All the choices we make, and the absolute control we each have to make those choices. Therefore we must ultimately take responsibility for the changes these choices can bring, no matter how big they might be. Even if the change demands your life as a reward. Hey, and who is to know, given the freedom of that choice, you can continue your life in the humdrum boring circles for ever and a day until, unfulfilled and tired of living, you die. On the other hand you could choose to have several weeks or hours during which your nerve-ends buzz to melting point as you drink every pleasure you ever dreamed existed and then you are no more.

What would you do?

It would be difficult, courageous even, to choose the latter. With hindsight the choice would have been easy. But while we are pounding the weary treadmill of life we are never going to sacrifice even a little bit of it, just in case paradise, if ever it existed, might be lurking somewhere around the next corner.

He was twenty-eight, she was thirty-five. They met by accident... but equally, who knows? Maybe they were destined to meet.

John Patrick King – Johnny to his friends – strolled over to the bar at the Landmark Hotel on Marylebone Road. The other patrons were few: two, in fact. A soft spoken Irish man and an exquisite thirty-something woman with a Beatle bob hair style. It was that time in the early evening, the mid point between winding up the after-office drinks and the start of early evening aperitifs.

Johnny had already savoured the cool pleasures of three glasses of white wine and consequently he was more relaxed than his usual self-conscious state. He was beautifully dressed in a cool, black, loose fitting, imitation Armani suit, white shirt with cut-away collar and blue tie. His shoes and forehead shared shine, one from spit and polish the other from the flush of alcohol. His ear length copper hair was beginning to lose the sheen from its daily wash. Johnny had but one blemish in his face; a small scar on top right hand side of his lip. This was a war wound he had suffered with pride when he was younger and out pushing a snow sleigh around the hilly streets of his native Derry. Unknown to Johnny, one of the sleigh's runners was resting against a large piece of coal lodged in a slight dip in the snow covered footpath. So when he pushed the sleigh for his one hundred yard ride, it was static, very static, and Johnny had flown over the sleigh, face first, taking the full impact on his nose and mouth.

He'd only managed to contain his tears – tears of embarrassment as much as of pain – until he caught sight of the crimson stains as the blood oozed into the snow. He figured from what he saw that he must be losing gallons of blood and not the several drops it actually was.

Johnny had gotten over that particular incident, not to mention quite a few others. He retained forever, though, a mark on his lip to remind him of the shock at the sight of his own blood. He had tried to grow a moustache to cover the scar but it wasn't that easy. Hair refused to grow out from the scar tissue and so all his moustaches were distinguished with a break, looking something like an aerial view of a river running through a forest. To be honest, he felt it had looked pathetic so he had never bothered to try and grow one again.

The barman, Scottish and full of it, was just about to serve Johnny King his drink – simultaneously refreshing the bar-take's best friend by topping up the salted peanut bowl – when a woman came and sat down directly beside Johnny. Strange, Johnny thought, as he surveyed the dozen or so empty seats at the bar. At that point he gave her little more than a brief consideration. His mind was more on the bowl of peanuts. He couldn't believe how customer after customer would dive into the bowl, fingers first, chasing away their hunger and increase their thirst. What he couldn't believe in particular, was that all of them seemed oblivious to the fact that their owners would visit the toilet, on average at least twice during the evening. Now Johnny had been going into men's toilets long enough to realise that the majority of visitors to the white-tiled establishments invariably do their business and return, avoiding the wash-hand basin, to another drink, banter with their mates, a beautiful woman, their wives or a combination of all four, and another handful of nuts. So, from Johnny's perspective, bar savouries, nuts, etc were to be avoided.

He couldn't avoid, however, staring into the mirror which was cleverly positioned behind the entire length and height of the bar. From it he could observe the back of the barman, his hair thinning on the crown; his own reflection, an amazing array of bottles of spirits; and the image of the stunning woman who was sitting down beside him. She was dressed in a tight-fitting crimson dress. The same shade of red, in fact, that had spoiled the snow all those years ago The sleeveless dress had a high neck collar. She arrived at the bar with a black cashmere overcoat draped casually over her right arm. Her left hand controlled a handbag whose strap appeared to weigh considerably into her shoulder.

Normally, one had to figure, she would have draped her coat over the bar stool she now occupied, and sat on the one next to it, placing a physical barrier between herself and the only other male at the bar. This achieved she could enjoy her 'space', the space solo women enjoy, and usually demand while waiting in public places for their partners.

The first thing Johnny discreetly searched out was a band of gold; the band that signalled she had committed herself emotionally and physically, to another. There were no rings on any of her slender fingers. After the initial brief glance at her well-manicured hands he found himself staring continuously at the mirror image of her face. She was quite simply magnetic. Full red lips, green eyes, marked by beautiful, natural shaped, eyebrows. And her crowning glory – an almighty mane of hair that fell naturally about her face and shoulders.

Johnny saw her reflection turning to her left. He panicked, realising she was looking directly at his side profile. She had the briefest of grins on her face.

He quickly averted his gaze trying to appear to be concentrating on the numerous bottles behind the bar. Each time he happened to glance back at her reflection she was still staring at the side of his face and her grin was growing and fast approaching a full blown smile.

In the background a compilation loop tape had begun to play *O Vulgar Abbeys* for the second time. The hypnotic song by the Babtirs was released by Camden Town Records and a mint copy would fetch up to fifty pounds up in Camden Market.

Johnny thought he recognised the woman in the mirror, at least the reflection of the woman in the mirror. Mind you, he thought, reflections were sometimes totally different from the real thing. Funny that, and something that should be totally impossible.

God, what was he to do? Was there a bogey hanging from his nose? Was there dirt in his ears? Maybe even a growth of hair? His father had suddenly, in his fifty-sixth year, started to sprout hair from his ears. The more he trimmed it the more it grew. Johnny hoped he was going to be spared this physical abnormality – at least for another ten years or so.

'I was just wondering how long it would take you to turn around and look at the real me?' Her voice, American – more Boston than New York – was soft and sensual to the extent that he was relieved not have been standing at that point, thereby avoiding severe discomfort in his trousers.

He figured that if he pretended he hadn't heard her or chose not to acknowledge the fact that she might have been addressing him, the embarrassment would pass and she would move on; move on to her next victim. This she undoubtedly would do, but not until such time as she had finished with her current one!

'It's a bit like watching traffic lights. The red one comes immediately and it seems the green ones take forever,' she continued, her voice so smooth, so controlled and barely above a whisper but each word succeeded in hitting his eardrum and exploding through every part of his brain as potent as any drink or drug.

'Ahm, sorry?' was the only grunt he could find to utter. Johnny wished she would go away and leave him alone. He was not equipped to deal with someone as absolutely gorgeous as the woman sitting beside him.

'Your voice. I heard you speak earlier with your friends – it's soooo beautiful! I absolutely love the Ulster accent, particularly in a man – it's just – oh it's… No, I shouldn't tell you. You'll think I'm too forward.' She folded her smile away and, straight faced, inquired, 'Where are you from, exactly?'

'I'm from Derry,' was Johnny's short and snappy answer.

As soon as he had delivered the line he thought, How stupid of me, here I was thinking – dreaming more like – that she was trying to pick me up and all the time she was a Yank with Irish roots. Johnny breathed a sigh of relief and continued, 'No, sorry. You see I'm from Derry City, not Derry County. Well actually,

Derry City is from, or in, Derry County, if you know what I mean.'

He was about to try and continue digging himself out of his babbling hole when she cut in with: 'Oh, it's so beautiful up there. I've been to Donegal a few times. I'm convinced it's God's own country.'

He turned in his chair now to face her full on and, if anything, the real thing was more exquisite than the reflection. There ain't nothing like the real thing.

'Aye, that might well be the case, but if it's true, it would seem he went on holiday in 1969 and has only recently returned.' Johnny responded. He was on safe territory here. God she looks so beautiful, he thought. Why does she look so familiar? 'Would you like a drink?'

She smiled a warm smile, which lit up her entire face again and revealed the most perfect set of teeth he'd ever seen. He wondered about his own teeth. If only he'd disappeared to his room when his colleagues did. He'd surely have brushed his teeth. But, then of course, had he done so, gone to his room to brush his teeth, he would have missed this delicious woman, wouldn't he?

'I was beginning to wonder what a girl has to do around here to get a drink?'

'Ah, Princess Di's famous line and look at the trouble it got her into with your man, you know, the rugby player?' he replied.

'I'm sorry?'

'No, it's OK. Can I get you something?'

'A glass of chablis would be perfect,' she replied demurely.

Now that he was finally sitting face to face with her, all his senses were being bombarded. His eyes would surely never again be witness to such perfect beauty. His ears no longer allowed his brain to put up any resistance as he surrendered to her voice. Now his nose was being caressed by such sweet feminine aromas which were so intoxicating, so furious that he felt involuntarily reaction in his nether regions.

Johnny swivelled his chair back towards the bar to hide any possible embarrassment.

'I'm John Patrick King,' he announced. Normally it would have been the simpler moniker of Johnny King but due to the fact that he thought she was a Paddy Groupie he threw in the Patrick to appeal to her Irish sensibilities. Patrick didn't really work well with John but as it was on his birth certificate it was his birthright.

'I'm Frances Michelle Bell,' she smiled as she offered her hand. Then they touched!

Her skin was cool, but not cold, soft and gentle and she caressed his hand sensually rather than shaking it.

This just isn't fair, he thought, experiencing yet another rush. He needed a distraction and quickly so he uttered the first thing which came into his head.

'So, when you marry and you have your first child you'll be Michelle Ma Belle,' Johnny laughed.

'Sorry?'

'You know? Just like the Beatles song?'

'Oh,' she said as the smile drained slowly from her face. 'Actually, I can't have children.'

'Oh shit. I'm sorry. I'm so sorry. Me and my big gob. I didn't know. Really honestly,' Johnny spluttered. He'd blown it now. There she was, inches away from him, the most beautiful woman he'd ever seen and she made all the running, but in one single second he'd blown it for a cheap laugh. *Idiot*, he thought.

'Just kidding!' she giggled, and then let out a hearty laugh which filled every corner of the bar. Her laugh was… well very nearly a *dirty* laugh. Yes, that was it: a dirty laugh was the best way Johnny could find to describe it.

Two glasses of wine (each) later, Johnny's friends arrived back to the bar en route to dinner.

'Oh, surely you're not going to take my new friend away from me so quickly?' Frances said coyly.

At that point, seeing her in conversation with the others, Johnny realised exactly who Frances reminded him of. It was Rosanna Arquette, or at least the character Ms Arquette played in the movie *Black Rainbow*. Frances certainly could have played her double and neither the camera nor the actress' co-star, Jason Robards, would have been disappointed.

'Why don't you join us for dinner, then?' Robert (the longest married and biggest letch of the group) suggested.

'Nah. We're OK here,' Johnny cut in, with unnecessary speed before she had an opportunity to reply. 'Maybe we'll follow you later.'

'Yeah, and pigs will fly!' Robert replied smarmily as he and the others departed the bar.

'Why are you staring at that couple so much, Kennedy?' ann rea whispered, her Beatle bob tossed like she was about to hit the Yeah, Yeah, Yeah refrain.

'I'm just intrigued at how quickly they seem to be getting to know each other. All of it instigated, I hasten to add, by the lady,' Camden's indomitable detective replied.

'That's no excuse for staring so, Kennedy.'

'I mean, I was thinking... sorry, I know it's no excuse for staring... but I was thinking that they know next to nothing about each other at this stage. They are simply attracted to each others packaging. He, because she looks like that actress, you know the one...' Kennedy struggled, he was hopeless at remembering the names of celebrities. These days there were simply just too many and the breed was growing daily.

'Rosanna Arquette. Surely you remember *her* name, you fancy her, don't you?'

'Come on, please.'

'You do, don't you?'

'You see ann rea, that's my point. I may be attracted to the overall package, but I know nothing whatsoever about her. We allow ourselves to have these fantasies, but how often do we remind ourselves that the object of our attention is always only one-dimensional? As long as it remains like that we're never going to be disappointed because we'll never have to deal with anything other than the perfect picture. You see that couple over by the bar? They're about to live out a fantasy. They are about to step out of from their illusions. They are about to step down from the picture to reveal themselves, flaws and all, to another person,' Kennedy mused.

'And what's wrong with that?'

'Nothing. Absolutely nothing. But I was just thinking that they know nothing about each other, they are destined to disappoint. They are also, potentially, putting their lives in danger, aren't they?'

'Ah, come on Kennedy, you don't have to be looking for a potential crime everywhere we go.'

'Yes, OK. OK, but that doesn't mean it's not there. Don't go mistaking paradise for that place across the road. I mean, some people hurt and some people are hurt. They all have to be out there, or here, somewhere. Hey, but you're right, it's probably just chapter one of another romance. They just caught my attention, that's all, probably nothing.'

'Probably nothing my foot, you and your Rosanna Arquette fixation. Stop trying to disguise it as something else; pretending you were detecting a crime. Would you like me to go and chat up your man so that you can step in and play out one of your fantasies?' ann rea jested.

'I think I'll stick to my last fantasy, if you don't mind, thank you very much. I'm enjoying it too much to want to stop,' the detective replied, playfully caressing the back of her neck.

'Are you sure this is OK? I mean, I'm being positively selfish, but I'm having such fun. You will tell me if you need to go...' Frances began.

'Nah. Nah, it's OK. There'll be too much drink, too much Indian food, too much talk about cars, football and girls. Not to mention too late a night,' Johnny replied, draining the remainder of his glass.

'Good. Great. My round. Same again?' And before he'd a chance to protest, she added: 'Look, let's find a table. Somewhere a bit more private?'

The bar was filling up fast, becoming very noisy.

Johnny surveyed the bar space. 'There's not much room anywhere in here, it's turning into a bit of a zoo. Why don't we go to my room? It'll be a lot quieter there and we can have a bottle of wine and drink it in peace.'

It had taken all of the young man's confidence to make the offer. He figured she could only say no. And anyway, she was the one who'd suggested finding somewhere more private. He felt stupid to think he'd had a chance with this goddess in the first place. Secretly he thanked her for the opportunity to make the invitation. If she said no they could have another polite glass of wine and he would chase his friends. He knew exactly where they would be; a few streets away in the excellent Viceroy Indian Restaurant. The food wouldn't make up for the loss of Frances but it would at least satisfy another hunger.

She looked at him with neither smile nor frown of reproachfulness on her face. At this point should she have replied either to the positive or the negative he would not have been surprised. Well maybe that's not the complete truth, if truth be told!

Because Johnny Patrick King was astounded, as in gobsmacked, when eventually Frances Michelle Bell replied: 'Yes, that would be nice. I'd like very much to go to your room with you.'

Johnny told Frankie that he was a draftsman, a bachelor, a vegan; a fan of *EastEnders, Cheers* and *ER;* that he played football at weekends; that he lived in Manchester, loved Oasis, Paul Weller, Ocean Colour Scene and Sinead Lohan; worked for British Rail (who incidentally used to own the magnificent building in which they were now entertaining themselves) until his section was sold to Virgin; never been in love; didn't go to church anymore, although he like to would to believe in God; had two brothers and two sisters; was close to his parents and visited them in Ireland whenever he could; liked good clothes; never smoked, although occasionally he indulged in a little cannabis; had tried E, but felt it was a waste of money; had ambitions to travel; wanted to own his own business, although he hadn't as yet worked out what business that should be; went to the movies a bit; read a little (mostly Dick Francis and American detective fiction); and would love to move to London.

Frances told Johnny that she was an only daughter (put up with her mother, hated her father); had been married (once) and her husband had died leaving her in the very pleasant state of being independently wealthy; lived in New York but was on an extended stay in London where she was staying with friends in Hampstead; loved the music of kd lang, Roy Orbison, Patsy Cline, The Blue Nile and Frank Sinatra; liked *NYPD Blue*, *Cracker* and *Friends*; had been a teacher in her early twenties; hated all and any drugs; loved wine; practically lived in the cinema; read a bit, mostly biographies and poetry, especially Seamus Heaney; and she had a hobby she just *might* tell him about sometime!

'You still seem distracted, Kennedy,' ann rea whispered, trying to ascertain just how distracted he really was.

Kennedy didn't reply at first. They were still in the dark corner at the far side of the bar. It had been ann rea who had decided that they should meet there before joining some friends of hers for dinner in a a nearby Italian restaurant. A journalist, she had been to Wimbledon to conduct an interview with a footballer who'd lost his memory. His partial lapse had been especially evident on the football field the previous Saturday when he'd been sent off for repeatedly (five times) lifting the ball and running up the field with it in the direction of his own goal. Anyway, ann rea had suggested Kennedy meet her at the Landmark to save her going the whole way back to Camden Town and then retrace her steps again back to Baker Street. Her interviewee was still apparently suffering from his malady; he'd forgotten to turn up for the interview. ann rea consequently was looking for, and in need of, some attention.

'Sorry,' Detective Inspector Christy Kennedy grunted after a while, thereby admitting he hadn't been listening to her.

'Where are you, man?' she said, snuggling up close to him.

'It's just that our two friends are on the move. I can't believe how quickly she picked him up,' Kennedy replied, nodding in the direction of Frances and Johnny who were clearing up all their belongings as they prepared to leave the bar.

'Hey, maybe your fantasy is a hooker?'

'No, she's definitely not a prostitute,' Kennedy continued, as he watched them perform their leaving ritual, double checking all their pockets and the seats they were vacating to make sure they were leaving nothing behind.

'Maybe she just fancied him. Hey, even Rosanna has to like *someone*. How do you *know* she's not a hooker?' ann rea quizzed, getting into the watching game now.

'Well, I think she would have been a little more sure of herself before she moved in on him if that had been the case. You know, she didn't even let him catch her eye, she just went straight for him. He could have been a policeman and she'd have made the first move. No, if she was a professional she would have been a lot more cautious. Another thing: if she was a hooker, she wouldn't have spent as much time with him before something happened.'

Now something was happening: Frankie and Johnny were leaving the bar, together.

'There, look at that – she's holding his hand. She'd never do that if she was on the game. Also, look at her, she's not really body confident enough. Prostitutes cruise with more self-assured swagger.'

The detective and his journalist friend scrutinised the departing couple. Kennedy noticed how tight the shoulder strap of her bag pulled on her dress.

'So…' ann rea began, stretching the word into about three syllables, 'can I assume from all of this, that you are something of a scholar in the field of prostitution?'

'I'll never major in it, I can tell you. No. No just a policeman's intuition.'

'Why were you so intrigued by them?' ann rea inquired. *She* was obviously intrigued by Kennedy's behaviour.

Kennedy's only reply was, 'Excuse me for a moment, won't you?' and before ann rea could reply he very subtly moved from the corner of the bar and casually and unobtrusively glided in the general direction of the hotel lobby, looking very much like someone about to visit the toilet.

Three and one half minutes later he returned, stopping off at the bar to pick up two fresh glasses of wine.

'What on earth was that all about, Kennedy?' ann rea inquired, drinking and smiling at the same time. 'Do you know them? Is one of them a criminal?'

'No and no.' Kennedy took a rather large swig of his cold crisp wine. 'It's just that I'm convinced that only half an hour ago neither of them knew each other from Adam and Eve. Yet in that short time, a sufficient connection has been made to entice them to head off to a hotel room together.'

'So? Kennedy, you're still such an innocent. Men and women do this kind of thing. It happens all the time.'

'Either, or even both of them could be a murderer, you know.'

'Oh, for heaven's sake! Come on, please!' ann rea laughed. Her laugh was so loud that several heads at the bar turned in their direction. 'Oops, sorry,' she said to the room in general.

She dropped her voice to nearly a whisper before continuing, this time for Kennedy's benefit only: 'I mean, come on. You have to leave your work behind some time. I would have thought getting you out of Camden would…'

'We're hardly out of Camden, ann rea,' Kennedy smiled.

'OK. If you want to be that technical, then out of Camden *Town*.'

'No, it's OK, I know. Sorry It's just that he seemed like an average kind of guy and she was a bit of a stunner…'

'Ah yes, we'll always get back to that, don't we? I think you fancied her quite a bit yourself and now that they're up there doing extremely naughty things with each other, you're annoyed.'

Kennedy flushed with what could have been envy but was probably embarrassment. Possibly from the fact that deep down, yes he did find her and Rosanna Arquette positively attractive. He still wasn't confident enough to admit things like that to ann rea. He felt there was nothing wrong in recognising somebody's beauty. He even figured it was perfectly natural to think of the aforementioned actress when intimate with ann rea. If he was brave enough to mention this to his partner, he'd then have been able to inquire as to her sexual distractions. ann rea was self-assured enough to say things like, 'Oh he's gorgeous, delicious, my kind of man,' and when she did so, it wasn't in any way a threat to their relationship. She'd never do anything other than address what was on her mind. Kennedy wished he had that kind of confidence in their relationship. Not for now though. Maybe not ever.

'Sure, I only have eyes for you,' Kennedy joked in a mock Scottish accent.

'I'd be flattered if only you didn't have to throw away that white stick,' ann rea replied, elbowing him playfully in the ribs.

'Seriously though, my point is that they've gone upstairs together to a hotel room and they know not a lot about each other. He could be a serial killer; she could be a front for a black-mailing operation…'

'Well, she's on a definite loser with him anyway,' ann rea announced confidently.

'How so?'

'For starters, he's dressed well, but not expensively. He's got the taste but lacks the money to pay for the real thing. Secondly, he's not old enough to hold down a powerful position in a big company. On top of that, he's obviously not a big tipper. Did you see how the bar man turned up his nose at the loose change left as a tip? He handled the coins like they'd just been retrieved from a toilet bowl. And finally, Watson...'

'And finally, Holmes?' Kennedy probed. He was enjoying the fact that ann rea was fast developing her own powers of detection.

'And finally, Watson, our young adventurer had neither an engagement ring nor a wedding ring upon his finger, so there would be no obvious opportunity for blackmail.'

'Excellent! We'll have you in Camden Town CID yet!'

'Oh, that would be nice,' ann rea said seductively. 'You've had me nearly everywhere else.'

'And on that note, I think it's time for our meal. I'm starving,' Kennedy said, choosing verbally to ignore her last remark. But mentally, well now, that was a different matter altogether. He couldn't help recalling the catchphrase from some TV show or other: *Wait 'til I get you home...*

At the same time, he couldn't help pondering on exactly what might be going on a few floors above them.

No sooner had Frances and Johnny entered room 502 of the Landmark Hotel than Frances was at the bedside radio and tuning it to Classic FM with all the ease of a Hampstead resident. As she did so she carefully deposited her bag on the bedside table, close to the clock-cum-radio, and was sure not to knock the table lamp over. The lamp's cream hues blended with the shades of brown and cream in the room. Meanwhile, Johnny began awkwardly to uncork the wine, studying her every movement.

Frances interrupted his bottle opening. She took the bottle , with corkscrew protruding like a strange flower, more suitable for the set of *Blade Runner*, and placed it on top of the television cabinet. Then, very gently, she took him in her arms and led in a passionate but gentle kiss. Her tongue doing the exploring, and Johnny felt all reserve, if any existed at that point, melt away. He was hers to do with as she pleased.

As they concluded their kiss, their first kiss, she sang wistfully:
No body would ache so much
Yeah no body would ache so much
Ache so much for you.

The melody was so powerful he felt a lump rise in his throat. He wanted to ask her what she was singing but his concern that he might appear out of touch and spoil the moment, spoil a special moment. Had he known the lyrics were from Tanika Tikaram's classic 'Harm in Your Hands' he may have proceeded more cautiously. On the other hand, he may have already been beyond the point of no return.

'I think,' she began, 'that we're both old enough to forgo the "will we/won't we?" prelude. It can introduce a bit of erotic tension at times, but it also gets in the way of genuine pleasure, so let's both savour the moments knowing we're eventually going to enjoy ourselves fully. OK?'

'Great,' was the single word in the entire English language Johnny could find to utter (barely) in reply.

'OK, I think you should finish opening the wine now.' And with that she returned the futuristic bloom to Johnny.

By the time he had uncorked the bottle of Bergerac 1997 – not so much cheeky and crisp as ill-bred and brittle – she had removed her red dress. Johnny very nearly dropped the offending bottle at the sight.

She was standing in her full glory in black lace bra, panties, suspender belt and stockings. Brave? No, not really. Provocative? No, definitely not. Sensational? Definitely YES! The Ulsterman's heartbeat was as solid as that of the Lambeg drum and very nearly beating as fast as the war drums.

Johnny could just not believe his luck. Things like this simply just didn't happen to him. Hell, they rarely even happened in the movies. Again he was reminded of the scene in *Black Rainbow*, the one where Rosanna undresses slyly for a young journalist. That one scene had sent Johnny to sleep on many a lonely night with a smile on his face.

But now he had his own vision, a vision which was being branded into his own brain by the power of sheer desire and lust, and which would comfort him for the remainder of his life; no matter how long (or short) such a life should be.

His first reaction was to want to kiss her again, only this time with him taking the lead. He resisted, knowing that should he step so close to her to share another kiss he'd lose the sight of the heavenly vision before him.

Frances seemed to sense this because she said, 'Slowly, Johnny, slowly.' He loved the way she pronounced his name. She made it sound more like a sexual challenge than a moniker. 'I want to enjoy this, I love to kiss, I like to prolong, I love to delay but first of all I'd love a glass of wine.'

Johnny was fully dressed. Frances was barely dressed. In point of fact 'barely dressed' is quite an apt term in the circumstances. Johnny wondered what he should do. Should he start to remove his clothes? If so, in what order should he do so? He'd always remembered hearing that men look hideous if they strip to their shirts and socks.

He needn't have worried. Following their glasses of wine Frances started to undress him. Slowly. Kissing him with long and lingering moist kisses as she did so. Then he started to worry about the length of time he could remain... er... manly for her. He needn't have worried. She led them both through blissful highs and lows before they both, at her boisterous, desperate and very vocal urging, enjoyed the ultimate human pleasure. Both clung on to each other for dear life, as the waves gently subsided and the ripples became less and less frequent until, eventually, they disappeared altogethe. All that remained of their spent passion was the afterglow of their perspiration as it mixed together.

Johnny had never ever known anything so exquisitely beautiful... well, that was until about twenty minutes later, when it was even better... or until about thirty five minutes later again, when they tasted the best that it could be. The best that it would ever be for him. He seemed to recall in a haze Frances departing the bed as he drifted off to deep, peaceful, contented sleep.

Frances, however, had not yet completed *her* ritual. No, she had much more to do. She removed the remainder of her clothes, which at this point were her stockings and suspender belt, and she took her bag into the bathroom. She took out a pair of surgical gloves and put them on, her blood-red nail varnish still visible though the plastic. She removed a little bottle from her bag, unscrewed the cap and tipped two capsules into her hand. She broke the capsules open and poured their contents, white powder, into a glass of water, which she stirred with her sheathed index finger. Her finger moved around the cloudy water like a small red fish, darting first this way, then violently that, until all the power had dissolved and her glove-covered finger could again be seen clearly.

She returned to the bedroom and gently nudged Johnny to partial consciousness. In a stage whisper she told him how thirsty she was.

'Fancy some beautiful, ice cold water?' she encouraged through his half sleep.

He raised his head a little from the pillow, looked around the room and at her, and convinced himself he was in a dream, it had all been a dream. A thirsty dream though, so he greedily gulped down all the water and fell back on to his pillow.

Frances fetched her bag from the bathroom and produced a plastic sheet. She unfolded it to its full extent, eight foot by six. She removed the bed covers, rolled Johnny to one side, stretched out her plastic sheet and rolled the co-operative victim back on to the centre of the bed.

She then secured the safety latch on the door, returned to the bathroom and looked at her self in the mirror. She was quite shocked at the sight that greeted her. She appeared to be a woman in heat or someone longing for their ultimate fix.

Her reflection frightened her. It scared her, because she was in the strange surroundings of a sterile hotel bathroom, and it scared her because she realised her actions were now beyond her control. She had long since passed the point of no return. It was as inevitable as the sun coming up the following morning. She had to continue.

She returned to the bedroom. Johnny, lying docile on the bed, drew no sympathy from her. He was harmless, he just hadn't known what had hit him. He'd certainly just enjoyed the most pleasurable experience of his life. Why should she pity him? Better to leave it this way. There is nothing better than the best, so why waste time trying?

Very simple words, but true, she thought as she removed her prized stainless steel instrument from her bag of tricks.

It took a few additional minutes to position herself astride his body. Her weapon caught the rays from the dim bedside light, reflecting shimmering beams all over Johnny's naked torso.

She located the position on his chest, directly above his heart. Frances appeared to be savouring these moments for as long as possible. She had told Johnny that she liked to delay, she liked to prolong. He'd never have guessed that this is what she'd meant. She was now teasing herself towards her ultimate experience.

The stainless steel tip of her weapon was no more than a quarter of an inch above his skin. She moved it slowly around and around an imaginary spot, pinpointing the exact point, the final point, the point of penetration. She knew from her previous experiences that the rush she was about to feel would be far superior to any penetration Johnny would ever feel.

The sharpest of tips touched his skin.

Frances applied pressure to it until she had broken the skin and she could feel her weapon slip through his body towards his heart.

Then she was in heaven. She experienced her fourth orgasm of the evening. It was neither better nor worse than any of the three she had enjoyed with her partner from Ulster. Suffice to say it was different and equally rewarding to her in an altogether different way. Rewarding in the way an artist, a great artist, takes pride in their work.

The following morning, about three miles south of room 502 of the Landmark Hotel, Detective Inspector Christy Kennedy and ann rea woke up together in Primrose Hill. Frances Michelle Bell had left not a trace in the hotel room of what had occurred the previous evening.

She was long gone, and with her went the evidence of what had taken place while the majority of Camden slept peacefully. All the evidence, that was, apart from one item: the body of Johnny Patrick King. His form bore the mark of exactly what had occurred the previous evening. But even a detective as experienced as Kennedy, had he been aware of all that had happened, would not have been able to track down Frances. Not in a million years, even considering the fact that he had actually seen her, face to face, less than twelve hours earlier. All traces of her were gone, gone for good and she was off in search of another victim.

Surprisingly though, something on the bed moved. Johnny had been rolled to one side, obviously to enable Frances to remove her plastic sheet. He was so close to the edge, in fact, that at exactly eight-forty-five am, his arm fell out on to the floor. The change in the equilibrium of his body caused him to roll in that direction. Before the body had a chance to completely roll out of bed however, his head hit the bedside table with an almighty bang and he sprang up to be greeted with the mother of all hangovers.

He stumbled to the bathroom to get a damp towel to try and control the pounding in his head. He blinked feverishly at his reflection trying hard to get his eyes to focus. Everything was a blur. He bathed his head in a sink full of cold water and as he stood up his focus returned.

The first thing he noticed were marks on his chest. It was a weird combination of reds, blues, greens and blacks. He stared closer and eventually deciphered the mirror image of a tattooed American stars and stripes flag with words written across it.

Johnny realised he was marked, branded for life with print right across his chest close to his heart. Future girlfriends, should there ever be any, would always quiz him about exactly was meant by the words:

Michelle Ma Belle these are words which go together well.

HR McGregor

Notes

Genres are breaking down, becoming slippery and shape-changing into new and strange hybrids. Genres are labels, marketing devices. They exist and have purpose for the distributors and exhibitors, the marketers (those that *££profit££* most from the work) but operating as a straightjacket they do not serve the interests of the creator or the consumer. Genre, like language itself, is organic; it lives, it adapts, it transmogrifies, and grows. The best work transcends genre. I read British crime fiction because I find in it some of the most critical and compassionate portrayals of class conflict, hardship, deprivation and the causes of crime in any literary form. The best crime (and horror) fiction faces up to all those dark aspects of human behaviour that society – and other genres – need to repress.

The marketers and brand-namers seem to believe that consumers want exactly the same thing over and over again. Do we? Do we really?

The Confession

by HR McGregor

I will go to the police.
I will confess everything.
I will go to gaol.
I will not pass Go.

These were my thoughts and had been since I picked up the
sports pages of *The Guardian*, chucked them on the floor in the
direction of the bin and picked up the local paper that had been
lying underneath.

On the front page there was a photograph of a boy. *The* boy.
Then I saw the headline.

BOY DIES OF WEIL'S DISEASE

I might as well have had Weil's disease myself, so violently was
my lunch spewed over the floor. By the time I had cleared it, and
myself up, I was calmer. And curious. I read on.

*A boy died in the John Radcliffe Hospital last night after a week long
struggle against leptospirosis or Weil's disease. He was admitted to the
hospital last Thursday when his flu symptoms worsened and he collapsed at school. It is not known how the boy contracted the disease
which is caused from water contaminated by rat's urine. There has not
been a fatality due to Weil's disease in the county for twenty years. See
page 4.*

I didn't need to read anymore. I must go the police, I must go
straight to gaol, I must not...

I put the paper down and covered my head with my arms.
There was a loud clump, a jangle of bells and a short trill. It was
the Shogun, and her brother, Pharaoh, was fast behind. I stared at
the cats, the sleek black and his fat tortoiseshell sibling.

It is not known how the boy contracted the disease.

Oh, but it is known. *I* know.

It seems as though I must reassess my image of myself. It seems that I must incorporate the fact that I am a murderer into my spiritual self-assessment. I will go the police. I will confess everything. I will not p...

I stood up and stared out of the window. The waters of the canal were a muddy green and the trees on the far bank were stark and bare where only a week ago they had been covered with their gold and russet canopies. How quickly winter had taken autumn's baton to finish the year's relay. Was it really only three weeks ago that I stepped out of the boat into all that mellow fruitfulness and caused someone to die?

I turned to the starboard porthole and peeled back the curtain to look at the mooring station. Everything was as it should be and I was disappointed. I was hoping for the world to have rearranged itself so that I could believe that none of this was really happening to me. If there isn't a towpath anymore then I needn't go the police, there is nothing to confess and I can pass Go after all. But there it was, same as ever.

I put on my coat and left the boat, but standing on the towpath I had a panic attack and had to rush back inside in order to be able to breathe. I did some alternate nostril breathing and tried to remember the name of the nice police, the one who came to our monthly boat-dwellers meeting in the Boatman's Arms. He came to talk about the crime wave and offer advice in dealing with harassment from minors.

'Oh for the days when you could clout them round the ear with immunity and send the little buggers to bed without any supper. Better still, keep them in exhausting employment – chimney sweeping and the like,' he said with a gentle twinkle in his eye.

Remembering the policeman's joke turned the air in the boat to mud and I ran back out on to the towpath and took great gulps of oxygen. I began to feel faint, but I couldn't go back in the boat. I couldn't breathe in there. I wouldn't be able to breathe until I was where I belonged. At the police station.

I looked around me and was momentarily calmed by the tranquillity of the scene. A picture-postcard stillness that was broken only by the frenetic flow of the water in the middle of the image. Only the river was real to me and, as I stared, I felt myself become hypnotised by the flow and found that I was breathing normally again.

The towpath is a causeway that separates the canal from the millstream, an inlet that links the river to the canal via a lock. When I moved here six years ago it was as pretty a place as you could imagine. A rural haven in the town; no sight of building, only water and greenery. The narrowboats are moored on the canal, across which is the grandiose estate of a major public school. The beautiful buildings of the old school, where generations of the richest in the land had been educated, could only be seen in winter when the trees were stark and bare. We were grateful to the old place. There was no fear of development there. At least on one side, our environment was safe.

On the other side of the millstream there used to be the remains of an old Abbey. The river's edge was lined with willow and sycamore and beyond there was bush, a green wasteland leading to the railway station. No more. The building started three years ago. It was halted for a while because they were building on contaminated land, but it recommenced in time.

I didn't mind about the social housing, high-rise flats which went up first, along the town end of the canal, close to the road and station. I've seen the homeless all over the town, I've sometimes responded but mostly ignored their whiny pleas for any spare change. Not without the middle class pang of guilt, followed by resentment. Why do they whine so, surely they could try a more up-beat approach in pitching their need? The man who cheerfully stands on his head in a bucket outside Marks and Spencer makes a great deal more money than the whiners. Someone told me he was on the Enterprise Allowance scheme.

We were all pleased about the social housing. Good. Why shouldn't the poorest of the poor enjoy the loveliness of the water and the trees? But then the posh houses went up, down at the end, overlooking the winding-hole and lock. The prettiest part. That really pissed us off.

The town crept up around us and suddenly there was far less green. No longer an idyllic backwater, the towpath became a major thoroughfare. And then the rats came. Four years on the boat and not a rat in sight, then suddenly six, in one week. The cats killed them of course, that's how I found them, chewed and disembowelled in the engine room.

'It's the rubbish from the houses,' the boaters said. And we laughed because we are well used to the derision of those who regard us as wild water-gypsies, travellers, spongers and drug addicts, one and all. It had taken a long battle to secure the permanent moorings along the final stretch of the canal and there were many whose interests would be far better served by driving us away.

I was so deep in thought that I didn't realise I hadn't exhaled for several minutes.

I rushed back into the boat for my inhaler. I would just have to alternate locations until I found the strength to go the police station. That was when I decided to write it all down.

A statement that the police could read rather than have to deal with the hysterical gibberish of a guilt-deranged boater.

Writing it made it real. More real than it had been at the time, but of course, hindsight has more depth than experience. I tried to record each moment as it lurched towards the next tranche of unlimited possibilities. I wrote of how bright the sun was, of how the sky was as blue as it gets and the canal was covered with leaves, so much so that you could not tell which was water and which was towpath. Vivaldi played in my mind's CD and I decided to go for a walk. I headed north up the canal, looked up at the golden brown trees lining the far side and then across the millstream to the new houses beyond. A group of youths stood on the edge of the winding hole throwing sticks into the river. I recognised one of them. How could I forget his satanic grin as he leered at me through the hatch a few weeks ago, picked up my hat from its hook on the engine room door, spat in it and said something about my cat being fat.

I ignored him. We boaters were used to it although we collectively grieved the loss of our haven, our secluded water-world. The level of abuse, harassment and crime had steadily grown and it was due largely to the kids from the flats. We were all embarrassed to admit this. Let me explain here that the majority of boatdwellers on the towpath were professional people. There was a social worker, two teachers, a local radio DJ, three Oxfam workers, a journalist, a homeopath, a PhD student and part time lecturer, a computer programmer, a performance poet. For the most part Guardian-readers-against-the-military-industrialist-machine types. Greens or Labour voters (at varying degrees between extreme 'Old' and 'New') who didn't want to admit that people whose side we thought we were on were making our lives hell.

Break-ins and thefts. Vandalism. Underage couples having sex on the Elsan disposal unit. Beer cans, condoms and hypodermics on the towpath. Verbal abuse:

'Can't you afford a fucking house then?'; 'Show us round your boat or we'll set fire to it!'

The only thanks I got for telling a pair of twelve-year-olds that the structure on which they were about to lose their virginity was in fact a sewage disposal unit was the venomously decried information that they knew my boat and they knew my cats and then I would see.

In one week there were two break-ins and three bicycles, a paddle for a canoe, a sack of coal and a watering can were taken from the towpath. The canoe had been vandalised and sunk. And, as any river or canal dweller knows, to a certain mentality there is only one thing wittier than throwing a shopping trolley into a stretch of water and that is unmooring a boat, especially if it is wired to the shore so the electricity cable and phone line break.

We tried not to take them seriously. We tried to be on their side and to understand that their delinquency was a function of their deprivation.

I walked on towards the lock and I registered him without really seeing him. He was a figure on the towpath, that's all, and I was distracted by noticing that Louise's bike was missing. She was away and I was keeping an eye on her boat. I went to investigate. Had it been stolen or merely thrown into the canal?

It wasn't in the water. I looked up, and this time I really saw him. He was standing, legs apart, throwing stones into the river. All the energy in his throwing seemed to come from his groin which was thrust forward and made a circling movement as he swung his arm round to fire his missiles. I found his movement interesting – it had all the frustration, rage and torture of adolescence in one gesture. Then I felt guilty for observing him but instead of making me stop my guilt only drove me to conceal myself further and I edged towards the young willow tree where the missing bike should have been tied.

He threw one last stone, more viciously, and with more power from his groin than previous and then stopped. I hadn't seen him before, he wasn't one of the usual gang of towpath tormentors. He turned and walked towards Katie and Nick's boat. He said hello. Blandly. The large sycamore in front of me obscured the boat and I saw only his arms reach out to take something from it. The little bastard's helping himself to one of Katie's Geraniums! But before that thought had time to fully realise itself, I saw that he had picked up the Pharaoh and held him gently, stroking him and saying something.

Ahhhh, I though, but that *ahhhh* died before it reached its final aitch as I saw him turn and run and with a great, dramatic, discus-throwing body-swing, he hurled the cat into the centre of the millstream, his crotch thrusting out in the direction of his aim as though it was desperate to follow that trajectory. As though it was fucking the event.

I felt something very large and offal-like appear at the back of my throat. The boy sauntered on up the towpath without looking back. I ran to the river's edge. The Pharaoh was struggling with the current. His little black, otter-like head struggling to stay above water. I scrambled down the bank and with what little voice I had, given that I think my spleen was sifting on my larynx, coaxed him towards me. He gave a little cry as he neared the shore and I waded in and scooped him into my arms. Then he stared at me and gave a *great* cry, a wail of anguish that I could only anthropomorphically interpret as a profound existential crisis.

As I carried him back to the boat I wept. There, I wrapped him in a towel and opened a tin of tuna, his absolutely favourite thing. He sniffed it, turned his hugely dilated eyes towards me and gave another great miaow. I took some deep breaths and then I left the boat and walked up the towpath. I wanted to tell someone, I needed to speak to someone. I was, I am sure, in a kind of shock, but instead of having any of my customary respiration problems, I appeared to have stopped breathing altogether without any panic or discomfort. When I saw him my lungs took in a huge gulp of air which seemed to scream as it made its passage down my throat.

He was standing on the hump-backed bridge, looking down at the lock beneath. My first impulse was to shout and run towards him, my anger was so great. I kept seeing the Pharaoh, his fur spiked, twisting himself around, panic stricken. But I was too stunned for action and I walked slowly towards the bridge. When he noticed me he made no indication of recognition and I realised that he probably had not seen me cross the towpath to rescue the cat and that I would have been entirely concealed from his view once he reached the lock. The little bastard had just nonchalantly wandered off not knowing or caring whether the cat lived or died.

He looked through me and he turned and walked on over the bridge and up the canal. I followed. My blood seemed heavy, solid. He quickened his pace and I ran to catch up with him. I was going to grab hold of him and confront him, I wasn't going to take that, what I had just seen, no way. The little shit was going to have to face what he did. I was going to take him back to the boat and make him see the cat, make him see what he has done. I was going to find out where he lived and inform his parents; people who are cruel to animals can be cruel to humans. This has now been proved scientifically, though why anyone should waste time and money researching something that has been obvious since the infant Vlad started impaling small mammals and birds is beyond me. The boy's phenomenally sexual stick and stone throwing was normal adolescence, but to throw a trusting creature into the centre of a fast flowing river is sick. It must be nipped in the bud. I slowed down to calm my breathing. I wanted to be authoritative and powerful and I had to control the wild anger that would sabotage my intent.

He is probably from the flats, he probably has a horrible home life, was abused, is abused.

I think in those moments I felt that I was going to save this boy, I was going to use my outrage to reach him, to make him accountable, and to show him another way, to introduce him to his empathy quotient.

When I was about five or six feet behind him, I noticed his school uniform and all my smug projections evaporated and my blood felt light again, incredibly light. It felt as though I soared through the air while my hands were clenching themselves into the tightest fists. I smashed them hard into his lower back. His blazer gave him some protection but nonetheless I think I must have hit his kidneys because he doubled over, or rather back, in pain and, taken by surprise, was not prepared for being hauled up by his blazer lapels and hurled into the muddy and putrid waters of the canal.

'You little bastard,' is what I think I said. 'You animal, you and your posh public school and your rich parents and you're nothing but a savage, a bullying toff of a future serial killer.'

I can't be sure of the exact words, I have a feeling that the heat of the anger might have been much more gratuitous, I'm sure all those words were there but with perhaps some stronger ones as well. While I screamed my rage out at him, he clambered about in the slimy, but shallow, canal, spouting out water great gobfulls of water, shaking, spluttering and looking in complete disbelief at the harpy on the towpath. He started towards the bank but thought better of it and waded across the canal to the other side. He scrambled out and only then did he turn back to face me.

'You are fucking nuts,' he said, and then he ran away.

A cyclist went by. All was quiet at the boat yard opposite and no-one had observed us. I walked home with great sobs welling up inside me. The Pharaoh and the Shogun were sitting on the sofa together, in spite of being sworn enemies. Pharaoh was still shaken, tense and needy. I poured myself gin after gin. I cried. Several times I went to phone a friend but each time I didn't get beyond the first few numbers. It won't help. Talking won't help. After the fourth gin, I began to see the funny side of the situation. Even Pharaoh's outraged journey through the air seemed cartoonish enough to warrant a giggle and as for my furious revenge – well it was rather hysterical perhaps, but the little shit deserved it.

I told no-one about the incident. Was this out of some pre-cognition of the potential outcome. Shock had made him swallow huge mouthfuls of canal water liberally dosed with rat's urine and it would seem that he had told no-one either. Was this out of shame? What were his last few weeks like? Didn't he know about

Weil's disease? He should have made a connection between his flu symptoms and his intimate contact with the dubious consistency of the Lower Oxford. Was he too ashamed to tell anyone that he had been pulled up by his lapels by a small blond woman and hurled into the canal before his adrenaline had time to signal danger?

I can see him sneaking into the dormitory to change his clothes before questions could be asked. I can see his flu worsening and his guilt and misery growing with the infection. By the time he collapsed it was too late. The disease must be treated in the early stages and the boy had passed this cure by date. Did he know at the end? He must have been questioned and informed of the causes of his demise. He must have made a connection and still not told. Why?

Questions, questions, questions.

I must go to the police. I must confess everything. I must go straight to gaol.

I had almost finished writing when the Pharaoh jumped up on to my desk and walked over my keyboard. #[;.dx,okvjbznv

L;K N
*4yrvdpo:; frfs xiktezitf m
'/hkckc\   'LOjOdc\n

I pushed him aside and he started purring very loudly and nudging me with his face.

'Oh you are so beauooooooooootiful' I murmured into the backs of his ears, 'did my poor baby get thrown into the river by a horrid boy?'

I deleted my confession, opened a tin of tuna for the cats and phoned a friend to arrange to go the cinema. On the way down the towpath, I saw two uniformed boys sitting cross-legged by the edge of the canal. I crept up behind them silently and gave them each a little push. They went over so easily. Plop. Plop. But I didn't stick around to see how they surfaced and struggled out. Nor whether or not they had swallowed any water. I crept off, unseen in the dark shadows of the towpath.

Peter Guttridge

Notes

Crime writing came through the movies. B movies on a Sunday afternoon when I was a kid: Rathbone and Bruce, of course, looming out of the mist; Bogart on rain-slick LA streets; Mitchum in *Build My Gallows High*; Farley Granger in *They Live By Night*; *Double Indemnity*, *The Postman Always Rings Twice*, and Aldrich's extraordinary *Kiss Me Deadly*.

Then later, in the early seventies, a golden age of crime moviemaking: *Badlands The Honeymoon Killers*, *Charley Varrick*, *The Friends of Eddie Coyle*. Mitchum as Marlowe twenty years too late, the ineffable *Chinatown*.

The movies led to the books – Chandler and Hammett and John Franklin Bardin. And, yes, you could say that American culture colonised my imagination. But that was no help for *this* wannabe writer – if I tried to transplant that American sensibility to the places I knew best (we were talking the mean streets of Accrington, Nottingham and Oxford at the time) I'd end up sounding like some dire DJ with a phony mid-Atlantic accent.

Plus there was something faintly ridiculous about all these hardboiled macho characters. (I'd been a big fan of Richard Stark's Parker series as a teenager but I was through puberty now and Nietzschean supermen didn't have the same appeal.) So my first attempt at a crime novel, in my late twenties, was a post-modern Sherlock Holmes pastiche in which he gets involved in an adventure with a guy who knows the Great Detective is just a fictional character – and, yes, it was as bad as that sounds.

Then I drifted into journalism, interviewed contemporary US crime writers, read their work (it helps). Ellroy's books were the real thing but I had a fondness for the wit in the work of Crumley, Leonard and, especially, Hiaasen.

And I realised that alongside Rathbone and Bruce I loved the partnership of Crosby and Hope in the *Road To* movies. That whilst I enjoyed Bogart, I loved Albert Finney in Neville Smith's *Gumshoe*. And that whilst *Get Carter* counted among my all time greats I also delighted in *Pulp*, the comic crime film *Get Carter's* director Mike Hodges and star Michael Caine made the year after.

I became a comic crime novelist. It has the advantage that there aren't many of us doing it compared to the hundreds (thousands?) writing straight crime fiction. It has the disadvantage that not many people read us. But since a sense of humour is an infallible sign of high intelligence, comic crime writers at least get quality, if not quantity from their readers. I mean that very sincerely. Quantity, however, would also be good...

The Postman Only Rings When He Can Be Bothered

by Peter Guttridge

Mrs Spring was floating face down in the pool when her gardener found her. She hung there, half submerged, tangled in a length of filtration pipe. It was Tuesday, ten thirty am. Each morning in the warm months Mrs Spring came into the garden at seven, disrobed and gingerly lowered herself into the chilly waters. The pool, installed for status not swimming, was circular. For fifteen minutes Mrs Spring laboriously circumnavigated it.

From my study on the first floor of our cottage I occasionally had the misfortune to see this ritual. It was a terrible spectacle. Her body had known better days. At least for her sake I hope it had. If my window was open, I would hear gargled gasps as she breathed with her head sometimes above, sometimes below the water.

On that Tuesday morning, I didn't know anything was wrong until I heard a commotion around eleven. I was having my ear bent, as usual, by my cleaner Donald about Roger Moore (as usual).

Rural unemployment being what it is round here, you can virtually enslave the yokels and they're poor enough to be grateful. Donald does us twice a week for less than the cost of my daily Scotch bill. And I certainly don't intend to do it myself – I'd given up my job to write, not to take on domestic duties, despite what my lovely wife Ruth might sometimes hope.

Unfortunately, he has several drawbacks, one of them being that he can – and does – turn any conversation round to Roger Moore within moments of it starting. He'd been telling me of another driver coming to grief on Century Lane, an accident blackspot two or three miles away. A 2CV had skidded off the road and been totalled against a tree. He'd immediately segued to a car chase in a Bond film in which 007 had been driving such a vehicle. And, *voila*, there he was on Roger Moore.

'See, Mr Stewart, people don't realise what a range he has,' he was saying as he pushed a duster in a desultory way along my bookshelves. 'Some bloke down the pub said he was just a pair of raised eyebrows. But I told him he's played in a lot of different movies, more than you'd think. He was a German officer in one.'

'Did he do the accent?' I said wearily, scrolling through the text on my computer screen.

'Well, no, but that's not my point. My point is—'

'Leave the desk please, Donald.'

'Sorry, Mr Stewart,' he said, rifling quickly through the papers he'd picked up before putting them back on my desk. 'See you got another letter for The Forge. That postman should be shot, then I could do his job. I'd—'

'*Thanks* Donald,' I said sharply, though he was right about the postman. We lived in The Old Forge whilst just down the road the Parkers lived in The Forge. The postman regularly mixed up our mail, though in fairness that was also because Ruth still went by her maiden name of Parkin, which provided an additional complication for the short-sighted old gent.

Aside from being an anorak about Roger Moore – a little perverse these days wouldn't you say? – the other drawback to Donald is that he is incurably nosy. He has a habit of rooting through the things on my desk if I'm not around to stop him.

Donald droned on, then interrupted himself.

'Lummy,' he said (he has a fondness for Fifties Ealing films too). 'Come and look at this, Mr Stewart.'

I joined him at the window and looked down at two stocky men standing in Mrs Spring's pool. Stripped to their underwear, they were manhandling her body through the water towards a stretcher at the side of the pool.

Beside the stretcher were two neat piles of clothes, topped by police helmets, truncheons and other crime-busting paraphernalia. There was also a set of false teeth. Mrs Spring wore ill-fitting dentures that whistled when she was agitated. She took them out before swimming, since underwater they produced a kind of death rattle. Aptly enough, it now seemed. The body is a temple, Mrs Spring used to declare to those people who still had anything to do with her. Hers was devoted to excess. When she rolled out of the policemen's exasperated grasp just as they had her feet hoisted on to the bank, the consequent displacement of water more than proved Archimedes Principle. It soaked a third man in a smart suit who was taking down notes as he listened to the white-faced gardener.

I sent Donald away, telling him to finish off the next day, then phoned Ruth with the news. It took five minutes to tell her, given that she put me on hold every couple of syllables.

A heart attack, we supposed, my neighbours, the Westwoods, and I, an hour or so later. We had congregated with virtually all the rest of the hamlet on the grassy track that runs from the church between our adjacent gardens and Mrs Spring's. Word spreads quickly in a place like ours, cut off as it is from neighbouring villages. We occupiers of these houses huddled round the Saxon church and Jacobean manor house may be solidly middle class but we gossip like fishwives.

Murder, Mr Deacon the newspaperman announced the next morning. I met him at the post-box just after seven. He saw me crossing the lane from the track and clanked to a halt on his decrepit three-gear bike, the basket of newspapers swaying drunkenly before his handlebars. A bike with three gears is all you need, Mr Deacon insisted, even though everyone else in the Western Hemisphere was whizzing past him on multi-gear mountain bikes. Only after many years of nagging had his wife persuaded him some months before to invest in a car, a second hand Fiat Panda. He bought it, reluctantly, but refused ever to drive it.

The road into Novington from his shop at the base of the Downs was steep; he was as usual red-faced and panting. He was a short man, rather too short for his bike. As he sucked in air, his body rose and fell awkwardly on the crossbar lodged perilously between his thighs. 'The police phoned last night,' he gasped, 'whilst I was out at darts. Mrs Deacon took the message. They want a statement from me this morning. Tell them if I saw anything yesterday morning.'

'And did you?'

'Well, I saw you, Mr Stewart, with that parcel in your hand. I thought to myself, he'll never get that in the post box.' He looked at me as if I must be mad even to try. 'You didn't, did you?'

I shook my head, hiding my surprise behind a smile. Although my wife, Ruth, and I had moved down here two years before I was still unused to the fact that in such a small community it was impossible to do anything unobserved, even at seven in the morning. I had seen Mr Deacon from a distance when I took the parcel to the post-box on the other side of the lane but he had given no indication that he had seen me.

I wasn't mad, however. I had discovered by chance that the door to our local post-box had a faulty catch. It didn't always lock when the postman closed it after emptying the box. Parcels that wouldn't fit in the narrow slit at the top would easily fit through the door. Inconveniently for me the box had been shut tight the previous day.

Mr Deacon, inhibited by his crossbar, made a token effort to lean conspiratorially towards me. 'And I saw that Edith Macrell loitering by the church. She'll be the *prime suspect*.'

With that Mr Deacon straightened his basket of newspapers and set off down the lane to the houses on the far side of Novington Place. I watched him go. Mrs Spring murdered. I had heard nothing. Nor had I seen Mrs Macrell. I wondered if she'd seen me.

The third policeman in his smart suit came to see me on the Thursday. He introduced himself as Sergeant Pratt and watched closely to see my reaction.

'Would you like a glass of champagne?' I said, successfully controlling my smirk and waving the half empty bottle vaguely in his direction.

'Celebrating are we, sir?' he said, frowning.

'Something like that,' I said, sneaking a guilty glance at the huge pile of branches the tree surgeon had left by my garden shed about ten minutes before.

The timing of Pratt's visit was a bit of an embarrassment to me. As we stood on the terrace looking across Mrs Spring's vast, well tended gardens to the sparkling waters of the English Channel I was uncomfortably aware that until this morning I had not had this view.

I should really capitalise the word 'view'. Novington is famous locally for its unparalleled vistas. The View of the dramatic chalk cliffs and the vast expanse of the foam-flecked sea beyond is a constant subject of conversation with those who have the misfortune not to live here but who come humbly and enviously at weekends to see it.

Novington itself is pretty enough, with its jumble of Tudor cottages and grander Georgian villas, but it is the view that both nourishes the spirit and enhances the house prices.

Mrs Spring had access to The View from every part of her exceedingly large garden. We house-owners in the four cottages on the ridge behind her garden were less fortunate. Mrs Spring, a staunch Christian, passed over the Love Thy Neighbour bit of her religion. She did not wish to be overlooked anywhere in her acreage, even in areas where she never ventured. Some years before, therefore, she had planted fast growing firs, forsythias and rhododendrons to screen us from her sight. In consequence, we lost The View.

The Westwoods had been the most affected. Two years before they had resorted to copper nails in the bases of the trees but the killing process was a slow one and the Westwoods were not in the first flush of youth. The day after Mrs Spring's death they sneaked into her garden to lop three feet off the forsythia and rhododendrons that had grown wild and high, then celebrated this partial reappearance of their view with dry martinis on the terrace.

When the tree surgeon the Westwoods had ordered came on Thursday morning to lop down the fir trees entirely, I called him over. I thought he might as well also raise the skirts of the huge chestnut tree whose lower branches obliterated the view from our garden as convincingly as its upper obscured the sun. Job completed, he got the first glass of fizz.

Cynical? Frankly, nobody cared for Mrs Spring. (It was only in the newspaper report I learned that she had a first name – Dorothy. I'd never met anyone who had the temerity to call her anything other than Mrs Spring). She was cantankerous, vindictive, spiteful, malicious, snobbish and bullying. On a good day.

Sergeant Pratt accepted my offer of champagne then walked slowly from one end of the terrace to the other, looking thoughtfully down at the grassy track, a public right of way that separated Mrs Spring's garden from the cottages on the ridge. He sniffed the champagne, more suspiciously than appreciatively, as he looked at The View.

'Lovely view of the sea,' he observed, narrowing his eyes and finally taking a drink.

'We like it,' I said nonchalantly. 'Can you tell me how Mrs Spring died?'

'It will be in the coroner's report next week so I think I may confide in you, sir. We thought at first it was a heart attack but Mrs Spring's heart was in good repair. Except that is for the fact it had stopped beating forever. Nor had she drowned. A suspicious pathologist, noticing slight bruising on her neck, found evidence that she had been strangled.

'What kind of evidence?'

'It's rather technical, sir. Suffice it to say we estimate the time of death at between seven and seven thirty on Tuesday morning. Can you tell me anything of interest about that period of time?'

'Not really. I'm sure Mr Deacon is a better bet,' I said. 'When I spoke to him yesterday he said he was going to make a statement. What has he got to say?'

Sergeant Pratt tilted his wine glass thoughtfully. 'He hasn't got very much to say at all, sir. Unfortunately, Mr Deacon was knocked off his bicycle by a hit and run driver early yesterday morning at the bottom of Novington Lane. Mr Deacon is dead.'

'What time?' I asked weakly.

'Between seven fifteen and seven forty five. Do I understand that you saw him yesterday morning?'

'I spoke to Mr Deacon at the post-box around seven. A hit and run driver? But the road to Novington doesn't go anywhere – we never have any traffic.'

'Precisely, sir,' Pratt gave me another searching look. 'Did you see or hear the noise of any kind of motor vehicle around the time you were talking to Mr Deacon?'

'I think I may have heard something afterwards, when I was having my breakfast in our garden. You know, Mr Deacon told me he had seen Mrs Macrell out and about on the morning of Mrs Spring's death.'

Pratt cast a baleful glance on me.

'Did he indeed? Thank you Mr Stewart. Tell me now, do you happen to own a red car?'

I shook my head.

'Not any more. I sold Edith Macrell my Golf last year. That's red. Lots of other red cars in the village. Wing Commander Westwood, Patrick Ferguson at Novington Place. My wife's car is red, too.'

'Would your wife mind if my men came to take paint samples?'

'It would be unwise for me to speak for her but I can't see she'd object.'

When he'd gone I phoned Mrs Deacon to offer my condolences. She was tearful but hard at work. 'Nobody else will do it if I don't. As Wing Commander Westwood made clear. He's the limit he is. He phones me up yesterday to say he hasn't got his newspapers. I say, "I'm ever so sorry Wing Commander but I've just heard that Eric – Mr Deacon – has been run over." The Wing Commander's quiet for a moment then he says: "So who's going to deliver my paper today?" '

Sitting on the terrace I thought about Mrs Macrell. She'd been very close to Mrs Spring at one time – they were both widows. Then Mrs Spring had Mrs Macrell's chimpanzee put down. The chimp lived in a foetid room of its own in Mrs Macrell's ramshackle Georgian farmhouse. It cavorted there day and night, swinging off the central light fitting, relieving itself on the furniture below.

The chimp was playful and loved to nip. One day it mistook Mrs Spring's earlobe for some tasty titbit. The amount of blood an earlobe can produce is disproportionate either to its size or its usefulness. And that amount of blood on a silk blouse, of however overbearing a pattern, is difficult to disguise.

So Mrs Spring, one hand holding a lump of Mrs Macrell's

hastily proffered kitchen towel to her ear, the other clutching her handbag to her extravagant bosom, insisted Mrs Macrell pay for the cost of a replacement blouse. Mrs Macrell – a wealthy woman who in common with many wealthy women didn't like spending her money on anything but herself – refused.

Mrs Spring, dentures clacking, threatened to have the chimp put down. Mrs Macrell threatened to set the chimp on more than Mrs Spring's ear. Mrs Spring thought it wise to withdraw. The very next day her solicitors went into action. A long legal battle was expected. Then suddenly Mrs Macrell backed down. Paid up and acquiesced when Mrs Spring vindictively insisted she have the chimp put down.

This was particularly strange as Mrs Macrell had often declared that the chimp was like a son to her – a worrying thought, especially for her actual son, Jonathan, a good-natured non-achiever in his early forties.

'She probably had an unhappy life,' my wife remarked when we discussed Mrs Spring's policy of always kicking opponents when they were down. Ruth always looks for the best in people – she'd qualify for sainthood if saintliness allowed for an active sex life.

I finished the champagne thinking about the police setting a Pratt to catch a Macrell. I can't help thinking in newspaper headlines. After 25 years as a sub-editor – during which time my main functions were making the illiterate scrawlings of our celebrity columnists readable and finding puns for headlines – it's in my blood.

I enjoyed subbing – I've always liked to be thorough about details – but I was happy to throw it in when we came down here in favour of the writing I had always intended to do. I had a commission to write what I assured my publishers would a millennial domestic version of *A Year In Provence*.

The parish of Novington, some three miles long and half a mile wide, contains more millionaires than you can shake a stick at, if, as Groucho Marx once said, that's your idea of a good time. There are retired racing drivers and jockeys, celebrated chefs, former actresses and a world famous artist. There are also a great many weirdos.

I'd outlined the idea of writing about this peculiar congeries over a boozy Soho lunch to a friend who had recently started an editing job at one of the new publishing conglomerates. My pitch was that I, Metropolitan Man *par excellence*, would live among country folk who would be as alien to me as Parisians were to Amazonian Indians. Of course, that was before I discovered just how alien they really were.

I was reminded at Mrs Spring's funeral. For someone who was so unpopular she got a very good turnout. Ruth and I could scarcely find a seat. 'They've all come to make sure she's really dead,' I whispered to Ruth. She looked very fetching in black seamed stockings and a short black linen dress – the only black dress she had. She shushed me, then tugged ineffectually at the skirt when she saw me leering at her thighs.

During the service I looked from one to the other of my neighbours wondering. They were all glancing at Mrs Macrell, clearly convinced she had killed Mrs Spring. Mrs Westwood also had her down for Mr Deacon. 'Maybe not deliberately,' she'd said to me the previous day. 'But she is a terrible driver.'

The pall-bearers, buckling under the weight of Mrs Spring's coffin, led the way out of the church. Two chubby men I assumed were Mrs Spring's sons comforted a bowed old lady. She shuffled on spindly legs, clutching her handbag. If Mrs Spring had lived to be a shadow of her former self, this is who she would have been. It was Winifred, her sister. I met her at the house later.

'Dorothy was never the same after her husband died,' Winifred confided to me. 'She loved Frederick so. They'd been married 35 years when she was told he had cancer. He was dead a week later. She mourned him for two years. She was under the doctor with depression. When she came out of it her personality had changed. She resented everyone else's happiness.'

There were tears in Winifred's eyes. 'She made herself very unpopular, I know. But that was because she was so unhappy herself.' She looked me straight in the eye. 'Do you know who killed her?'

I shook my head slowly, looking beyond her to Mrs Macrell, flushed with sherry, over by the mantelpiece.

Although she only lived three houses away along the track, I'd met Mrs Macrell about six months after we moved in. I'd put an ad in the local paper to sell my car and she'd phoned me. She wanted to buy it for her son. No, not the chimp, the other one.

I'd gone round to Mrs Macrell's house to deliver the car at nine in the morning. Mrs Macrell came to the door in a rumpled night dress. A thin stick of a woman in her early sixties, she had in one hand a small cigar, in the other a glass of red wine.

'Is this a bad time?' I said.

'Any time's a bad time,' she said, taking a swig of her wine. 'I'm a manic depressive.'

'That's nice,' I said, momentarily nonplussed. She looked at me. I stumbled on: 'Are you having a bad week?'

She sniffed. 'Bad year.'

We stood in her doorway as she haggled about the price

because I could only find one set of car keys. I promised I'd bring her the other set when I found it – I'm hopelessly untidy – and made good my escape. 'Would you like a glass of wine?' she called after me. I shouted back my thanks but declined the invitation. It was a bit early in the day, even for me.

Janet, my first wife, always used to say drink would be the death of me. If your cooking doesn't get me first, I used to snarl back. She was a vegetarian, so every meal was pulses or beans, pulses or beans. A dinner party at our house could be a hazardous affair. Our guests were discouraged from going anywhere near a naked flame for at least an hour after the main course.

Our attitude to drink – I drank, she didn't – was one of many areas of disagreement between us. But her death affected me more than I thought it would – I suppose because we had been together fifteen years. The Years of Struggle we used to call them. I used to call them. I was in genuine mourning when I met Ruth. I was fifty and here this beautiful brunette, eighteen years my junior, came into my life.

We got on well, even though we had little in common. She was an MBA and had the work ethic very badly. An ambitious East End girl, still trying to earn her father's approval. He was a scrap metal millionaire and very dominant in her life.

However, I soon discovered there were two Ruths. One was a tense driven senior executive, the other was a soft sentimental woman who loved nothing more than cuddling up in bed for hours on end. For years she had been struggling to merge the two.

This second Ruth was hopelessly impractical in other endearing ways. She was a living rebuttal to Pavlov's theory of conditioned response. No matter that she must have used a seat belt thousands of time, when she sat in the passenger seat of a car she never, ever remembered to put the seat belt on unprompted. At home she had been using my computer for four years now but still had to ask me how to print documents off.

Our first months in Sussex were blissful. Candle-lit dinners on the terrace, Chopin and Satie drifting through the French windows into the night. Walks at dusk through the fields, arm in arm.

It was only later that friction developed because of her gung-ho attitude to work. I have my own simple rules for life. They work for me. I sleep at night. But there was no way I could advise Ruth. She read California-speak self help manuals about excellence, being a complete person and getting in touch with the universe within but she scorned my advice as offering simplistic post-hippy placebos.

She was after all living in the real world. She commuted each day to London from Chiltington and some evenings, fraught from work, she drove home far too quickly in her Renault turbo to find me sitting with a bottle of wine in the garden after a creative day writing in the sunshine. She didn't always conceal her irritation.

We didn't go to Mr Deacon's funeral on the following Wednesday, though we sent a wreath. The day after the funeral Mrs Deacon turned up to deliver the newspapers in a gleaming new car, a shiny blue Japanese job. I tried to remember what colour the Fiat Panda had been. Surely it had been red?

'Have the police managed to find anything out about the motorist who knocked over poor Mr Deacon?' I said when she came to the door.

'Not a thing,' she sniffed, handing me the newspaper. She didn't seem overly concerned.

'New car?' I said politely. 'Nice colour.'

'Brand new, Mister Stewart, thanks. It's not all that's going to be new either. Mr Deacon was so mean he'd skin a flea and tan its hide. For twenty years he had me believing we were one step away from the bankruptcy court. When he died I found out how much he'd really got saved up in the building society. Now I intend to spend some of it.' She walked over to the car, calling back over her shoulder. 'And if he's watching from wherever he ended up, I hope it drives him mad, the miserable old sod.'

The Westwoods threw a drinks party that Sunday lunchtime to show off the magnificence of their view. Mrs Spring's death had given them a new lease of life – they looked ten years younger. Their house was one of those that made me want to take a bin bag and fill it with every junky knick-knack in sight so Ruth and I stayed out on the terrace watching the seagulls wheeling above the cliffs.

I got involved in the usual fatuous conversation with Mrs Westwood, who always felt she had to talk to me about literature. From the other end of the terrace she honked, in great excitement: 'Donald, do you think Shakespeare wrote the plays?'

'Frankly, Mrs Westwood, I don't give a flying fuck.' Well, no, I didn't say that, but I wanted to. I was cheesed off because we were stuck with David Parker, the blacksmith with artistic pretensions who lived at The Forge. He was a big man with powerful hands. He had one of those silly beards that don't have moustaches and in his black roll neck sweater he must have looked just the thing in 1959. Shame it was forty-odd years later.

He was married to Lucy, a sparky woman in her early fifties, who we always thought was so *together*. Yoga, pottery, herbal tea and *The Guardian*. Clearly, however, a panic had set in about an imagined lonely old age and she had married this oik. We saw them casually almost every week because of the regular mix-up over mail.

'We've got a letter for you,' Lucy said now, rummaging in her handbag and producing a square brown envelope.' It came about a week ago but I put it somewhere safe then couldn't find it. Sorry.'

Ruth took it from her outstretched hand, glanced at the handwriting on the envelope and quietly stuffed it into her own bag. I thought I saw her colour slightly.

As I was trying to extricate us from the Parkers, the Wing Commander bore down.

'Phone,' he said. 'Jonathan Macrell. He and that woman can't make it. Taken in by the police for questioning. Deacon's death. Maybe Spring's too. Police have the car. Paint samples. Looks bad. Allowed one telephone call. Used it to send apologies about drinks. Ass.'

When we got back to our house, Ruth, looking distracted, excused herself and went up to the bathroom, taking her handbag with her. When she eventually came back down, she avoided my eyes and went out into the garden. I found her bag upstairs. There was no sign of the letter Mrs Parker had handed to her.

I watched Ruth in the garden from our bedroom window. She looked like she was settling in for an afternoon's work. I made a phone call then went over to the local stables for my regular Sunday hack. It was a hobby I'd taken up when we first moved here. I used to do a lot of things then.

When I was made redundant – excuse, me when I was *downsized* – I sold the house in London and bought a cheaper one down here – that's to say, I *downshifted*. I got the minimum pay-off, might I add, so I lived on the profit from the house for a while. It didn't go far.

I couldn't get an advance on my book – first time author – so I borrowed money from Ruth's father to live on whilst I wrote it. He thought the loan was for an extension to the house. He could well afford it, but he set it against Ruth's eventual massive inheritance.

Ruth was very good about it, but the situation caused strain between us. After all, why do women go for older men if not to be taken care of, financially and emotionally? She didn't expect to be keeping me. I think she respected me less.

Maybe that's why the affair began. About three months before Mrs Spring's death, Ruth began coming home late. If I asked, she'd say she'd been working. If I said I'd phoned her and there had been no answer, she'd say her secretary had forgotten to switch the calls through when she left for the night.

A few times at home the phone rang on the answering machine but there was no message. We got lots of wrong numbers. The phone had rung at six thirty on the morning of Mrs Spring's death. Ruth had just been going out the door – she usually leaves for work about six but she was late that morning. She said the caller had hung up when she answered it.

The police let Jonathan go on Monday, although they still held his mother. The same day, Donald the cleaner delivered some hot news. He had his own key to the house, so as usual I had retreated to my study in advance of his arrival.

First he asked me if he could do the study and the other rooms upstairs the following morning as he was running late.

'Sure,' I said, pleased to postpone the inevitable monologues about Roger Moore. Even then, he wasn't quite ready to go.

'Crikey, Mr Stewart, a woman in Chiltington has died in suspicious circumstances,' he said, hovering in the study doorway. 'That makes three.'

My fingers stopped clacking on the keyboard of my computer. 'I'm sorry to hear that. How did she die?'

'Riding accident. Fell off her horse and broke her neck.'

'How ghastly,' I said, with feeling. Unpleasant memories stirred.

'You might have known her,' he said. 'Valerie James. She used to keep her horse at the stables you go to.'

I said nothing. He sniffed. 'How's your riding coming along?'

'Fine, thanks,' I said absently. I was thinking about my first wife, Janet. She had been a keen horsewoman. She used to ride in Richmond Park when we lived in Twickenham. Every Tuesday and Thursday, rain or shine. You could set your clock by her. She too had died in a riding accident. The coroner had concluded that her horse had refused a low jump, she had toppled over his head and broken her neck.

I had begun to learn to ride as a way of exorcising my first wife's death. I'd taken it up when we first moved down here, in what Ruth called my period of second infantilism. But then she didn't know about Janet and I didn't feel I could explain to her.

Ruth had been remarkably incurious about my life before her. She had never even asked how Janet had died. But then, if I'm honest, Ruth was always too self-absorbed to bother much about anyone else.

I picked her up from the station that evening. It was close, with black clouds massing and thunder growling ominously. We

were going to dinner with some friends in Chiltington. Ruth had
been acting oddly towards me since the Westwood drinks party
but tonight she seemed particularly subdued.

'Seat belt,' I said, as we waited at a set of lights. She reached
for the belt but didn't speak.

We drove home in silence. Ruth went straight upstairs for a
bath. When she came out of the bathroom, wearing only a towel,
she came into my study, dropped an envelope on the desk
without speaking and went to our bedroom.

It was the envelope Lucy Parker had given her at the
Westwood's drinks party. I'd been expecting it. I flipped it over,
lifted the flap and took out a second envelope. White, good
quality. I looked at the familiar handwriting on the front.

There was a card inside. I began to withdraw it then stopped. I
knew what it was. I dropped it back on the desk and went into
our bedroom. 'Do you want an explanation?' I said.

'There isn't time,' she said, fiddling with the zip of her dress.
'We've got to be at Tony and Ellen's by eight.' She brushed past
me. 'I just want you to know that I know.'

I guessed she wouldn't leave it at that. In the car, sitting stiffly,
she said:

'So where did you meet her?'

'Seat belt,' I said, glancing across. 'Look, I sent her a birthday
card, I admit that. But that doesn't mean anything. Certainly not
what you're thinking.'

'Don't demean us by denying anything,' she snapped at me.
'What about those wrong numbers, those abruptly ended phone
calls whenever I came into the room, those guilty looks? I've suspected for a long time. I pressed the redial button on the phone
once after you'd been having a whispered conversation. I got
through to a woman.'

I didn't say anything. I was thinking furiously.

'What I don't understand is why she sent your birthday card
back to *me*,' she went on. 'What did she hope to achieve? Did she
think I'd leave you because of her? Or was she being spiteful
because you had finished with her? Had you?'

She fumbled in her bag for a cigarette. Her occasional cigarettes were a habit that annoyed me, but now didn't seem the
time to make a fuss.

'Are you still seeing her?' she said, exhaling smoke.

OK, OK. Time to come clean. *I'd* been having an affair, not
Ruth. It didn't mean I didn't love Ruth. It just meant that I was
bored. Bored senseless.

Have you ever tried living in the country? Oh, it sounds wonderful when you're living in the city. And at first it is. Every

daybreak is magical as you wake to the birds singing in the trees, the sun burning the mist away over the sea.

You look forward to the long peaceful day stretching ahead of you. But God, do those days *stretch*. They are interminable. After a month I was praying for the pitch black nights to fall. Some mornings, at the thought of another slow, empty day ahead I wanted to strangle those bloody birds for being so cheerful.

I was a city person. Always would be. I loved the buzz of city life, loved working on a daily paper, always up against the clock. When those bastards sacked me and I had to move down here, it was as if they passed a life sentence on me. So I started an affair. And just as easily ended it.

'No,' I said truthfully. 'I'm not seeing her.'

The dinner went well, considering Ruth drank too much, laughed too loudly and was too nervously exuberant – but then she was always like that. I drank only mineral water. I observed Ruth distantly. I was sorry that I had hurt her but I was not distraught. I didn't care enough about her.

Don't get me wrong. I loved her – in my way. But my way isn't other people's way. There's always been a coldness in me, a chilly core. I can be gregarious, I can be concerned. But it's all pretence. At a fundamental level, I just don't care.

Tony had a friend who was a policeman. He had the latest news about the murder inquiry. The paint found on Mr Deacon's bike matched samples taken from Mrs Macrell's car. She was going to be charged.

As we were leaving, Ellen said: 'You know, we had our own gory death here last Sunday.'

'I heard,' I said, guiding Ruth towards the car.

'A woman broke her neck falling off her horse,' Ellen continued. 'You might have known her, Donald, she used your stables.'

'I heard,' I repeated. I opened the passenger door and helped Ruth get in.

'Valerie James,' Ellen said as I hurried round to the driver's side and opened that door.

'Who—?' Ruth said, leaning across towards Helen, as I closed the driver's door behind me.

'I heard,' I said as I turned on the engine and the lights, put the car into gear and set it in motion.

Ruth was quiet for the first hundred yards. Then she laughed and said: 'Not the Valerie James who had a birthday recently. Not the Valerie James who was my husband's mistress. The one he said he wasn't seeing any more.'

I automatically glanced down. She hadn't put her seat belt on. I started to say something but she continued talking drunkenly.

'No wonder you're not seeing her.' She stifled a laugh. 'It would be a bit difficult. And probably illegal.'

It remained an oppressive evening. Storm clouds were massed in the sky above us. I had opened the sun roof and now drove slowly through the winding lanes, pleased to feel the breeze on my face.

'Did you love her very much?'

'Don't be absurd,' I said, after a moment.

Ruth leaned her head against the side window and tucked her feet beneath her. Without looking at me she said dully: 'Janet rode, didn't she?'

Ever since Ruth dropped the card on my desk, I'd been trying to work out what to do. Ruth was huddled on her seat, gazing blankly at the scenery rushing by. I looked fondly at her. How I loved her, in my way.

And how little that meant. I signalled a left turn.

'That damned birthday card!' I said. 'Everything followed from the fact that the postman doesn't always lock the post-box properly. I thought I was the only one who knew this. But Mrs Spring knew it too. She regularly stole letters from the post-box to discover her neighbour's secrets. That must be how she got something on Edith Macrell, to make her destroy the chimp. Anyway, Mrs Spring stole my birthday card to Valerie, ten minutes after I'd put it in the box.'

Ruth stirred in her seat. I could tell she was looking at the side of my face.

'Mrs Spring?' she said cautiously. I glanced at her. Suddenly she looked sober.

'Yes, Mrs Spring, darling. Do keep up. When Valerie complained she hadn't got a card from me I thought it had been lost in the post. Frankly, I was relieved – never put anything in writing if you want to avoid getting caught. Then, at the summer fete, whilst I was on the bookstall selling twenty-year-old *Readers Digests* to an old buffer from Elam, Mrs Spring flourished it in front of me.'

Ruth began to breathe shallowly but said nothing. I think she was beginning to feel frightened. I took the next right turn. 'She was a nasty old woman, you know. *She* sent it to you, not Valerie James. Sent it out of sheer malice. I couldn't have that. I love you. I don't want to lose you.'

A car passed on the other side of the road, its headlights dazzling. I looked away. 'Or your inheritance.'

I took the third exit off a small roundabout on to Century Lane. I slowed down and reached up to close the sun roof. It had started to rain.

'So you…' Ruth's voice trailed off.

I smiled. 'You can say it, darling. I won't be upset. Yes, I killed Mrs Spring.'

Ruth laughed. Rather harshly, I thought. 'You won't be upset. Now I've heard everything.'

I smiled again.

'No you haven't. You haven't heard the half of it.'

The rain fell in earnest now, hammering on the roof and windscreen. 'Valerie phoned me that morning to warn me. Remember the six thirty call? She'd had a call from Mrs Spring the night before. Mrs Spring was gloating. She'd just posted Valerie's card to you.

'I went round to the post box to retrieve it before the postman arrived but the post-box was locked. So I went to see Mrs Spring as she was about to go for her swim. If I'd known I was going to spend a fruitless week trying to intercept the bloody card maybe I wouldn't have bothered.'

Ruth was looking at the road ahead again. She was wringing her hands. She still hadn't put her seat belt on but now didn't seem the time to say.

'I didn't necessarily mean to do it, darling. But she was so awful to me. I thought she was going to start shouting about it. And then the Westwoods would hear. I tried to stop her shouting. That's all I was trying to do.'

'And on Sunday when you went for a drive – you went to see your mistress?' Ruth whispered. 'Why did you kill her? Had she threatened to tell me about your affair?'

'Not exactly, no,' I said. The rain was falling so hard, the wipers could scarcely cope. I slowed down to twenty. 'Some storm, eh? Valerie thought Mrs Spring's death was fishy and she threatened to go to the police unless I left you for her. Well, I ask you, have you met her? Oh, no, of course you haven't. Well she's attractive enough but she's also a crashing bore about horses. Always rambling on about gymkhanas. I swear I usually had sex with her to shut her up.' I glanced at Ruth. 'Sorry darling, that was insensitive of me.'

'But why did Edith Macrell kill Mr Deacon if she hadn't killed Mrs Spring?' Ruth looked at me. I heard her gasp of realisation and felt her shrink against the passenger door. '*You* did it.'

'Clever girl,' I said.

'But how? Oh God – you found the other set of keys to the Golf you'd sold Mrs Macrell and drove into Mr Deacon in that.'

We'd reached a straight stretch of road. I steadied myself and put my foot on the accelerator. The windscreen wipers pumped rapidly.

'I regretted Mr Deacon. But when I went down the next day to intercept the postman and retrieve that damned birthday card he told me he'd seen me the previous day. I couldn't take the risk, you see. I thought I'd have to pop Mrs Macrell too, just in case, until I had the idea of using her car to kill him.'

'You killed three people so you wouldn't lose the chance to get at my father's money,' Ruth said flatly.

'Well, your father's money is one of your most attractive features,' I said cheerfully. 'But I hear what you're saying. Thing is, it gets easier every time. And the irony is, I'm not going to get the dosh after all.'

It took a few moments for that to sink in, then Ruth grappled with the handle to the passenger door.

'Child proof lock, love.'

She looked at me fiercely then subsided into her seat. 'How did your first wife die?'

'I know, I know. I've no imagination. Riding accident again. But it's terribly easy to mock up you see. Much better than other methods. I felt such a fool when the police spotted the clumsy way I killed Mrs Spring. I hoped they'd think she'd got tangled in the filtration pipe.'

The rain showed no sign of slackening. The lane began to wind again. We were approaching the accident black spot.

With Ruth dead there would be no way to link me to the other deaths because nobody else knew about my affair with Valerie. Nobody alive anyway.

It was going to be dicey for me when we came off the road and hit a tree but for the sake of verisimilitude I was prepared to spend a week or so in hospital. I figured that at thirty miles an hour I would easily survive the impact, given the driver's airbag and my seatbelt. Ruth, sadly, wouldn't be so lucky.

It was a shame I wouldn't be able to get at Ruth's inheritance. But at least there was the insurance money. I'd test negative for alcohol in my blood so the insurance company would have to pay up. And I'd learned from the meagre pay-off I'd got after my first wife's death not to under-insure my second one.

I slowed, spun the wheel and took the car off the road. I was trying to think of a headline. *Author Writes Second Wife Off*, perhaps. Time moved very slowly. I heard Ruth scream. I think I felt her hand clutch my arm. I braced myself as the thick trunk of a tree rushed towards us. A split second before we hit I thought of Donald the cleaner. Coming back to do my office in the morning. Nosing around. Reading the birthday card for Valerie James lying open on my desk.

Denise Mina

Notes

The story *Helena And The Babies* came about as the result of my first job, as an auxiliary nurse in private nursing homes in Kent. It was fascinating work. The residents, predominantly women, were often extraordinary, women who ran their own businesses, worked in the diplomatic service, women who fought and won the war. One resident's photographs showed herself and Nellie Melba sipping long drinks on a shaded porch. Another had been the most sought after furrier in London for two decades. Yet another had worked in the diplomatic service and lived in Hong Kong for thirty years. Regardless of their mental state they were often treated like children, as unreliable and simple minded, consigned to spend all day sitting in orthopedic chairs being coaxed to eat their greens with the promise of spotted dick for afters and a lovely lie down. The saddest aspect of it was that so few of them had the energy or wherewithal to resist infantailsation.

The story is also intended as a twist on the traditional country house mystery. Such stories require a backdrop grand enough to allow all of the characters to remain in one house while we meet them, a murder takes place and everyone wonders about it and, finally, the murderer is discovered. The traditional explanation for such grandeur is inheritance but, in a changing age, such stories often struggle to incorporate celebrity and stock broking, both of which are fictional tags for limitless funding. This shift has fundamentally altered both the form and the place of the house in the country house mystery.

Helena And The Babies is an attempt to address both of these strands.

Helena And The Babies

by Denise Mina

Auxiliary Nurse Bentham unpacked Helena Lawrence's suitcase. They were fine clothes, silk slips in peaches and pinks, cotton blouses and linen suits. Bentham stroked the beautiful clothes as she stacked them on the bed.

'I'm sure she'll like it here.' Allison Tombery was talking to Matron, ignoring Bentham. 'She chose this very bed for Grandma.'

'This must have been a very hard time for you,' said Matron gently, 'you have my sympathy.'

'Oh, it has,' said Allison tearfully. 'First Grandma dying and now Mum getting bad so suddenly. At least she's somewhere familiar.'

The room was at the very top of the big house, called 'The Babies' Room' by the nurses because the room had been a nursery and the occupants were all confused and doubly incontinent. The ceiling was a low arch, giving the large room a cosy, enclosed feel. It was well lit with broad windows on two opposing walls. The tops of trees filled the windows, keeping the room cool in summer. There were six beds in the room. At the end of each sat an old woman in a comfy, urine-proof armchair. Creeping blindness and wild confusion meant that, despite months of intimate proximity, the Babies were hardly aware of one another.

Helena's own mother had spent three months sitting at the end of this bed by the window. Helena adored her mother and had chosen the home and the bed carefully. The summer light had warmed dear Elizabeth's feet at tea time, just as it did Helena's now. The tapping of the tree branches against the window caught Elizabeth's attention, as it did Helena's now. Elizabeth had died within three months of moving in. It was often difficult, said Matron, for many older residents to make the transition from home. And now, only one month after her death, Elizabeth's only daughter was here to take her place.

Allison bent down to the wheelchair and took her mother's hand. The bones and veins and sinews were visible through the paper thin skin. Helena looked vacantly upwards, her mouth hanging open, aware that her hand was being touched but not knowing by whom, or why.

'Mum,' said Allison, 'it's me, Mum.'

Matron noticed the likeness between them, from their slight physiques to their long, angular faces and coifed white hair. Matron was secretly surprised that Elizabeth had declined so quickly. Elizabeth was a robust little woman with a strong heart and a will of iron but she slipped away over a cold winter weekend and died of a sudden heart attack.

A young nurse bustled into the room. She was short and had a punky black hairdo. She blushed when she saw Matron with a visitor. 'Sorry, Matron. I'm... I'm here to do the afternoon teas.'

'Very good, Nurse. Nurse Thomas, this is Helena Lawrence and this is her daughter, Mrs Tombery.' Matron turned to Allison, 'This is one of our newest nurses. Nurse Thomas looks young but she has a lot of experience, don't you, Nurse?'

Nurse Thomas smiled shyly as she moved quickly around the room, clearing the tables for the tea trays.

'Where did you work before this?' asked Allison.

'Oadby Hospital,' said Nurse Thomas quietly.

'Well, I hope you're happy here,' said Allison kindly, 'and I hope you'll take good care of my mum.'

Allison looked at her mother and took her hand again. Sour, hot urine flooded Helena's wheelchair and cascaded on to the linoleum floor, splashing on Allison Tombery's linen dress. She dropped her mother's hand and leapt back from the splattering spill, frantically brushing the piss off her dress. She looked at her wet hand and laughed weakly.

'I'm so sorry. It smells terrible.'

'It smells like that because Helena's slightly dehydrated, Mrs Tombery.'

'I don't understand, she used to be such so fastidious.'

'Incontinence is never deliberate.' Matron cupped Allison's elbow. 'You mustn't feel ashamed. Let's go downstairs and finish the paper work. Nurse Bentham will help your mother get cleaned up.'

Matron lead her from the room, nodding to Bentham to attend to Helena.

'Thomas,' said Bentham when they were out of the room, 'take your break before the afternoon tea.'

Thomas cleared the final table and went upstairs to the locker room to get her cigarettes. Bentham was left alone in the room.

She dropped the clothes on the bed and leaned over Helena, stroking her face slowly with the back of her hand.

'I knew your mother,' she said.

Thomas was hiding in the staff toilet, smoking a cigarette. She couldn't smoke in the staff room. The other nurses stopped talking when she went in there, and sat looking at her, waiting for her to leave. They knew about the Annex, they knew about the alleged beatings, they knew nothing was proved and they knew that Thomas had left the Annex suddenly. Thomas couldn't take it any more, that was why she left. She found herself unemployable, everywhere she applied to knew about the Annex. But she was desperate to remain in nursing, so desperate that she offered to work at Roseybank on a voluntary basis for three months. If it went well she would be offered a job. Otherwise she could leave with new references. She was spending all her savings on bus fares.

The staff didn't want to work with her because she was working for free, because she had come from the Annex. She spent the first month working as a floater between the floors, fetching and carrying from the kitchen, making the beds and toileting when the other shifts were running slow. She had been there for a month when Bentham actually requested her as a shift partner for the Babies' Room. Thomas was amazed, no one else wanted to be associated with her. Bentham was miserable to work with and she didn't trust Thomas at first. She wouldn't let her do any patient care, not even the bed baths. She made Thomas do all the heavy work, the bed changes and the laundry. But after the first week Bentham came around: every afternoon, without fail, she left Thomas alone for an hour to manage the afternoon teas. Thomas was grateful for the trusting gesture. It sent a message to the others.

So Thomas hung on. In less than two months she'd be out of there, she'd have references and she wouldn't need to mention the Annex on her CV or get references from Staff Nurse Evans. She heard the other nurses talking about Bentham. They said she was a misery because she'd worked the Babies' Room for so long and so many of them died.

The urine was seeping into Helena's legs, burning her. Without a word, Bentham slipped both her arms under Helena's and lifted her up, perching her on unsteady legs. They staggered slightly, locked together like marathon dancers, while Bentham reached behind and tugged down Helena's sodden pants.

'Dirty, dirty,' murmured Bentham. 'Dirty, dirty bitch.'

She lifted Helena's dress, baring her backside to the world. A hot flannel hit Helena's back and the nurse scrubbed hard, washing, drying and dusting her. She pulled clean incontinence pads on to the chair and sat Helena down, pulling her wet dress up at the back, sitting a crocheted blanket on her lap to hide her naked legs.

'Don't be a dirty bitch like your mother,' Bentham's face was inches from Helena's. 'D'you understand? I looked after your mother. She was a dirty bitch as well.'

She reached down below the arm of the chair and pinched the skin on Helena's boney hip, twisting it between her fingers. Helena jumped, not knowing what she was feeling but feeling something very unpleasant.

'Yes,' said Bentham softly, 'you understand that, don't you?' Bentham walked over to a fat woman sitting directly across from Helena.

'This is Mrs Hove. And this is what happens to dirty old bitches.'

She slid her fingers deep into Mrs Hove's white hair. It was as soft as duckling fluff. Bentham tightened her fingers into a fist and tugged, jerking Mrs Hove's head back. Mrs Hove squealed with surprise and swung her arm around, trying to knock off her assailant. It was the wrong arm on the wrong side and Nurse Bentham sniggered.

The door opened. Matron came in followed by Allison Tombery. They saw Bentham standing by Mrs Hove, holding her hair, and stopped dead.

'What are you doing there, Nurse?'

'I was going to set Mrs Hove's hair this afternoon, Matron.' Nurse Bentham stroked Mrs Hove's hair. 'But it doesn't seem to need a wash.'

'Good, well, perhaps we could leave it until tomorrow.'

Helena was staring at the crocheted blanket, picking at it with her arthritic fingers.

Allison Tombery came to visit on the second day, fussing around her mother and trying to feed her lunch. Helena wouldn't take anything. Allison smiled at Bentham. 'Is she eating, Nurse?'

Bentham walked over and looked at Helena. 'She isn't eating much but she's drinking a lot, aren't you, ducks?'

'Are you all right, Mum?'

Helena smiled to the air, showing off her ragged yellow teeth. The summer light played softly through the trees outside the window and Helena lifted her hands, reaching out to the thing she was smiling at. The backs of her hands were peppered in little purple bruises, like splashes of ink on tissue paper.

'What happened here?' Allison asked Bentham.

Bentham held Helena's fingers and looked sad. 'She banged them on the cot sides last night. We tried putting padding on the bars but she pulled it off.'

'Oh dear, poor thing. What have you done to yourself?'

Helena looked Allison full in the face and smiled, drawling a strangled: 'Yaaaaannng.'

Allison sat back and looked despondent.

'She wasn't always like this. She was a journalist, you know. The first woman ever to edit the *Leicester Mercury*.'

'We have many professional ladies in this room,' said Bentham. 'Mrs Hove over here was a furrier. Mrs Clutterbuck over there,' she pointed to a skeletal woman slumped in an arm-chair in the corner, 'was a GP.'

'Illness is a great leveller, isn't it?'

'Yes,' said Bentham. 'It is.'

Allison Tombery didn't come on the third day. Or the fourth. Or the fifth. She phoned on the sixth to say she was going on holiday and wouldn't be in for a week, could Matron phone this number in Portugal if her mother's condition changed?

Helena Lawrence had been in the Babies' Room for a week. Thomas was in a good mood. She had counted the days and had exactly one and a half months left before she could leave. She wanted to leave Roseybank, the staff hated her. One and half months and the Annex would be behind her, Staff Nurse Evans couldn't touch her.

It was early morning. Thomas was making the beds up while Bentham washed and changed the babies. They were waiting for the breakfasts to come up from the kitchen. It was quiet in the room, the babies were gurning contentedly as warm water sloshed in the basins and fresh sheets flapped over beds. Quite suddenly a shriek erupted in the far corner. Thomas dropped the clean sheet and spun around.

Bentham was standing over little Mrs Clutterbuck, holding her arm. Mrs Clutterbuck was in so much pain that she couldn't speak, her eyes stared blankly, her mouth opened and moved, as if she was trying to speak.

Bentham turned slowly. 'Go back to your work, Thomas.'

Horrified, Thomas walked over to Mrs Clutterbuck. 'What on earth are you doing to her?'

'Go back to your work.'

Mrs Clutterbuck's arm was wrong, it was hanging wrong, at an absurd angle.

'You've dislocated her shoulder, Bentham, how the hell did you do that?'

Bentham let go of Clutterbuck's arm carelessly, it fell into her lap at a crazy angle. Mrs Clutterbuck closed her eyes, tilted her head back and let out a high, shrill whinny. Bentham didn't seem to have heard it.

'Go back to your work. Mrs Clutterbuck fell over.'

'How could she fall over?' Thomas snorted indignantly. 'She's sitting down!'

Bentham didn't look away from Thomas's face as she yanked Mrs Clutterbuck out of the chair by her dislocated arm and dropped her on the floor. Mrs Clutterbuck landed on her good shoulder and panted with pain. She stopped panting abruptly, stared under the bed and gurgled. Her good arm crept up to her chest, her little hand contracted like a dying flower. Expressionless, Bentham watched her and looked up.

'She's fallen over now,' said Bentham slowly, 'you better go and get Matron.'

Thomas staggered backwards out of the room, running when she got to the stairs. She came back with Matron.

'What has happened?' demanded Matron.

Thomas didn't know what to say. 'She's on the floor,' she said stupidly.

Matron saw Bentham at the far end of the room, crouching next to the body by the bed. She moved Bentham aside and took Mrs Clutterbuck's pulse. Thomas looked at Bentham. She didn't seem to understand what had happened. She had *murdered* Mrs Clutterbuck.

Matron stood up slowly. 'How did she manage to fall?' Her voice was hoarse. 'She couldn't stand up.'

Thomas paused, waiting for Bentham to own up. She didn't. 'I was making the beds,' explained Thomas finally, 'and Nurse Bentham was washing her—'

'No,' interrupted Bentham, turning to Matron. '*I* was making the beds. *She* was washing her and then I heard a terrible noise. I came over and she was lying on the floor.'

Thomas staggered back. 'That's a lie, Matron! *I* was making—'

'First,' Matron held up her hands, 'let's get her into bed and pull the screens.'

Matron pulled the screens around the bed as Thomas and Bentham lifted Mrs Clutterbuck's body into the bed, her dislocated shoulder hanging wildly at the side.

'You bloody idiots,' muttered Matron. 'Do you two have any idea how serious this is? She's had a heart attack. Her children and her grandchildren are doctors, they gave her a medical a month ago and there was nothing wrong with her.' She rubbed her eyes hard and sighed. 'Thomas, undress Mrs Clutterbuck and lay her out. Bentham, you come with me.'

Matron stormed out with Bentham at her heels, leaving Thomas alone with Mrs Clutterbuck. She only had a month and a half left. If they pressed charges Thomas would lose more than her references. Mrs Clutterbuck lay on the bed, tiny and helpless, her gumsy mouth hanging open like a baby bird waiting to be fed.

Gently, Thomas rolled the nightie over Mrs Clutterbuck's legs and up to her waist. She slid her left hand under the small of her back and lifted her slightly, pulling the nightie up with the other hand. She stopped. Mrs Clutterbuck's skinny legs were covered in bruises, bruises shaped like four fingered slaps, bruises like knuckle dents and small cuts like compass scratches. Losing her breath, Thomas pulled the rest of the nightie off Mrs Clutterbuck's broken body and stood back. Mrs Clutterbuck's sagging tummy was worse. A large, deliberate cross was cut into the blackened skin. Mrs Clutterbuck's chest heaved and she burped a stinking black liquid, it splattered out over her lips. It smelt like liver. Thomas blinked and it came to her: Bentham had asked for her, knowing about the Annex, knowing that Thomas would be blamed when Bentham was found out. She left Thomas alone to do the tea so she would have had time to do this. She darted across the room to Mrs Hove. Mrs Hove looked up at her, smiling kindly.

'Mrs Hove,' she whispered. 'Mrs Hove, let me see you.'

Thomas took the travel blanket from Mrs Hove's lap and lifted the dress. Above the knees, around her groin, rolls of flesh were covered in red and black welts.

'Oh, Mrs Hove.' Thomas took her face in her hands. 'Poor dear, Mrs Hove.'

Thomas went over to Helena, who was picking at an invisible thing on the table. 'Can I see...?'

She lifted the dress. Helena's hips and thighs were red and yellow. Matron came through the door, looking stern, with Bentham in tow. They stopped and stared at Thomas.

'What are you doing?' demanded Matron.

'I was looking—'

'You're in a lot of trouble. Get back behind that screen. Small wonder you're crying.'

Thomas hadn't noticed that she was crying.

Bentham pulled the screen back and gasped dramatically, 'Oh. My. God,' she said and slapped her hand over her mouth.

Matron looked at Mrs Clutterbuck. She stepped forward,

gently closing Mrs Clutterbuck's eyes. She paused. 'You evil little shit,' she said.

'It wasn't me, it was her,' gabbled Thomas, 'she wouldn't even let me wash them, Matron, I swear to you, Matron, I swear on my life!'

'How dare you…' Matron was beside herself, 'with *your* history…'

'I didn't *touch* anyone in the Annex. I told on the others and they couldn't prove anything and I had to leave because they made my life hell. Matron, I told, that's why I had to leave.'

Matron wasn't listening. She was staring at Mrs Clutterbuck, 'How could anyone… Unbelievable.'

She pulled the sheet over Mrs Clutterbuck's face. Bentham patted Matron's shoulder and Matron acknowledged the kindness with a slow nod.

'I'm going to phone the police,' she said. 'Nurse Bentham, bring Thomas to the office.' Bentham wrapped her big hand around Thomas's upper arm, digging her nails into the skin, as venomous as a playground bully, sneering at her when Matron wasn't looking. She dragged Thomas down the short flight of stairs to the small office.

Matron picked up the phone and dialled.

Matron couldn't bear to stay in the same room as Thomas. She was downstairs, waiting by the door for the police. Thomas was looked out of the window trying to think. She heard Bentham hissing at her, 'You're the next Beverley Allit.'

Thomas looked at her. 'You *are* fucking Beverley Allit.'

'They'll hate you, the police, when they find out what you've done.'

'*I* haven't done anything, Bentham. They'll find out it was you when they measure the bruises. My hands are too small to make bruises that big.' She could see Bentham glancing at her hands and thinking about it. 'You're a mental case, Bentham.'

Bentham slid towards the door and took hold of the handle. She turned and grinned. 'Be a shame if you got away, wouldn't it?' She opened the door, looked outside and crept out of the room.

Thomas could run. If she got down stairs she could get out of the kitchen door. Over the back wall. She stood up suddenly but stopped at the office door. If she left they'd think she was guilty. Bentham would never get caught. She sat back down. That's what Bentham wanted, that's why she left her alone. She'd be standing in the kitchen, waiting to catch her and make herself a hero. Thomas looked out of the window. The fire escape. Thomas leapt to her feet. There were fire exits all over the house, Bentham couldn't cover them all. She was standing behind the door, sweating and tremorous, wondering which exit to take, when the door opened. Matron was there with two policemen. Her face was very red. She raised her hand and slapped Thomas across the face as hard as she could.

'What,' screamed Matron, 'have you done with Helena Lawrence?'

Beyond the door, Matron was ticking Bentham off for leaving Thomas alone and the nurses were gathering, quizzing each other and expressing dismay. The sun shone in through the office window, yellowing one of the policemen's trousers. He fumbled in his pocket and leaned across the desk. 'Cigarette, Miss?'

Thomas took one and the policeman lit it for her.

'We know you can't have taken her far,' said the policeman, 'you were only left alone for three or four minutes.'

'I stayed in here,' said Thomas, knowing they wouldn't believe her, knowing they would have checked with Staff Nurse Evans at the Annex and knowing Evans would relish the chance to put her in it. 'You want to talk to Bentham, not me.'

The policeman sighed, 'You know, in ten minutes we'll have a full team of officers here and we'll find her anyway. You might as well tell us.'

'I don't know where she is. Ask Bentham.'

'It'll look better for you if you do tell us.'

'I don't know where she is, I swear.'

He sat back in his chair and looked out of the window. 'What happened at the Annex, Sarah?'

'You mean you haven't already phoned them? Don't listen to Staff Nurse Evans, speak to someone in admin.'

'I'd rather *you* told me.'

Thomas slumped back in her chair. It sounded ridiculous. 'I reported senior members of staff for hitting the patients. The inquiry couldn't prove anything and I was hounded out of my job.'

'You didn't hit them yourself?'

'No.'

'Why didn't you tell Matron that when you came for the job here?'

She shook her head, 'It's harder to get a job as a whistle blower than as an abuser.'

The policemen didn't believe her.

'If you were management,' she said, 'would you give a job to someone who snitched on their last boss?'

'Yes,' said the policeman, without pausing to think, 'yes I would. Where is Helena? Is she in a cupboard somewhere?'

They didn't believe her. The inquiry didn't believe her and Matron didn't believe her and the police didn't believe her. Thomas couldn't even think of any words to say. 'Can I have another fag, please?'

'Did you kill her, Sarah?'

'I know—'

The policeman cut her off with a raised hand. He cocked his head and listened as a small army jogging noisily up the stairs.

'You've nearly missed your chance, Miss, d' you want to tell me now?'

The army arrived outside the door and Matron squealed. A silence fell over nurses. The policemen in the office looked at each other. The chatty one stood up and opened the door a crack, peering out into the hall. Thomas could see Matron's back. She was standing with her arms out at the side, frozen, not knowing what to do. The door swung open revealing four tall uniformed policemen standing around Bentham. Two of them were holding her by the arms while another recited a warning about rights. Bentham was frozen just like Matron. They were staring at something on the stairs.

'You're on holiday,' said Bentham.

Allison Tombery slid into view and smiled as Helena Lawrence stepped into the doorway. She was still dressed in her nightie, but was standing tall, wearing incongruous court shoes with a low heel.

'And what,' said Helen, quite clearly and distinctly, 'did you do to my mother?'

Paul Johnston

Notes

People often ask me why I write crime fiction. The question usually conceals the following sub-text – why are you wasting your time on mass-market rubbish when you could be working on the great political/social/philosophical/psychological etcetera novel? Here, in no particular order, are some of the reasons:

1) Crime fiction is not a ghetto. All narratives contain crime of some sort – so I am writing the great etcetera novel after all.

2) Crime fiction gives the writer the opportunity to abuse the political and social establishment without fear of reprisal. (Yeah! The ultimate power without responsibility.)

3) Large numbers of people enjoy crime books.

4) Large numbers of people buy crime books.

5) Some of the most notable writers of the twentieth century have given us crime stories – Hemingway, Faulkner, Chandler, Hammett, Highsmith, Ellroy. Too many Americans? All right, go back a few years to Conan Doyle, Stevenson and Wilkie Collins. Then highlight the greatest novelist of all time, Charles Dickens – there are dozens of academic studies devoted to his abiding interest in crime. (Shame about Inspector Bucket's name though.)

6) Crime stories provide insights into the nature of knowledge and the extent to which you can trust the evidence of your senses. They also examine the roles of causality, logic, time and the imagination. (End of pretentious philosophical interlude.)

7) Human behaviour is inherently ludicrous. Crime fiction is particularly well placed to point this out. (Article of faith number one – take the piss relentlessly.)

Enough reasons?

Oh, in case you were wondering, 'Crime Fest' is *not* autobiographical. Trust me on that. I make things up for a living.

Crime Fest

by Paul Johnston

Parker's standing at the entrance to the venue. The rain's dripping off the trees on to his number-one-clippered head and he isn't happy.

'Come on, Shirley, we'll be late,' says a woman with an upper-class accent.

Parker steps out the way to let the blue-rinses past then makes up his mind. The sharpeners he had in the pub wouldn't need topping up for an hour or so. Might as well take cover from the poxy Scottish weather and have a laugh.

'Yes, sir?' The guy at the till is spotty and keen. 'How can I help?'

Parker looks at the programme he found on the bar. The rain's almost turned them into pulp. 'This Crime Fest event, any tickets left?'

Spotted Dick gives his lip a chew. 'I'll just check for you, sir. He's very popular, you know.'

'Oh yeah?' Parker's never heard of the author who's doing the reading. Parker reads *The Sun* and that's about it.

'Ah, you're in luck.' The dick's in heaven. 'I can give you the very last seat.'

Parker looks at him. 'Give me it?' he asks slowly.

Double-take from the ticketseller. 'I beg your pardon? Oh, I see.' He laughs. 'I mean sell you it, of course. That'll be six pounds, please.'

'Six quid?' Parker gives him the eye. 'It had better be good.'

'He's the best, sir, take my word for it. I've read all his books.' Dick takes Parker's tenner and hands over ticket and change. 'Enjoy,' he says with a smarmy grin.

Parker shakes his head and sets off towards a tent. A large banner draped over it tells him the festival's been sponsored by a beer company, but there doesn't seem to be any of their product about. A girl in a blue sweatshirt points to the only vacant seat in the house – white plastic, far end of a row, right behind a thick pole.

'Six quid?' Parker says under his breath. 'They're pulling my plonker.' He pushes past women in flash coats and men in suits and ties. Christ, there must be a couple of hundred of the buggers. In the bright stage lights he can see steam rising from their damp clothes. Makes him think of the Turkish bath down Bethnal Green Road. Wishes he was there with the boys.

A bloke in a red tartan shirt gets up and starts talking into the microphone. 'Ladies and gentleman, I'm delighted to welcome you to tonight's event in the Crime Fest series. I'm sure I don't need to introduce our star guest to you.'

Parker squints round the pole and clocks a weedy-looking specimen in a leather jacket that's at least two sizes too big for him. Steel-rimmed glasses and a moustache that's a total waste of space. He smiles at the audience and they all start clapping. Jesus, some of them are even cheering.

The MC is over the moon with the crowd's performance. 'This writer's novels have won numerous awards,' he says. 'A Hollywood film of the latest in in preproduction.' Pause for applause. 'And no less an authority than the Prime Minister admits to reading them avidly.' Even more clapping.

Parker doesn't reckon that's much of a vote of confidence but what does he know? Then he notices the girlie in the sweatshirt going up to the author and handing him a bottle of the sponsor's lager. That makes him thirsty. Jealous too.

The tit in tartan hasn't finished yet: 'And so, ladies and gentlemen, it's my enormous privilege to ask the country's leading crime writer to read from his forthcoming work, *Blood on the Pages, Blood on the Wall*. I'm sure you'll give him a rousing Caledonian welcome.'

Everyone else is clapping and cheering, but Parker's got his thick-fingered hands spread over his heavy thighs. He's thinking about the blood he splattered on the wall in Deptford a few days ago. There was a fuck of a lot of it. That's the way it goes with a sawn-off. It wasn't just the red stuff though. He saw lumps of the Dutchman's brains on the bricks round the back of the warehouse too. And hair, not that you could tell it was blond any more. And bone. That ought to stop any other fucker putting the squeeze on Big Tel's operation.

Four Eyes with the eyebrow on his upper lip and the bottle of lager has started reading. He's got his papers on a raised thing like the vicar spouted from when Parker was a kid – he's trying to remember what they're called but he has to give up. His old dear used to take him with her to the church in Bow every

Sunday. He can't remember her face either, hasn't visited her in the old folks' home for donkey's years.

He has a go at listening to the author. Has a big problem working out what he's on about. Some bollocks about a bloke who spends most of his time at a typewriter. And there's a bird who's got her nose seriously out of joint. She seems to be after the bloke. There are a lot of words that Parker hasn't heard before, but the gist of it's that the bird wants to stop him writing whatever he's writing. So what does she do? She puts a contract out on him.

Parker bursts out laughing. That makes the writer break off and peer shortsightedly into the audience. Looks like he didn't mean to be funny.

'Do you mind?' The old bloke in the seat next to Parker is staring at him like he's just gobbed in his lady wife's face. He's wearing a light brown jacket made out of some hairy cloth and he's got dirty yellow teeth. Colonel Mustard.

'Yeah, I do actually,' Parker replies, staring into the old bugger's crusty eyes. Then he remembers that Tel sent him to this shithole of a city to keep his head down for a bit. So he lays off the colonel and tries listening again.

But all that does is make Parker lose his rag even more. Christ almighty, what is the tosser on about? People putting contracts out on writers? What kind of bollocks is that? Dealers who nick the supply, yeah, Parker can see them being targets. Or scumbags who grass the big man up to the rozzers. But writers? You can leave them right out. Who gives a shit about wankers who tell lies for a living?

The reading continues on but Parker's ears are giving it the body swerve. He's wondering when Tel will let him go back down to the smoke. Tracey'll be thinking he's giving her the runaround again. Christ, she's probably shagging that arsehole Colin by now. Parker knows for sure no one saw him at the warehouse. Only that pillock from Amsterdam and he wasn't going to be telling tales. Blood on the wall.

Parker tunes back into the reading. He hears something hot. The writer's got to the big scene, he's talking about a fight. The bint's hitman has crept up on the guy at the typewriter. And what's he brought to do the job? A fucking fruit knife.

Parker just manages to swallow his laughter. Colonel Mustard next door's giving him another heavy look. But the old geezer gets away with it. Parker behaves. Big Tel said no drawing attention to yourself. Or else.

But it's not that straightforward. Parker feels the blood begin to rise in his veins, it's boiling hot like it is before he goes out on a job. The dickhead with the nun's moustache and the hard man glasses is really getting to him. Film in Hollywood, books earning a fortune, people queuing up to hear him rabbit – and what about? Parker's business, that's what. How come a baby-faced writer knows anything about the business? He's got a nerve, making a mint out of us.

Parker takes a deep breath, then another and another. That's what Lenny One Thumb taught him. Fill your chest and empty your mind. Something the old guy learned in the war. He para-chuted into Arnhem, or so he said. Arnhem, Holland. That makes Parker think of the Dutchman again. What happened to him was a real hit. Nothing like the bollocks this idiot's on about. Knife in a writer's back my arse.

But Parker stays calm, he's got a grip. He lets the words flow over him and drifts back to the smoke. To Tel and Trace. And Jan with his head blown off. The mess on the warehouse.

The voice stops for a bit as the writer takes a suck from his bottle of lager. That winds Parker up again. The pissy Scottish beer he sank in the pub down the road wasn't having much effect. Christ, the prat makes a fortune writing about our business and he also gets the only fucking beer in the tent to himself. That does it. Time for a plan.

Parker's generally not much good at plans. Big Tel tells him what to do and he does it to the letter. But he's not thick. He can think for himself. And what he's thinking right now is that the ponce in the pig-eye glasses needs to be taught a lesson. That's all there is to it. Once you know what you're going to do, you just need the nerve to pull it off. That's another of One Thumb's favourite lines.

The reading ends and the goon in the tartan top is asking for questions from the floor. Parker's got several but he'll sit on them for the time being. An old biddy starts the ball rolling by asking if the scribbler has any experience of real life crime – because, she says, his descriptions of criminal activity are so wonderfully con-vincing. Parker nearly chokes and gets a thump on the back from Colonel Mustard that's harder than necessary.

'It isn't a question of experience,' the jackass in leather replies. 'It's all down to the power of the imagination. How many crimi-nal masterminds did Sir Arthur Conan Doyle know? How often did Raymond Chandler get coshed and drugged like Marlowe does in the books?'

Parker doesn't know who these geezers are but he gets the drift – Four Eyes makes it up as he goes along and he's proud of it. The bastard reckons he knows it all. We'll see about that.

Eventually the questions dry up and a frothy cow comes on and tells people that copies of the author's books are available to buy. Apparently he'll be happy to sign them too. Parker wonders if he charges extra for that.

The crowd around the stage thins after twenty minutes. Parker's taken advantage of his seat behind the tent post to keep a low profile. Soon there are only a few groupies left. He sidles towards the exit.

'How about a drink?' Parker hears Tartan Top ask the writer.

'Sorry,' he says, 'no can do. Got to get back to the flat the publishers have rented for me.' He taps his nose like a wide boy from south of the river. 'Expecting an urgent fax from LA.' He hands over the half empty bottle of lager. Christ, the tosser couldn't even finish it.

Parker follows him out on to the street. At least the bleeding rain's stopped. Still no chance of finding a taxi though. Our hero stands on the corner waving like a scarecrow in a hurricane for five minutes then starts to hoof it. There are enough people around to make it easy for Parker to tail him unnoticed.

They walk along a street full of the usual rip-off chainstores, Parker keeping thirty yards behind. There's a terrible racket coming from an open-air concert hall down in the gardens. Parker can't believe it. Pissing with rain for most of the evening and the arseholes in charge expect people to turn out and listen to some godawful South American goatherd music.

It takes about ten minutes for the pork pie pedlar to reach his pad. It's in a tall block made of grotty grey stone. To reach it you have to go down a narrow passage off the main street. This is shaping up nicely.

Parker makes sure there's no one else around then heads off after his prey. He waits for the outer door to slam and watches the leather jacket move upwards in the stairwell windows. Typical Scottish skinflints. Even the nobs' places haven't got lifts. Seventh floor, lefthand door.

Right, sunshine. You're mine.

Parker glances round then runs a credit card down the space between the door frame and the lock. Clickety click, straight in. He's away up the stairs, driving his legs like he does in Stavros's gym every day back home. He gets to the seventh floor quickly, pleased that his breathing's still under control. Here we go.

He knocks on the door. No plastic this time. He wants to see the look in the tosser's eyes. But there's no answer. Where is he? Parker knocks again, harder.

'Just a moment, I'm busy.' The writer's voice is all high and mighty.

OK, sonny, if that's the way you want it. You're only making it worse for yourself.

Then the door opens. Wonderboy's got all four of his eyes focused on a couple of sheets of shiny paper. He's still wearing his leather jacket. 'Yes?' he asks, eyes staying down.

That's enough for Parker. He shoves the scribbler into the flat, hard. 'Avon calling, dickhead.' He kicks his victim in the balls, sends him crashing to the floor.

Parker bends over him. 'What you got there, smartarse? Your fax from Hollywood?'

Four Eyes is moaning, his mouth open and his tongue sticking out.

'What you saying?' Parker gives him another kick. 'You're not making any sense.'

The author twitches his head. There's something nasty on his chin, the remains of the lager.

'Gonna give you lots of lovely dosh for your fairy stories, are they?' Parker grabs him by the shirt and hauls him up. 'Well, you're in luck. You're about to find out what a *real* crime fest is.'

'What… what do you mean?' The scribbler's not looking at all happy. 'Who are you?'

Parker laughs, decides an introduction isn't required. Then slams the tosser into a chair next to a table with a big bowl of fruit on it. 'Who am I? I'm your worst fucking nightmare, mate.' Leans over him. 'Not even *your* imagination's good enough to come up with what I'm going to do to you. Or why.'

'What?' The author's squinting up at Parker through his round glasses, looking even more worried now. 'What's this all about?'

'It's about the bollocks you palm off on your adoring readers, big boy.' Parker sees his spit spray over the pillock's face. 'It's about you messing with the business.' A couple of slaps to his face. Glasses not looking too clever now. 'That isn't allowed.'

'Look,' the crime expert says, sounding seriously desperate, 'why don't we have a sensible chat about this? How about a drink?' He points over Parker's shoulder. 'There's some whisky over there. Or vodka if you prefer.' Parker keeps his eyes glued to him. He's not planning on getting distracted. 'Sensible chat?' he says, giving his death's head grin a test drive. 'Oh yeah, we'll have one of those all right.' He bends lower. 'And after that I'm gonna break every bone in your body.'

Smartarse isn't looking well. In fact, his face has gone as white as a Spurs shirt and sweatier than Big Tel's when he's with his tarts.

'Look, I don't get this,' he says in a squeaky voice. 'What have I ever done to you?'

Jab to the gob, lots of ketchup.

'What have you done to me?' Parker asks. 'You've taken the piss, my son. You've written a load of old horseshit about the business.' He grabs the tosser's chin. 'You've made us look like plonkers.'

Four Eyes, or rather Three Eyes – one of his lenses has gone walkabout – is shaking like a leaf. 'They're only stories,' he gabbles. 'They're not meant to be real life.' He tries smiling but his lips are too bloody for that to be much of a success. 'Something for people to read on the tube.'

Parker pulls the fax from the writer's hands. 'And something for the whole wide world to see at the flicks,' he says, waving it about. 'Like I say, you're taking the piss.'

The scribbler shakes his head frantically. When Parker drops the fax on his lap, he grabs it back. 'No, no, I'm not writing about real life,' he says, eyes sticking out like a frog's. 'It's just entertainment.'

'That's entertainment,' Parker sings, 'that's entertainment. Know it? The Jam. Bloody good band.' He peers at him. 'I suppose you listen to ponce music with violins and flutes.'

Head shaking again. 'No, no, I like popular music. The Doors, REM...'

'Who are they then?' Parker's grinning, playing dumb.

'Look, have a drink,' the bleeder says. 'I could certainly do with one.'

Parker gives him another slap and sees red stuff from his nose spray over the wall behind his head. 'All right. Let's have some vodka. You can stick that Scottish firewater up your arse.' He goes to the far side of the room. Unscrews the cap from the bottle and takes a drink. Lemon flavoured, not bad.

Parker goes back to Three Eyes. 'Here you are.' Slops some voddie over his face. A fair amount of yelping. 'Stings, does it? Good. Let's get back to business. To my business.' Parker leans over him and puts a hand on his throat. 'Taking the piss out of the business is bad. You've got to pay.'

Sudden movement lower down.

Parker freezes then falls backwards. Lands on his arse, goes flat out.

'Fuck,' he says. 'Fuck.'

Looks up and sees the scribbler looking down at him. He's still holding the pages of his fax. Now they've got blood all over them too.

Something sharp in his guts, something very sharp. 'What is it?' Parker asks, feeling himself beginning to float away.

'Fruit knife,' says Three Eyes.

Parker laughs. And dies.

The writer phones the police. Pours himself a quadruple whisky while he's waiting for them.

Then he dabs his nose with a tissue and sits down in front of his lap top. He starts on a story. He has the title already – *Crime Fest*. It'll do for that anthology he was called about last week. He's been stuck for a plot line.

Rob Ryan

Notes

Why would a father of three from Muswell Hill via Liverpool choose to set his first three books in a mythical America a couple of years hence? Perhaps because when I was a tiny baby, half my family emigrated to the USA. The wrong half, I always figured. They would come back once a year, impossibly glamorous, affluent figures.

Enamoured and envious in equal measure, I decided to become American without crossing the Atlantic. Everybody else made Airfix kits, I used to badger my relatives to send Monogram and AMT. I would only read *DC* or *Marvel* comics and my favourite '60s programme wasn't *The Saint* or *The Prisoner*, it was *Man in a Suitcase*, because the protagonist was an American adrift in Europe. I knew just how he felt. I even tried to subscribe to *Guns 'n' Ammo* once.

My family were not readers, and it is still a mystery how a paperback with a missing cover (when I eventually saw the raunchy jacket I knew why) turned up in a drawer when I was twelve or thirteen. It was the first adult book I ever read. Had it been Waugh or Conrad or Greene, things might have turned out differently. It was Mickey Spillane's *One Lonely Night*. I was doomed.

So when, much later, I had the nagging feeling that the location I had found in Seattle would make a perfect setting for a thriller, I decided to celebrate my cultural confusion. *Underdogs* became *Alice in Wonderland* as rewritten by John Carpenter. The second, *Nine Mil*, is *Winnie The Pooh* meets *Taxi Driver*. The third will be Peckinpah's take on *Peter Pan*.

While researching *Nine Mil* I spent a drunken evening in New Jersey with a very flirty High School teacher (I was not the object of her desire), who told me she was a little worried whenever she strayed, as her old man was a State Trooper, which meant he was required to be armed 24 hours a day. But, hey, she said, shit happens. I left before it did.

Shit Happens

by Rob Ryan

John Mitchell could not get used to having a third person in the bed. OK, he couldn't see that person, or hear them, but he knew they were there, an invisible force pressing down on his ribs, making his breathing shallower, his sleep lighter, his whole being nervous. Jesus, he thought, what was he going to be like when the thing was actually born?

He heard Ruby's voice rebuke him: not thing. Person. But until he knew what gender it was he couldn't give it a name, an identity, a face, let alone a personality. He suspected Ruby knew from the scan, but wasn't letting on. Was this so he wouldn't be disappointed when it was a girl, or be pleasantly surprised when it was a boy? In truth he didn't care what it was right now, just as long as he could give it – him or her – a name.

He rolled over and flicked off the alarm thirty seconds before it was due to kick in with KNJR, blasting Bon Jovi or some other local-boy-made-good all over the bedroom. It was barely light, and that light was chill, bone-numbingly grey, dull like granite. Late November, the worst of the year to come, and already three feet of beach in front of their house had been sucked away by the avaricious Atlantic, stolen grain by grain to be dumped on the shores of Wildwood. If it got any more of his sand and it'd be a small desert rather than a beach.

He slid out of bed and listened to Ruby snore and snuffle as she tried to roll over, the swell of her belly preventing her from assuming her usual face-down position. A kid. Mitchell was finding it hard to take in all this meant. Worst of all was the job interview he was having to go for. A nice desk job in the city. Working as he did for what was now called SHED – the Southern Highways Executive Division, which covered the state from Trenton down to Delaware Bay – at least he never knew what any day would bring, and he got to be out on the road. How would he feel if he knew every morning, 250 days a year, meant a two hour slog into the city and stint at a desk? The thought made his chest tighten some more, like he was being suffocated. Still, he promised Ruby he would go to the interview. The least he could do is have a shave and turn up, see what they had to offer.

Thomas Earl liked to drive into the city. He knew it was madness, knew it meant leaving home an hour before he would if he got the train like every other commuter in his town, knew that the Lincoln Tunnel was bad for his blood pressure, knew that the parking charges he faced were tantamount to extortion. But the car was the only place he could think, could order his thoughts for the day. So he had to swallow the downside.

It was barely day when he walked down to the garage, and opened the door from the inside, shivering against the sudden thwack of cold which hit him. Sleet had fallen during the night, but had faded away to leave a thin, icy sheen on the roads. He backed the Chevrolet out and looked up at the window of the his house, worrying he would see one of the kids, woken by his nocturnal prowlings, staring out of the window, and at the same time half hoping for a last glimpse of their faces before another day of papers and meetings and arguments.

He turned up the heat, switched on the car lights – he reckoned he would need them for another fifteen, twenty minutes, pulled out on to the street and headed for the highway. He decided that, this morning, he would take the George Washington Bridge, just in case the construction that had clogged the tunnel on Friday was still in place. He had checked at the office, knew it was meant to have finished over the weekend, but it had looked way behind schedule to him. He glanced at the clock on the dash. Nobody would be in the engineer's department yet to confirm or deny.

As he made a left out of his street, he checked his mirror and saw the white Dodge van pull out behind him. It registered, but barely – mainly that all kind of folks seem to be starting work earlier and earlier these days.

Aware that the roads were deceptively treacherous, he gingerly made the right and a left that got him on to the highway, and slid into his lane. Once he was settled down to a safe cruising speed he hit his voice mail recall on the car cell phone. A dozen calls had come in overnight, mostly petty complaints about projects he had slowed or stopped altogether and a couple about the one he was sitting on – legalising a casino in New York City.

They had ground the others down. No, that was the wrong expression. There was nothing down about what they were doing. Seduced was more apposite he decided. As usual, there was too much money sloshing around this scheme, money that was there for the spending, but not upon anything concrete, on things such as familiarisation tours – let's go and see how Nassau does it, or Monaco or Macau or, of course, Reno, Vegas. No, thanks, guys, it'll make a shit load of money, but we already got Atlantic City, and as far as Earl was concerned that was as near to crap tables and slots as he wanted to be. Earl knew the others thought he was being priggish, that with New York hit hard by the post Y2K downturn it needed all the dollars it could get, but he thought it was like the city going out and turning tricks when the going got tough. Undignified.

He was just working himself up into the kind of righteous indignation he needed to face the day when the fuel warning light flashed at him. Damn, just when he had got the temperature up inside and his breath had stopped coming in clouds. He signalled, moved lanes, and swung into the gas station.

Inside the Dodge van Pretty Boy Penn tried hard to fight the seething mass of dull, ill-focussed pain behind his eyes. As usual his self control had let him down the night before. He had known he had to be clear headed this morning. But one beer led to another which led to brandy and then that guy had offered him a line and in the john he had pulled out too much in the semi-darkness, and spent a couple of minutes trying to scrape it back into the wrap, but all that did was flick more out. In the end he had shovelled it all into one big mass and done the lot. It had kept him talking 100-proof crap until two in the morning. A few hours ago, really. And now the toxins from that and the brandy were busy trying to find a way out of his brain via his eyeballs. He felt as if even his sweat was some kind of industrial waste, sitting on his skin in a sticky, sickly sheen. And although the sky was the colour of pewter, he needed sunglasses to be able to half open his eyes.

To cap it all the guy in the passenger seat was being a real asshole. Maybe he knew Penn was feeling fragile, but he had been on him ever since they met at the rail station, when the guy came in on the milk run. Had he done this kind of thing before? Was he clear that they were meant to make this an accident? That it might take two, three, even four of these runs in different vehicles before they were actually sure how to pull this one off? Maybe even a home or office visit? You're too close. You're too far behind. Move up. Move back. Pull over on the left. Slow up there is ice. You got a piece? Well keep it hidden. It got history? Better hadn't have. Where did you get the van? Is it crystal you follow my lead? Yak Yak Yak.

Edgar. He remembered now. It was the guy who frisked him back at the Paladin office when he went to the interview. Pretty Boy felt like telling him who he was, that he was blood, not some hired hand, but suffered in stoic silence instead. Skinny, weasely looking guy, but kind of hard with it. Well Penn had rolled more people than Edgar he would bet – he was doing it once, twice a week up until earlier this year, hitting all those private poker games in Atlantic City, the ones where the guys like to play with a little toot and twat on the side, the ones that go on for twenty four, forty eight hours, without any interference from the casinos. They had hit four games before anyone got wise and upped the local security. It was just a shame in the last one that the guy managed to hit him across the nose with the length of pipe before he dropped him. Kind of ruined his nickname now.

Still, if Pretty Boy was pretty dumb, Paladin was absolutely stupid. Even he knew what it referred to – it was that guy with the face that appeared to be made out of vegetables. Real ugly.

He looked at Edgar. It might be worth being sociable, after all, this gig might last a few days: 'What was the name of the actor in *Have Gun Will Travel?*'

'What?'

'*Have Gun Will Travel?* Paladin? TV series?'

'What the fuck you talking about? Keep your eyes on the road.'

Pretty Boy shook his head and regretted it when his peripheral visions degenerated into flashes of silver light. How come Edgar didn't know it? They were both way too young for the series first time round, but he had seen it on cable. Maybe Edgar didn't watch TV. Maybe he couldn't read. Boone. Richard Boone, it came to him out of his foggy brain. That was who the agency was named after. Paladin – the Richard Boone character in *Have Gun Will Travel*. So if anyone on the East Coast wanted a job done, they called Paladin – arson, kidnap, beating, robbery, extortion… and so on. One stop shopping, and just like any respectable agency Paladin supplied the talent, and took a cut. Fine, but if he could figure it out, what was to stop some smart ass Fed with a copy of *TV Guide* doing the same?

He shivered and reached to turn up the heat, but it was already on full. This guy they were tailing so fucking early in the morning was some kind of councillor, and he was in the way. They had to to take him out of the way, but without being too obvious about it. That was the brief. Hardly *Mission Impossible*. Pretty Boy felt a wave a nausea grip him, and he closed his eyes for a second. When he opened them the the mark was indicating and moving over into the gas station. He stomped on the brake, felt the van fishtail on the icy surface, corrected the skid and pulled over to follow. He looked at Edgar who tutted at the manoeuvre and then shrugged. Maybe he was thinking the same thing – this could be an opportunity, a chance to cut all the cat and-mouse shit down to just one day. After all, it was a one-off fee, no overtime involved. Penn nodded his head as if he could fling off the dull, thudding coke headache. He had to stay alert.

Earl groaned when he realised there was no full service isle. It meant he had to get cold again. He popped the gas flap and stepped out of the car, rubbing his hand together to try and generate some warmth. Just as he was about to close the door and walk around to the pump, he heard the sound of an engine over-revving, the valves bouncing as the driver floored the accelerator until the kick-down came in, and the tyres finally gripped on the ice-slicked asphalt, hurtling it forward. It was a moment, a fatal moment, before he realised all that noise, the screeching, the smoke, it was all coming right at him. His brain refused to move his limbs, all it took in was a frozen framed image, like a movie still imprinting into his visual cortex, the last neural composite it would ever form, the contorted face of the driver, partly hidden behind sunglasses and a passenger yelling and spitting wildly at him.

This was not going to be John Mitchell's morning, he knew it. It was bad enough having to go into the city, but finding out that Ruby had all but drained the gas tank was the final straw. There couldn't be more than a tea spoon left in it he realised as he tapped the gauge. Ah well, they say pregnant women get forgetful. She had even forgotten he had the interview with the postal department over at Federal Plaza – she woke up and asked him where the hell he was going so early when he was on afternoon shift. He thought about pressing on – he only had a couple of miles to go before he could park up and catch a train, but he daren't risk it. He decided to pull in and fill up. He swore he felt the first hiccup as the carb – probably fuel injectors he corrected himself – sucked air and he eased off the gas to let it roll into place. He had just switched off the engine when he heard the painful screech of an accelerator being floored.

The fender smashed into Earl's solar plexus, arching his back through the glass of his door seconds before it tore off its hinges and spun away. The door was thrown clear, spinning in a crazy unbalanced arc, sparking on the floor as it bounced, but Earl wasn't so lucky. Caught by the front tire, he was pulled under as if on a conveyor belt, and the weight of the truck burst his abdomen like an overstuffed sausage then crushed his rib cage, spearing his heart and lungs in a dozen places. The double rear wheels that clumped over his inert form just made sure the job was done.

Inside the van Edgar smacked the driver on the side of his head, and Penn angrily yanked the wheel as he felt it thump over the body. 'What? What?'

Edgar felt the anger building. He had known this guy was a fuckup, boss' nephew or no. He thumped him again, and felt the front tyre lost grip as Pretty Boy jerked the wheel. The Dodge slid towards the gas pump island, just catching the rim hard enough to peel it back and break the tyre seal. They both heard the loud pop as the air fled through the new opening. The front of the vehicle dropped and started to vibrate wildly.

Pretty Boy looked at Edgar in horror, his throat tightening with the realisation of what he had done.

Yeah, he's gonna panic, come to pieces all over me, thought Edgar. 'Stop, we'll get another car,' he said coolly.

As soon as the van slithered to a halt Edgar put the big .45 to Pretty Boy's head and pulled the trigger. The driver's side door window shattered and turned red at the same instant and the blast threw Pretty boy's head out into the cold morning. A crimson mist seem to hang in the chill air, like a dying breath.

Edgar stepped out of the van without a backward glance at Pretty Boy. Nephew of the boss. Could be trouble. Well he'll get the story straight later. Right now he had to get as far away as possible. He quickly surveyed the scene before him. There was nobody in the gas station office that he could see – probably lying down. There was a guy over at another pump, car keys in hand, getting ready to fill up. He hoped the guy was the cautious type who topped up whenever the needle went to half. He had to get going. He needed that car. As he strode across the forecourt he raised the Colt auto and aimed it at his head to let the guy know his intentions were strictly dishonourable.

Edgar couldn't believe it when the man raised his own heavy duty weapon and let off two rounds, with the kind of grouping in the chest that Mitchell excelled at on the range. Edgar felt the two big punches in his chest, but didn't even have time to register the pain of the bullets tearing his insides to mush. He simply felt the blackened shutters come down even as he staggered back towards the abandoned van.

It all happened so fast, so automatically, that John Mitchell barely remembered pulling the Smith and Wesson and firing, but the ringing in his ears and the small twirl of smoke looping out of the barrel confirmed what he had done. Body count: two, one of whom looked partially like hamburger after the truck had finished with him. Hang back from that one – bit early in the day for insides. Leave it for the medics to scoop up. He kept the Smith at chest height and took three paces forward, peering over at the cab of the van. No, add one more – there was someone slumped in the Dodge. Well whatever that little scene was, the guy he dropped was not on the side of the angels, he was sure of that. Right there and then he suddenly knew he was going to call Federal Plaza and cancel the interview with the mail fraud department. The adrenaline coursing through his blood, making his senses pin sharp, confirmed what he had always known – he loved this job. He knew what the jokers claimed SHED stood for – Shit Happens Every Day. But wasn't that what being a State Trooper was all about? His kid would thank him for it one day, for having an old man who made a difference. He holstered the gun, walked back to his car, and slid inside to call it in.

Manda Scott

Notes

We live in a world of grand crimes and misdemeanours, a place where a collective society genuinely believes that it is worth the entire eastern bloc trade deficit to find out what two consenting adults thought to do with a cigar. I live in a different world, one where the far larger, far more damaging crimes and misdemeanours go unnoticed and unrecorded. So this – for the record. All of these cases are real. I have changed the necessary details to protect the guilty but the basic facts come from life. All bar the final event happened to me and the last one stands at only one remove. I have no reason to disbelieve the colleague who reported it, she doesn't have the mind of a crime-writer, she couldn't have made up anything this warped. I'd like to think I couldn't either, but I may be wrong...

99%

by Manda Scott

'N

ine out of ten get better in spite of you.'
'Anaesthesia is a modified form of death'.
'BSE will be the making of the farm side of the profession.'
These are the things they taught us in college. Not everything,
clearly, I have folders full of other notes: the clinical pathology of
malignant catarrhal fever in the suckler cow, signs and symptoms of diabetes in the dog, management of dystocia in the sow.
But it's the passing aphorisms that we remember, the pearls of
wisdom cast at random before the student herd, forgotten by
those who speak them before they ever pass their lips. I am
developing my own pearls for the time I choose to spread them
before the gilts and boars of the future:
*'Seventy per cent of the population can't give directions to their own
front door.'*
'Ninety per cent can't tell left from right. '
*'Ninety nine per cent shouldn't be allowed to share their lives with
any other living being.'*
The last one has changed recently. If you'd asked me this time
yesterday, it would have been seventy per cent and I would have
confined the restriction to animals, that being my field. Tonight,
five minutes ago, I revised it. This is why:

To understand, we have to go back a full twenty four hours. Last
night was not the best of nights to be on call. One football team
was playing another football team for the right to sell more repli-
cas of their strip. I know nothing about football and have no
interest in finding out. I knew about the match only because
every client who came through the door made a crack about my
missing the 'entertainment' for a calving or something equally
heroic. Being a small animal practice we don't do calvings but I
would gladly have taken a call if it meant guaranteed freedom
from football. Sadly, match night never quite works out like that
and this one was no different to all its predecessors.

Evening surgery was virtually empty – few folk were interested in staying late to have their dogs stitched up or their hamsters' teeth clipped. Even after closing time, the phones stayed quiet. I drove home with the mobile switched on and had to check the battery as I walked in the door in case the unthinkable had happened and someone had tried to get through on a faulty line. No dice. The line was fine, it was just that the nation was glued to the screen. I made dinner, walked the dog, made coffee, drank it and the only disturbance was the occasional roar through the walls as the six foot, flat screen digital technological monster next door was turned up to full volume the better for Jeremy and Martin to appreciate some artful piece of legwork.

Half time came and went and not one single call-out – unusual even for match night. This is the kind of thing I have nightmares about. I wake up at six am, sweating on the afterwave of a dream where I have sat all evening by the phone, not knowing that the wires have been cut and the Royal College is about to strike me off for failing to provide a full 24-hour service. I checked the land line and re-checked the mobile and found both intact. I was beginning to contemplate the possibility of an early night when Jeremy next door turned the sound up further than should have been technologically possible to celebrate the end of the match. The squeal of the final whistle coincided precisely with the first buzz of the phone and we were back to service as usual.

The first two calls were straight forward. A request for our puppy vaccination charges: ('This is an emergency line, please call the switchboard in the morning') and a roadkill hedgehog, stretched out flat and not moving: 'How can I tell if it's dead?'

Count the tyre marks? Maybe not… 'Try pressing on its eyes.'

'There's only one eye left.'

That bodes well. 'But does it move when you touch it – the eye?'

…pause to test theory…

'No, it burst.'

Fine. 'In that case, I'd say it's been dead for a while. If you want us to dispose of the body, bring it in first thing tomorrow morning.'

I spent five years in college training to for this. I could do it all night. I probably will.

Number three was the one that hurt. The owner was drunk and I suspect his team had just lost. Either way, his dog had 'breathing problems' – the late night history from hell. 'Breathing problems' covers everything from a potentially fatal anaphylactic response to a wasp sting, down to a low grade, chronic asthma that's been brewing for weeks. We went through the usual questions and answers and it came out unnervingly close to the former: six-year -old Border Collie, female, spayed, fine this evening, now unable to rise, with acute onset laboured breathing plus the odd 'choking noise'. Bad news. This one isn't going to be sorted out over the phone.

We'll bypass the disagreement over whether it needed come into the surgery or not (emergencies need emergency equipment all of which is kept at the surgery. Drunks can't drive and aren't prepared to pay for a taxi. The dog is insured and all veterinary fees are covered. Taxis are not. End of discussion). Bearing in mind the 70 per cent theory (can't give directions to their own front door) and adding the alcohol factor, I gave a suitably pessimistic estimate of my arrival time. Final orders, issued as I dragged on my coat and found my keys, were to get the dog inside and keep her warm. Fairly basic, I'd have said, even for a drunk on the losing side.

Drunk lived in a six-figure house on the edge of the river with an Audi and a BMW estate in the drive. He had a 21" flat screen TV and it was still on. I could see the glare of it through the side patio windows. The faces of four earnest ex-sporting types performed their verbal post-mortem on the match over a series of out-takes that would keep Jeremy and Martin happy for days. Drunk's wife/mistress/woman-of-the-moment lay horizontal on the sofa, a tall-stemmed glass in one hand, her eyes glued to the screen. Drunk himself was not visible.

The collie was still outside, lying flat out in the centre of the patio, her head at an odd angle to the ground. He was right about one thing: she was in serious respiratory distress. I got to her before he knew I was there and did what any normal human being would do for an animal in that much trouble: I tried to lift her head on to my knee. Therein lay the problem. She was an outdoor dog (can't have dogs in the house) tied by forty feet of washing line to a ring-bolt sunk in the concrete. Somewhere, in the ninety minutes plus overtime of the match, she had wound the entirety of it into a hard-twisted spiral, tightening it as a slow garrote round her neck. The effect was much as you'd expect; she gasped, one breath after another, fighting to draw the air past blue, spit-frothed gums, over a tongue swollen to twice the size it should have been, through a larynx crushed to a straw and swelling with every minute. Her eyes bulged like a Pug, and a pattern of ruptured blood vessels tattooed the white surface of the sclera, new ones breaking as vivid scarlet ink blots with each pulse.

I laid her head back on the concrete. 'It's OK, kiddo. We're here. We'll sort you.' She whined, short and strangled, on the next outbreath.

The drunk was beside me by then, swaying in the breeze, smoking Marlboro Light and breathing vodka martini and brandy, one arm held out at right angles as if not dropping fag-ash on her coat mattered when lifting her up to carry her inside had not.

'Get me a knife.' Of all the dumb, stupid things not to have in my kit, I didn't have a scalpel blade.

'Wha'?'

'A knife. Get me a knife. Now.'

God, I have such a short, short fuse. Come the revolution, I will nail this one to the wall long before I blow his brains out.

The rope was tied at her neck, somewhere underneath in the mass of black fur. I found it with my fingers but I couldn't turn her over to see. I needed teeth on it, or a screwdriver in the knot, anything to prize her free.

He came back with a knife, a full-length Sabatier, blunted and badly re-sharpened but still with enough of an edge to do the job. There was barely room to slide the blade between her skin and the rope, certainly not enough room for a finger to take the pressure off her throat. I sawed and she breathed and then, as I sawed more, she stopped breathing. Too late, the last strands of the rope came apart and I had her head up, her tongue drawn forward and her mouth held shut, blowing down her nose like a trumpet, like a straw, like blowing up a balloon that's never felt air and doesn't know how to swell.

'Come back, damn you. You're not giving up on me now.'

'Wha'?'

'Shut up.' I blew again, settling into the rhythm of resuscitation: three big blasts and then feel for a pulse. I didn't do that before, there wasn't time for crap like pulses. She was alive when I got there, I know she was alive, she looked at me and she answered when I talked to her, stands to reason there was a pulse. But not now. The pulse died when her breathing stopped and she died with it.

I didn't have oxygen with me and that was the second mistake. From now, I will keep at least a small cylinder in the house for emergency call-outs but I didn't have one then. I had adrenalin for her heart and atipamezole, which sometimes works, but I didn't get her back. She had spent too long on too little oxygen and then the final pressure of the knife at the end cut off the last supply. So it was me that killed her. Without question, she would have died soon enough if I'd left her, but knowing that didn't make sleeping last night any easier.

I charged the drunk twice the normal call-out fee plus time on the premises and demanded cash. He paid. Both of us conveniently forgot about the insurance. He trailed me to the car, leering in through the window, breathing vapour that would have seriously compromised a breathalyser and delivered his final thoughts on the subject; 'Don't tell the wife, will you? She's devoted to the thing.'

I hit the button to wind up the window and reversed out of the drive.

So that was last night. On waking this morning, I changed the third of Scott's rules. Now *ninety* per cent of the population should be physically prevented from owning an animal and I am quite prepared to take responsibility for making the necessary decisions.

Morning consultations were harmless, on the whole. Dog vaccines, cat bite abscesses and the occasional renal failure. None of this is beyond the scope of general practice. Then I moved through to theatre and that's when the day really started to go downhill.

Jake had been operating for two hours by the time I finished consulting and he was not having a good day. Jake's a good friend and a spectacularly good surgeon but he has a list of pet hates, top of which come breeders of pedigree dogs, particularly the ones that look as if they've had a head-on collision with the breed standard's version of a number ten bus. Unfortunately, we work in an area packed full of Bulldogs, Pugs and Pekes and a significant proportion of the practice income derives from the surgery necessary to give them a reasonable stab at life. I walked into the back room to an atmosphere straight from the Arctic circle and found Jake doing his Shakespeare surgery (the Complete Works) on a bulldog: widen the nostrils, shorten the soft palate, take out the tonsils, excise the rancid skin folds and *lo*, you have a dog that can at least breathe as it walks up the stairs. You can't do anything rational for the Queen Anne legs or the pelvis too small to give birth but it's a start. And it makes us somewhere close to a week's wages for a nurse so I, for one, am not complaining.

I wandered over to the operating table to take a look. The dog was propped up on its sternum with its mouth winched open to full stretch and tissue forceps holding its cheeks out. The 'wide-mouthed frog' look. Even for a bull-dog it was stupendously ugly.

'Having fun?'

'Fuck off.'

'I'll take that as a yes. Anything I can do?'

'You can look at Casper Johnson's chest films and then you can pick up the phone and talk sense to the owners. I've had enough of practising defensive medicine.'

Oh shit. I really didn't want today to be like this.

I don't share Jake's loathing of squashed-faced breeds, I reserve all my breed-apartheid for the German Shepherds, or at least, for their breeders. I have no doubt that when the originals ran around the hills and sheep fields of Alsace that they were perfect specimens of a herding, guarding breed. Half a century of planned eugenics, however, has produced a medical and surgical nightmare. I challenge you to find me a German Shepherd that does not suffer from at least one of the following: hip dysplasia, elbow arthritis, allergic skin, ear and gut disease, anal furunculosis (nice one, that: long, tracking tunnels of infected tissue migrating in around the anus. Most GSD owners don't check under the tail of their dogs. It's usually a bleeding, ulcerated mess before they bring it in. I used to do a Saturday morning AF clinic. We saw between five and ten dogs a fortnight, every fortnight, for five years. All but two were German Shepherds. I leave you to do the arithmetic.) All of this is not a good basis on which to pick the family pet. Added to which, if they do, by some miracle, survive to middle age, arthritic hips and all, then they die early of splenic haemangio-sarcomas or a spectacularly nasty chronic neurological problem that leaves them paralysed in the hind legs. Anyway you look at it, you have a recipe for long-term pain and heartbreak. And we haven't even begun to think about temperament. It's amazing, really, how fifty years of selective breeding can do so much damage. You may wonder why most of my profession is terrified of the concept of genetically modified foods but you only have to look at what we work with. Examine a Bulldog, go for a walk with a Shar-pei. Perfect representatives of man's best efforts at genetic modification of the wolf...

All that said, Casper Johnson is one of the nicest dogs I know. He's a white German Shepherd of impeccable temperament and that puts him in a class of his own. Sadly, his owners inhabit the other end of the life-form spectrum, down there with the krill and the small things that smear on the sole of your boot. They're both lawyers, they have too much money and they have no sense at all of the fact that a platinum credit card and threats of litigation can't change reality.

I picked up the chest films and went through to the ward. The nurse sitting by the giant-dog kennel threw me the kind of look designed to slay at fifty paces. It would be so much easier in this kind of case, simply to fall over dead and let someone else deal with it. I walked through the glare and knelt down by side of her chair.

'How's he doing?'

'The same as he was doing yesterday and the day before that. If we drop the morphine off, he screams. If we keep it high enough to stop him screaming, he's unconscious. What do you expect?'

I don't expect anything except that he's going to die. He's been dying since the day last November when he walked into my consulting room, lame on his left hind leg. The x-rays showed the early stages of a bone tumour and we bounced him as fast as his paws would take him to the local referral hospital for their oncologists and orthopedic surgeons to sort out. They tried. I am sure they tried everything modern medical science has at its disposal. Still, they failed. These things happen. Science does not have all the answers. The up-side to being in veterinary medicine rather than the other sort is that we can make the decision to pull the plug when we can see the end coming and we know that it's going to be grim. The surgeons explained, very nicely, to everyone concerned that they had done all they could and it was time to terminate treatment and then, when the owners refused to give them consent for euthanasia, they sent him back to us for the final ending.

Or not. Mr and Mrs Krill aren't into euthanasia. Somewhere, deep in their collective psyches they can't handle the concept of death. I would like to offer both of them therapy but they wouldn't know what to do with it. They have spent their lives insulated from any kind of reasonable reality and they think their behaviour is normal. For whatever reason, they want their dog back, alive and well, and when he finally dies, which he will, they will demand an independent post-mortem on the basis of which, they will frame their demand for legal redress. If there is any indication whatsoever that we hastened his end, they will take us to the cleaners. As far as I can find out if they are prepared to pay for twenty-four hour nursing and full pain relief then that is their prerogative. I can refuse to treat him and make them take him elsewhere but that's as far as it goes and I am not prepared to do that. Whatever his owners are like, he's a good, honest, decent dog and he deserves better than that. We are therefore, as Pete said, practising defensive medicine, doing our best to keep him pain-free and praying for an early end.

I opened the kennel door and walked in. Casper Johnson lay flat out on the floor of his kennel, his missing leg hidden under the fleece of greyed-out, yellowing hair. A drip line ran into each of his fore legs and a catheter emerged from under the fur at the back, conveying urine to a bag on the floor. I reached back round the edge of the door and found his chart: temperature stable, fluid output balancing fluid input. Everything else within normal limits. No sign of him dying yet.

'You have to do something.' This from the nurse. She's in her thirties and she's been here since before I qualified. She's the best clinician we've got. 'We could give him insulin and send him home. They'd never know.'

'They might not, but Jack Donaldson would find it.' JD, the pathologist. The man who can detect foul play at a hundred paces. 'He'd nail us to the floor.'

'It's still worth it.'

'Maybe. We could all live without our licences. It might be time for a career-break. Jane reckons we'd make more per hour stocking shelves at Sainsburys anyway.' I lifted the envelope with the chest films and slid them up on the viewer. The cannon-ball masses of the chest secondaries showed stark against the relative black of his lungs. 'Maybe we'll try this first, huh? Lawyers think in black and white. If they see the facts they might change their minds. Jake thinks it'll work.'

Jake was wrong. They didn't even want to look at the films. In fact they refused to pay for an 'unnecessary procedure'. I spent an hour on the phone and I failed as others have failed before me, as I will continue to fail until the drugs and the cancer get the better of the big dog in the back ward and I have no idea how long that will take. I sat in the office, fighting the beginnings of a very bad headache and for the first time in years I wanted to chuck it all in and go home.

We were closing the doors at eight when Ray Matthews, the RSPCA inspector, turned up. Ray's your average Society man; six foot two, built like a lumberjack and fearsome enough to stop the dog-fighters in their tracks. He has hands that span both of mine and fingers that won't fit into our largest size gloves. Nevertheless, he handles fledgling robins and stray mallard chicks with a delicacy that puts me and most of my colleagues to shame. If he has a problem, it's that he's irritatingly cheerful and has a habit of talking right at the moments when the rest of us want some peace. But not tonight. Tonight, he stood in the back door of the surgery with his hands in his pockets and he looked sick.

'Are you on call?' he asked.

'No. It's Jake's turn. What's up?'

'Would you like to come out on a visit?'

Why do I feel there's only one right answer to that? 'You don't want Jake?'

'No.'

I don't think I've ever heard a single syllable sentence from Ray in the entire ten years I've known him. I reached for my car keys and dropped them back in my bag. 'You're driving?'

'I'm driving.'

'Let's go.'

He took me down into one of the urban death zones on the far side of town, the worst infliction of mid-sixties planner's blight: a maze of identical boxes, tacked together in terraced rows, each with their ten square feet of garden, front and back and the twitching net curtains keeping eyes on the neighbours. The street names have long ago been painted out or altered to something less appealing so that the only way to find your way round is to stop one of the locals and ask directions. Even when you've found the right street, the sameness of it numbs the mind. If they didn't have numbers falling off the front doors, you'd never be able to tell them apart. In the very worst of my nightmares, I dream of dying and being re-born into one of these.

Ray, quite clearly, knew the way. We reached one undistinguished pile of brickwork amongst the many and he stopped and parked the van on the pavement. The simple act of being there gathered a throng of snot-nosed, blank-faced kids, none of them ready to step out of the way to let us through. All of them stank. Everything stank. We walked up the garden path through a pervading smell of tom-cat which gave way, slowly, as we approached the house and became instead, a stomach-turning mix of rancid chip fat and cigarettes. The house number had fallen off completely but the imprint of it showed, dark against the bleached out brick: 79. There was no knocker, no bell. Ray lifted his fist to knock and then paused just before his knuckles hit the wood. 'Trust me on this,' he said. 'Follow my lead.'

'Whatever you say. You're the boss.'

She was in her late twenties, I would say, the woman who opened the door and she reacted in much the same way anyone here would react to the sight of a uniform – she tried to close it again.

'We've nothing here for you.' As if he were the rag and bone man.

'It's the lurcher.' He outweighed her two to one. He pushed in against the door and it opened flat to the wall behind. 'We've come to take the lurcher.'

He knew his way round the house as well as he knew his way round the streets. We walked through a hallway that was a repository for used cat litter and into a living room that housed the cats, four of them, a parrot in a terrifyingly small cage – and a lurcher. He was young, maybe two years old, a well-marked blue fawn brindle, about 24" at the shoulder, slim built with a lot of greyhound in him but something else to give the silken coat and the glorious, dark-rimmed beauty of his eyes. If I'm honest, I noticed him before I noticed anything else and even when I'd seen the rest, my eyes came back to him. Whatever else they did in that house, they looked after the dog. He lay on the floor in front of the television watching us with a kind of quiet, calm that still took in every movement. Beside him, petrified to silence by the presence of a uniform, sat a girl of about eight. Superficially, she looked much like her mother; anorexically thin with gaunt features and straight, dark hair cut hard into a fringe that lay horizontal along her eyebrows. The rest of her was more difficult to place. Her eyes, particularly, were not her mothers. They were dark grey, like slate with a paler rim that matched the blue-tinged shadows in the hollows beneath them. Later, I noticed her clothes. She was wearing shorts, which was fine – it was a hot day for the time of year – but over it she was wearing a sweatshirt and that was not fine at all. You don't wear a sweatshirt in this heat for the warmth of it, that's for sure. And then there was something about the way she was wearing it. From the moment we walked into the room she kept each hand tucked inside the opposite sleeve, mandarin-style. I've never seen a child do that except when they've something to hide. The television was on and she had been watching it when we came in. Now, she sat crosslegged, her back rigidly vertical, her eyes on the dog, her hands in the odd, daoist pose and I wanted, more than anything I've wanted in a while, to see what it was on her arms that I wasn't supposed to be seeing.

'The dog's fine.' The woman was desperate, haranguing, her voice rising through the registers with all the musical range of a badly tuned violin. 'You're not to take him.'

'He's underfed. This is the vet. She'll tell you.' Ray turned to me. 'Tell her the dog's underfed.'

Bloody hell. It's a lurcher, Ray. They're supposed to look like this. Half the dogs in the country would be better off if they were as fit as this thing. It's rangy, I grant you, long-legged, and lean. It may have a touch of saluki back there in the breeding, for the speed and the stamina. I have no doubt that he works well on the lamp and they probably use him on fox. If you were sharp and you knew where to wait, you could maybe get them for coursing deer. That, at least, is illegal. But I can't, in all honesty, say that he's underfed.

Follow my lead. Trust me on this.

You're the boss.

I stood near the back of the sofa, struggling to find something to say when suddenly, I had no need to say anything, no chance even to open my mouth.

'What the fucking hell is going on in here?'

The noise came like an explosion from the hallway. The front door hit the wall hard enough to break the plaster. The cats scattered. The parrot swore and then fell silent. The woman screamed a high, cut-off scream like a dying rabbit. The girl sat straight-backed and silent. The dog cocked its head to one side for a better look.

'The father,' said Ray. He didn't say whose. And then to the shape in the hall; 'We're taking the dog.'

It would have been easier, I think, if he'd said something back but he didn't. He stood in the doorway, easily two inches taller than Ray, broader, heavier, more vicious. This is the kind of man who hunts fox, who hunts deer, who fights his dogs and shoots the losers. But he isn't fighting the lurcher, I'd put my degree on that.

He stepped forward and he could have been the only one in the room. 'Who the fuck is that?'

'That's the vet.' Ray's eyes didn't move my way. 'She's here to certify you're mistreating the dog.'

Of all of us, the dog was the most relaxed. He stayed near the girl, but he had his ears up and his tail floated an inch of the floor, sweeping slowly across and across so that if you tied a rag to it, it could have cleared the floor.

'Fuck that. The dog's fine.' The shape turned my way. 'Tell him it's fine.'

Whatever the relationship, she got her eyes from this man: slate grey with great dark shadows underneath. Maybe he does drugs. Maybe they all do. That would explain why I'm not to see her arms.

'Ray? Can we go outside for a minute? I think we need to discuss this.'

'You go out, you're not coming back in.'

'We're not leaving without the dog.'

They said it together, twins in chorus, two bull-necked men, squaring up for the charge. If they fight in here, they'll not stop until we get the police. Every one of us knows this.

'Ray?'

'It's underfed. Anyone can see that. That counts as mistreatment. We have the right to take it in.'

'It's the best fed dog this estate's ever seen.' He thought about that and qualified it. 'He's better fed than you are.'

That, I doubt. But the principal was sound.

Trust me.

You're the boss.

I've never seen Ray wrong in anything he's ever done. But I have a degree and a profession and I can't let them both down.

'Ray, he's right. The dog's fine. We've got no reason to take it away.'

In the silence that followed, only the girl moved. She reached out and stroked the dog's head. He turned his neck and ran his tongue across her hand.

'You have to tell me, Ray. I can't do anything if you won't talk to me.'

We sit in my flat, either side of the kitchen table and my home feels as if it is turning into a war zone. I drink beer. He drinks coffee, black and sweet. He refuses my biscuits. Worse, he has said nothing since we left the house. If Ray monosyllabic is unusual, an hour of silence is unheard of.

'You should have let me take the dog.'

'I couldn't stop you, sunshine, but I can't say something that isn't true. The mastadon was right. The dog was fine.'

'It was being abused.'

'Well it was all psychological then because you couldn't tell on the outside.' I paused for another drink from the can. My second. I am not good with drink. I will regret this in the morning. 'Now the kid, yes. If you told me she was abused, I would believe you. I'd put money she had bruises on her arms.'

He looked at me the way my nurse looked at me this morning when I went to visit Casper Johnson. 'Tattoos,' he said. 'She has tattoos on her arms.'

I looked at him. I couldn't think what to say. 'Isn't she a bit young?'

'Depends.' He shrugged. 'There's a blue heart, apparently, with 'Dad' written across it in red.'

'Oh.'

Ray moved in his chair, the tail end of a need to stand and pace. 'The "mastadon" is her father,' he said.

'Poor kid.'

'He is also her grandfather. The woman is his daughter. She is mother to the child.'

'Ah.' The beer tasted sour in my mouth. I leant over and put the can back in the fridge. 'So can't social services do something about that?'

'Like what?'

'Take her into care.'

'Her and half the kids on the estate.'

'They're all his?'

'They're all related to their parents more than once in the family tree.'

'I thought that was urban myth.'

'You thought wrong.'

Fine. So we live and learn. 'I'm sorry, Ray. She was a nice kid. She deserves better than that. But I don't know what to do. It's not my field.'

'The dog was your field.'

'We've been through this. The dog was fine.'

He reached for my fridge, opened the door, took out my beer and finished the can. It took a good minute or two of steady drinking. He crushed the can single handed, then opened his fingers and held it out, balanced, as you would hold a peanut for a camel, or a mint for a Shire. We both watched it rocking back and forth on his palm.

'Very symbolic. What does it mean?'

'Nothing.' He reached back to the far corner of the room and dropped it softly into the bin. 'Forget it. It's gone.'

'And the dog?'

'The dog, as you say, will be fine.'

'The girl?'

'The girl will continue as she has done every night for the past year. Come nine o'clock, just before the news, she will be taken upstairs to the bedroom and her father will read her a 'bed time story' from his collection. When he's finished, he will call in the dog. She will kneel on the floor in front of him and she will masturbate it to orgasm. When she is finished, she will lick the semen from the floor, on the orders of her father, who is also her grandfather. God knows what he does to her if she refuses but I don't think it can be good.' Ray stood up. 'The care workers are on to him. If he lays a finger on the girl, they'll have her. But they can't get him for abusing the dog.' He stopped. His eyes held mine and I didn't know where to look. 'That was your job,' he said.

Phil Andrews

Notes

We like writing or reading crime stories because we are all criminals, and we enjoy investigating an area of human existence which few of us care to acknowledge openly. All that separates any of us from a serial killer is the seriousness of the offences we commit. The real deviant in our society is the person who never breaks the law, whether it is exceeding the speed limit or being economical with the truth on our tax returns (although Derbyshire traffic police and the Sheffield office of the Inland Revenue should note that the above does not apply to me).

What is more, most of us have a sneaking admiration for high-profile criminals. It is no accident that one of the most potent mythological figures in history, about whom more films have been made than any other character, is the medieval equivalent of a gangster from a Nottingham council estate who periodically goes with his mates down to the local branch of Barclays and props a shotgun across the counter. And if robbing the rich to help the poor is deemed all right for Robin Hood, we shouldn't be surprised if other people get the same idea, even when 'poor' is a relative term.

Of course, there is no such thing as crime in the minds of the perpetrators. All criminals have excellent reasons for deciding that a particular law should not apply to them. It may be social deprivation, sexual jealousy or – as in this story – the belief that the law is an ass, or that justice can only be achieved by taking the law into one's own hands.

My novel *Own Goals* is set in the world of Premiership football, and looks at the reaction of someone who has poured his own money into a club for years when others start creaming off the television and sponsorship millions with which the game is suddenly awash. One of the attractions of crime writing is to examine the circumstances under which people decide they can break the law in the interests of what they believe to be justice.

Because it deals with something of which we are all capable, crime writing is not really a *genre* at all. It is merely a way of observing human behaviour. The plot is an extra for which you should be grateful.

Cooler than Hitch

by Phil Andrews

'You're a smart bastard, Spence.'

Spencer knew he was, but he had to ask.

'What's that mean, Hugo?'

'There's a war on out there. Doormen the size of oil tankers controlling the business in every club, gang fights over territory, people getting beaten up with baseball bats, shooters.'

Hugo liked hard-boiled language. That was because he was an accountant and watched too many movies. 'And you sit outside it all, cool as fuck, with your own little private operation.'

This kind of careless talk in public places made Spencer uncomfortable. 'That's a different business. I'm not here to give people a habit. If I thought you were getting a habit I'd refuse to supply you.'

He had known Hugo since University. They shared an interest in movies. Hugo was a recreational user who enjoyed his recreation enough to be a good customer. And as a respectable professional man he had too much to lose to be indiscreet.

But Spencer knew it was time to leave, though he liked the bar of the arts cinema, with its understated lighting, minimalist decor and old movie posters on the walls. It reflected Spencer's lifestyle and self-image better than any place he knew.

He finished his espresso, picked up the copy of *Sight and Sound* Hugo had left between them on the table and went out to his American four-wheel-drive. Hugo was one of the few people he trusted enough to allow credit, but he flicked open the pages of the magazine as he drove to the bank, just to make sure. The money was there, laid neatly between the pages of an article comparing Alfred Hitchcock's directorial careers in England and Hollywood. Spencer preferred Hitch's later American movies.

Driving to the cash dispenser always set that old TV ad looping through his brain again, the one where the cool guy gets up late on Sunday morning, showers and strolls out for cash to

buy the Sunday papers and takes them back to his loft to chill out
with coffee and some West Coast jazz. Maybe, subconsciously,
that's why Spencer had bought the old Victorian mansion close
to the city centre, and why there was a plumber back there now,
fining a stylish new shower.

Strange bloke. Vaguely familiar, though Spencer hardly cared
to admit he might know someone in his fifties who wore work
overalls with his name on them. Frank something. They lived in
the same city but in parallel universes.

Spencer punched his PIN into the cash dispenser and fed in
Hugo's money. It was criminal the way banks encouraged you to
launder cash through these machines. They even bribed you to
use them with higher interest rates, as if Spencer needed an extra
one per cent. But the ability to feed notes in without contact with
a human being, and to print out a statement to tell him if, when
and how much someone had paid into his account, could have
been tailor-made for him.

Spencer hit the statement button to check that Matt had made
his weekly payment, and a sliver of paper curled out of the slot to
confirm that he had.

He drove to the laundrette and took the bin liner of washing
out of the boot. Matt was already there. When he saw Spencer he
started taking his stuff from the machine and putting it into the
Tesco carrier he had brought it in.

Spencer put a small packet of washing powder down on the
machine next to Matt's. It was already open, the torn cardboard
tab forming a little pouring spout. Matt used the same brand,
same size, tab torn open. He picked up one of the packets and
stuffed it in his bag. It was not the packet he had brought in.

White powder was white powder. Who would know the difference? Spencer did not acknowledge Matt, but loaded his
boxers and socks through the porthole of his machine, slid a
couple of coins into the slots and punched them home with the
heel of his hand. It relaxed him, just watching his stuff flop round
through the plastic window. It was even cool, since those two
lads had stripped down to their boxers to the sound of Sam
Cooke to advertise Levi's. Maybe 501s were no longer at the
cutting edge of fashion, but a laundrette still gave off the right
vibes.

He thought about what Hugo had said, the heavy mob taking
over his operation. He didn't think it was likely, because he
didn't flaunt it. He steered clear of the hubris that afflicted so
many successful people in his trade. No sharp suits, no flash cars.
The secret of long-term success was restraint. He rarely handled
the stuff himself, so there was almost no chance of being caught

in possession. He never accepted cash on delivery, but always kept the transactions separate.

There had been one incident, of course, but he had weathered the storm. He had emerged from it a wiser man and now he kept an even lower profile.

Like everyone else, Spencer had started experimenting at university, but he had been careful not to become dependent. Treated with respect it was a harmless branch of the leisure industry. He soon realised that by supplying a need to a discreet and discriminating group of clients he could avoid having to write all those demeaning letters begging someone not nearly as well qualified as him for a job. He was not in the mass market. He supplied students and a few people like Hugo with the money to support a lifestyle similar to his own. It was enough.

But if he did attract the attention of the hard men, he was ready for them. One of the pleasures of sitting here in the laundrette watching his Calvins go round was working out scenarios for eliminating someone quietly and efficiently, and leaving no trace. It made him feel like a film director. Not a splatter merchant like Tarantino; more like Hitchcock with a clever plot like *Dial M for Murder* or *Strangers on a Train*. Only Spencer's shooting scripts were cooler than Hitch's.

His current storyline involved a prostitute with a habit who would do anything he asked her for a few grammes of the right substance. He had a girl in mind, still attractive enough to lure a man to a hotel room. Spencer would be waiting behind the curtains with a length of piano wire and a wooden dowel to give him the leverage to twist it tight. The people who might want to muscle in on his territory did their dealing round the clubs and used doormen who pumped iron as their persuaders. Spencer was slim, light rangy, but they didn't worry him. Come up behind someone while he was on the job with a length of piano wire in your hand and he'd be dead before his dick went limp. He almost wished someone would give him an excuse to do it. It took the high-speed moan of the final rinse cycle to wipe the smile of anticipation from his face and bring him back to reality.

The plumber had backed his van into the drive, so Spencer had to park on the road. At least it wasn't the rusting old white Transit a cowboy builder would have turned up in, but a dark green Leyland van with the company name on the side in old-fashioned gold lettering. Spencer was using a reputable, long-established firm. Even they would come and do a job overnight if you made it worth their while. He didn't want somebody drilling and hammering during the day when he was trying to sleep or watch a movie.

The shower components were in the hall and for some reason the plumber had taken up some of the floorboards in the kitchen, though the shower was going in the bathroom. Spencer poked his head round the door.

'What's happening with the floorboards, Frank?'

'That's where the pipework will run.'

'You know best,' shrugged Spencer.

Frank wasn't exactly a bundle of fun. A bit surly, if anything. But spending your life removing other people's pubic hair from blocked U-bends probably explained that.

'You know I'll be out for the rest of the evening?' said Spencer.

'The office told me.'

Stiff old bastard. But Spencer was a forgiving sort of bloke. Live and let live was his motto.

'Help yourself to coffee if you want. Milk in the fridge.'

Spencer drove to the Sportsman. The younger City players and their girlfriends used it before they went on to a club. Twenty grand a week for kicking a ball around! Criminal. And they only trained for a couple of hours a day, so time hang heavy. But if they wanted a little something to spice up their leisure hours they needed to deal with someone discreet. There were always reporters sniffing after stories.

Spencer sat in his usual seat with his usual half of low alcohol lager. It was antisocial to drink and drive. He could see Mick Condon and Gerry Vizard at the bar with a couple of tarts, suits so sharp it made your fingers bleed to look at them. It was Condon who came over and handed him the envelope.

'Couple of tickets for Saturday, Spence.' Usual mantra.

'Thanks. Usual seats?'

'Yeah.'

He opened the envelope with the football club crest and there were the match tickets, with a wad of notes for company. He waited for the players to leave before finishing his drink and driving out to complete their order from his supplier. This week he might even use the tickets. City were playing Manchester United, so the seats would have scarcity value. Spencer wasn't a great soccer fan, but when your job had its perks, it was daft not to take advantage occasionally.

Frank's tools were all good quality, Sheffield-made. The firm let you keep them when you retired. It was a little perk of the job. He'd planned to go in for marquetry, keep him out from under Linda's feet a bit. No need for that now she was dead, of course. Now it would help pass his time on when he was on his own all day. But for the first time in months he felt no self-pity. His only concern tonight was to be finished before

Spencer came back. A bit of music helped while he was working, so he tuned to Radio 2 on the kitchen portable.

Spencer sat in the car, listening to the spare honking of Jan Gabarek's sax sounding like a lonely swan on the stereo and waiting for Condon to pick up his order. What this city needed was a decent jazz club where intelligent people could gather to listen to good music in a civilised atmosphere and indulge whatever other recreational tastes they had free from the constraints that applied to the kind of people who used this place, who could not be relied on to show restraint in what they inhaled and ingested.

When Condon finally came out and Spencer had handed over the goods he reversed into the quietest corner of the car park and went into the club. The doorman looked at him with that expression of friendly menace all doormen have. Spencer looked at his neck. He could tell by the bulging arteries that he was a body builder. How quickly they could be stopped off by a piece of piano wire applied with torque.

Spencer didn't like these noisy black holes with their naff lighting and synthesised pop and beer at a quid a pint but now he was ready for something he knew he could come by easily here. He saw the girl he was looking for near the bar. The strobe lighting made her face flicker like the picture on a faulty television screen. He had chatted to her once or twice before, and detected the signals. He could always tell when they were ripe. He knew he hadn't misread the signs when the friend she was with gave that knowing smile as he sat down and made herself scarce.

He bought her a drink and they sparred with words whenever the decibel count fell low enough. In between times, he watched the little deals going on in dark corners, transactions the Drugs Squad would spot a mile off.

She said something he didn't hear and he moved a lot closer to her and put his ear to her mouth.

'I said: 'What do you do?'

'This and that.'

'And the other?'

He laughed.

'Not short of dosh, are you? You a dealer?'

He didn't like this sort of talk in public, even when nobody else could hear. But it never did any harm to let a girl sniff a bit of danger. It always turned them on. Spencer shrugged. 'Half the kids in this place are on uppers or downers. There's nothing wrong with chemicals if handled properly.'

'There was that student who died after taking Es in here. What was her name?' Spencer's look said he couldn't remember. But he remembered. Jo-Ann Walker, shortened by the tabloids to Jo because it made a tighter headline. And there were plenty of those as she lay in a coma for a week before her parents switched the support system off. And again when the mother topped herself a few months later.

JO'S MUM DIES OF GRIEF, said the tabloids. Lying sods. The police had been under pressure to get a result on that one all right. But even though they had Spencer in the cells for 48 hours they made nothing stick. He'd been forced to lay low for months after that, until the all-clear sounded. But that was all behind him now, and he preferred to forget it.

'She should have taken more water with it,' he said, and the quizzical look on his face was intended to preserve his mystique, to keep her guessing. Well, she was trying to deceive him, wasn't she? Her blonde hair was dark at the roots.

'Ever had a ride in a Jeep?' said Spencer, sensing the moment was right.

She laughed, knowing what he meant. It was a better come-on line than: *Want to come up for a coffee?*

He passed her bag to her, running the long leather strap through his palms and thinking you could garrote someone nicely with that in an emergency, though piano wire would be preferable.

The air outside had a welcome coolness. He reclined the passenger seat. She got in and lifted her bum without any encouragement so he could slide her knickers off, and he nipped the teat of the condom between his thumb and finger and slid it on.

To screw through rubber with a steady pumping action was one of life's little pleasures. There was no chance of the rubber splitting. This was a top-of-the-range German shower cubicle with heavy-duty seals that were absolutely watertight And Frank was using six-inch screws straight into the floor and ceiling joists. The joists were solid oak in Victorian houses like this. No chance of anybody knocking this down, no matter how hard they hit it.

He'd always taken satisfaction in a job well done .He was enjoying the feel of the steel thread of the screw biting into the hard timber more today than he had for ages, even though he knew it may be the last time he would do it.

'Smoke?' she asked when it was over. He didn't, but he always carried a Zippo because he loved the *noir* effect of the flickering light on a girl's face in a dark place. He leaned over her and spun the wheel of the lighter with his thumb, thinking how vulnerable her young face looked in the flame.

The flame of the blowlamp, fiercely blue, licked round the copper pipework of the shower drain, forming a perfect seal. The pipework ran under the floorboards to the outside of the house. Frank's last job would be to connect it up when he was confident everything was watertight.

Spencer dropped her off on his way home. The plumber's van was still in his drive. Christ! How long did it take to install a fucking shower?

All the stuff had gone out of the hall. He shouted up the stairs, but there was no reply so he opened the kitchen door.

What the fuck!

Frank stepped out of the cupboard beneath the stairs, closed the door behind Spencer and slid home the bolt he had carefully fitted. He went outside, attached one end of a length of hose to the shower outlet and the other end to the exhaust of his van and secured them carefully with jubilee clips. Then he started the motor.

A side door from the garage led back into the kitchen. Spencer saw Frank come in.

'What the fuck are you doing? You've installed the fucking thing in the kitchen you fucking moron. And now the door's jammed. Fucking well let me out, you dickhead!'

Frank could only hear what Spencer was saying when he looked straight at him and read his lips. That helped him focus on what little sound penetrated the shower walls. Frank had never liked the Germans since the war but, you had to hand it to them. They were good engineers. He would take up Spencer's offer of coffee now, but not that filter muck he had left out. Frank rummaged in the cupboards until he found a jar of instant. Then he sat on the kitchen stool to watch.

Spencer had smelled the exhaust fumes now, and realised their were entering the shower cubicle through the drain.

'You mad fucking bastard. What's going on?'

He was banging on the toughened glass walls with his hands. They barely shook, but the outlines of Spencer's palm was printed in condensation on the glass like a halo. He put his foot over the drain to try to stop the fumes coming in, but the blue gas seeped round his shoe.

There was panic on Spencer's face now, the face Frank had seen through the spyhole in the cell door when the police asked if he had ever seen Spencer with his daughter. The face he next saw when he came here to measure up for this shower unit.

Spencer tore off a shoe and sock and jammed his heel down into the soakaway to form a perfect seal. Frank admired that. It was a sound technical solution. Except that Spencer would soon have used up the oxygen in that confined space and the more he shouted and tried to breakout, the faster it would go.

Spencer knew it, too. He was still now, staring out at Frank with a pleading look. He was already having to breath faster when he realised where he had seen Frank's face before.

How could he have forgotten all those photographs of Frank Webster and his wife Linda staring out from the papers and the television news after they had agreed to switch off the life support of their daughter Jo-Ann?

'I'm sorry,' he whispered with what breath he had left.

Spencer was in tears now, but Frank merely sipped his coffee and seemed to look straight through him. He'd been trying to think where he'd seen someone die in a shower before, and it had come to him. It was that Alfred Hitchcock film he'd seen on TV. *Psycho.* Very loud and American. All those screeching violins as Anthony Perkins repeatedly stabbed Janet Leigh through the curtain. Must have been very messy. This was better, Clean, Restrained. This was the English way to do it.

PLEASE! yelled Spencer, his face distorted as it pressed against the glass.
Please!
please...

But it was Jo-Ann's face Frank saw projected on the glass, so peaceful after the doctors had switched off the machine and taken those plastic tubes out of her nose. And then Linda's, though the overdose of barbiturates had left her eyes all blood-shot. But he had blanked that out, as you do with things you don't want to remember. And she would be able to rest in peace now. He felt very calm, and he went on seeing their faces on the shower screen long after Spencer had finally stopped gasping for breath.

Adam Lloyd Baker

Notes

How many crimes did you commit today?
Did you park on a double yellow?
Did you talk to some nice girl, get flattered by the attention, fold your hands to hide your wedding ring?

Did you take shit at work and vent it on a postal clerk or check-out girl?

Did you make personal phone calls from the office?

Did you steal stationary from the cupboard?

Did you phone in sick when you were not?

Did you tell the girl at the till she gave you too much change?

Did you ignore a begging hand?

Did you pick up money in the street?

Sniper. Serial killer. Gentleman thief. Consolation fantasies for every clock punching Joe who wants to be powerful, wants a little respect.

For the most part it is not the cruelty of evil men that makes living an ordeal, but the petty hurts and violations we inflict one on another each working day.

You might cheat on your wife, steal hotel soap, or sneak in late for work, but we don't call these transgressions a crime because they are too chickenshit to make it on the statute books and anyway we don't want to face how cheap our principles get sold.

Be honest with yourself. How many crimes did you commit today?

Atlantic City

by Adam Lloyd Baker

I've been watching that Korean guy, off and on, all night. He's sitting in the office, looking out the window. He was there when I went to get coffee and he was there when I got back. Doesn't read a magazine or anything. Just watches the sign say: *ROOMS... VACANCIES... ROOMS... VACANCIES...* and rain beat on the cars in the forecourt. I wonder what he's thinking.

Elmer and I came south to make some money. Saw the motel sign just as we ran out of gas. Ahead of us: Atlantic City. Behind us: unlit nowhere. I got a job washing dishes. Elmer hasn't got a job. He's kind of a broke dick.

We've been sharing this room for two weeks. He took the left side of the room to be close to the TV. I got the right side which means I got the window, the radiator, and a bed that vibrates if you drop a coin in the slot.

Maybe that Korean guy thinks we're fags. Maybe he doesn't think anything at all.

'This is latte.' says Elmer, peering at his coffee. 'I wanted *café au lait.*'

'That's what I asked for.'

'Well this is steamed milk. Look. It's settling. I've paid for half a cup of air.'

'Take it back.'

'Fucking spics. Spit in your food. Look how much actual coffee is in this thing. Half. Less than half. There ought to be a law. You're gonna serve the public then at least speak some fucking English.'

Me and Elmer have been in this room all day. We're going a little crazy.

I take a damp slip of paper from my breast pocket and put it on the radiator to dry.

'That the tickets ?' says Elmer.

'Yep.'

'For the concert.'

'Friday. Yeah.'

'What's her name?'

'Louise.'

Elmer lies back on the bed and puts his hands behind his head.

'Let me tell you how it is with women.' he says. Elmer is thirty years older than me and has White Power tattoos up his arms. We met riding box cars. 'Forget all the sensitive, changing the diaper, shit. The ladies want a man to be a man, all right? They want an alpha male. You watch wildlife programmes ? Lions, zebras, so on. The alpha male is king of the gorillas. The big-ass grey back.'

'You're full of shit.'

'No, really. You could learn something, kid. You see, your average chick is always on the look-out for good genetic material, right ? It's a biological imperative. That's why a Ferrari is a license to fuck. It proves you're a successful animal. You go out into the world and take want you want. Lord of the Jungle.'

'That's Tarzan.'

'Look, I'm trying to help. Now this Louise girl. She waits on tables all evening and every time she goes in the kitchen she sees you scrubbing pans. Just another kitchen schnook. So when you take her to this concert you have to show a better side of yourself.'

'I can't get a Ferrari by friday.'

'Maybe not, but at least get some snappy duds. I mean look at this.' He gestures to my ragged jeans and sneakers. 'I seen winos with more self respect than that. What were you planning to wear on Friday?'

'My boots, my good jeans, that grey shirt with the stripes.'

'You need a jacket. Black leather. Trust me on this. You'll look older, street tough.' Elmer points at his Harley jacket hanging on the back of a chair 'Leather gives off pheremones. Chicks are hot for it.'

'I haven't got any money. The tickets cleaned me out.'

'I thought of that. This is the plan. We get dressed and drive into town. Hit the casinos, right ? Win you that jacket and be back before your shift starts.'

'That's a fucked up idea.'

'Trust me,' says Elmer. 'I've got a system.'

Elmer's little Dodge, hammering through the projects, headed for the downtown lights.

'How much money you got?' asked Elmer.

'Fifty. You?'

'Ten. Lend me twenty then we split the winnings half and half.'

'Sure.'

'Say three, three fifty, for a good jacket. I think a plain, blazer style would suit you best.'

'If this system is so fucking bulletproof how come everyone isn't bleeding these joints to bankruptcy?'

'Greed. Fucker sits down at the blackjack table and starts winning big-time then every pit boss, every camera in the vicinity, is on him. Whatever scam the guy has going they get wise, drag him though a Staff Only door and snap his fingers. We got to be smart. Take a little here, a little there. It'll be like going to the bank.'

Elmer parked outside the Taj Mahal and threw his keys to the valet. We went inside.

A windowless, cathedral space. Row after row of inert slot machines and empty seats. The graveyard shift.

'OK,' said Elmer, 'the roulette tables are up ahead. Back here in an hour.'

Elmer's system went like this:

When you sit down at a roulette table you can bet your lucky number at fifty-to-one and maybe walk out a millionaire. If you're the conservative type you can bet black or red, odds or evens, at two-to-one.

Elmer figured that if you stood next to a table and watched the ball land on a black number ten times in a row then common sense tells you a red square is coming up any time and you should step in, place your chips, and double your money. That was his plan.

There were enough people working the tables that I didn't feel conspicuous hanging around, watching the ball. Everyone's attention was on this cigar chewing jerk in an Accapulco shirt who yelled, 'go, baby go' at the ball like he had been taking advanced asshole lessons somewhere. Eight reds in a row so I took a stool and changed my thirty dollars for three little green chips.

I put ten on black, ten on evens. The croupier rolled black 22. My hands were shaking when I raked in the chips. Bet black and evens one more time. Black 38. I walked away with ninety dollars in my pocket.

Three more tables, three more wins. I was on a streak. won so much they changed croupiers on me. A casino guy slapped my back and comped me free drinks at the restaurant. When I met up with Elmer my pockets were stuffed with chips.

'How much you got?' asked Elmer.

'Seven, maybe eight hundred.'

'You're fucking kidding me.'

'Swear to God. My money kept doubling.'

'Jesus. I didn't win a thing.'

'No?'

'Streaks. They happen. Spent the last half hour smoking in the bar.'

'Come on. Let's find a cashier.'

'Fifty-fifty. That's what we said.' Elmer standing on the pier, waiting for sunrise over the Atlantic.

'Yeah. That's what we said.'

I shuffled bills and peeled off four hundred.

'It's too cold for this shit. Let's walk.'

Elmer bought a pizza slice and I got coffee. We strolled along the boardwalk. The sky was light and the stars were going out.

'You see this is what I'm saying,' said Elmer, resuming a dialogue he'd been conducting in his head. 'You and me. A man travels through life, he needs friends. You can't make it on your own. That's what jail taught me. Alone, you're nothing. But a bunch of guys looking out for each other can push on through.'

'Yeah.'

'Believe me. In the wing, on the yard. Got to band together.'

'Didn't we park back that way?'

'I want to show you something, if it's still here.' The lights were down in Atlantic City Leathers but we could see the window display.

'This is where I got my Harley jacket.' said Elmer. 'Must be, Jesus, fifteen years ago.'

Boots, belts and gloves. A Harley Electraglide with leathers draped over it.

'See anything you like?'

'It's mostly biker stuff.'

I squinted at the price tags.

'Shit. Look at this,' said Elmer. 'You have to see this.'

The jacket cloaked the shoulders of a headless mannequin.

It shimmered in the morning light. The card said 100 per cent genuine rattlesnake hide. The tag said $900.

'My God,' I said.

'Maybe we should just break the glass.'

'Come on. I got four hours til my shift. Hit the tables, make some fucking money. We did it once, we'll do it again.'

Elmer picked up a girl and a bottle of Cuervo Gold on the way home. I'd seen the kid before. She was one of the sex-for-smokes chicks that hung around the bus terminal. Black, late teens. Today her name was Tracey.

'It's a question of perspective,' said Elmer, lighting a cigarette off the dash. 'You dropped three hundred but you're still one twenty ahead. You don't have a jacket but you didn't have one this morning either, am I right Tracey?'

'Yeah.'

'Comes down to the type of guy you are. Is the glass half full or half empty, you know what I'm saying? I mean you're not gonna sulk on me know, are you?'

Elmer threw his jacket over a chair and said: 'I'm gonna phone for burgers. I think that place up the road delivers.'

I swilled cups in the bathroom and heard the bedsprings creak. Elmer had his shirt off and was lying on the bed. Tracey massaged his back and shoulders. She ran her hands over the swastikas and Aryan Brotherhood tattoos.

'It's nothing, baby,' said Elmer. 'Just jailhouse bullshit.'

I gave them a cup of tequila each and sat by the window. I took a hit from the bottle.

Elmer's Harley jacket lay across a metal chair. The corner of his wallet protruded from the left pocket. The girl had seen it also.

'Oh, that's good,' said Elmer.

'Magic fingers,' said Tracey.

I went to the bathroom for a piss. When I got back Elmer was sitting on the side of the bed with his dick out. Tracey got down on her knees and licked his circumcised prick. Elmer laid back and let her suck.

I sat by the window. It was raining again. The Korean guy was still in his office. He was asleep at his desk with a pen in his hand.

'No good,' said Elmer. He sat up and pushed the girl away. 'Just not happening.'

'Did I do something wrong?'

'I'm tired.' Elmer took twenty from his pocket. 'Here. For your time.'

The girl took the money. She sat next to me on the bed. 'Anything I can do for you?'

'That's all right. You can get going if you want.'

Tracey looked out the rain spattered window.

'I got no place to go,' she said.

'No friends or nothing?'

'No.'

'You want to watch some TV?'

A knock at the door. A delivery boy with a bag of food. Triple order of cheese burger and fries. We crowded round the cupboard, using it as a table to squirt ketchup and shake salt. Sometime, while my back was turned, Elmer's wallet disappeared from his coat.

We sat in the cold light of television. Racing from Daytona. Tracey finished her burger and lay on the bed next to Elmer. She stroked his tattoos and said: 'How long were you in jail?'

'Eleven years.'

'What for?'

'Armed robbery. A cigarette warehouse. Me and a friend.'

'That's a long time.'

'A security guard got killed.'

'Did you shoot him?'

'I don't remember. The cops ask you over and over, and you tell so many lies the truth gets lost along the way.'

'What happened to your friend?'

'Well, out on the street you don't have no friends. Lesson number one. I don't need to tell you, right? The cops pulled us in on a rumour. If me and Billy didn't say nothing we'd walk. But they put us in separate rooms. Laid out the deal. You see, that security guard turned armed robbery to murder one. Capital crime. The trigger man gets the gas chamber but the accomplice might be out in ten, maybe less. So the guy who snitches first, who down-plays his own involvement, gets to live. What do you do in a situation like that? I told them Billy shot the place up. Everything between us, all the blood brother bullshit, didn't mean a damn thing. You do what you have to do.'

'That's a sad story.'

'Yes it is.'

Tracey put on her shoes.

'Thanks for the food,' she said.

'It's still raining.'

'I think I saw a bus stop by the diner.' Tracey walked towards the door and I followed.

'Maybe get some cigarettes from the machine,' I explained.

I stood with Tracey beneath the eves of the chalet, watching waves of rain wash over the forecourt. I wanted to tell this feral kid to stop turning tricks, to go to school or something. I wanted to say words that would keep her safe, but couldn't think how.

'You gonna be all right?' I asked.

'Sure.'

'I'd drive you someplace but I got to be at work in an hour.'

'It was nice.'

'Kept you dry at least.'

'Thanks.'

'I got to ask you for Elmer's wallet back.'

'I haven't got no wallet.'

'It's no big thing but I got to have it back.'

'Honest.'

'Don't shit a shitter.'

Tracey took the wallet from the pocket of her denim jacket and handed it over. I took another twenty from the wallet and gave it to her.

'Don't get too wet.'

She ran across the street to the diner. I went back inside the cabin. Elmer was snoring on the bed. I kicked him awake.

'What the fuck is this?' I demanded.

'What?'

'This money. In your wallet. There must be a thousand, maybe fifteen hundred here.'

I waved the notes at him.

'I was gonna give you some.'

'Fifty-fifty. That's what we said. You been winning all night. What's yours is yours, and what's mine is yours, is that it?'

'I was just fucking with you. You want the jacket? We can get it.'

I cuffed Elmer across the head and he fell to the floor, a jail-house bitch once again.

'Nothing but a ball and chain. When I finish work tonight I am out of here. I'm taking three hundred for the rent. Do what you like.'

'You aren't gonna leave, are you Johnny?'

I pulled my bag from under the bed and packed my clothes.

'I am so sick of your noise.'

'Come on, man. Amigos. You and me, huh?' Elmer sat down on the edge of his bed. 'Johnny, I ain't got nobody. Nobody in the world. Don't go.'

I packed my books.

'You want some coffee, huh? To set you up? I'll get some coffee.'

Elmer held a newspaper over his head and hurried outside.

Alone again. I sat on the bed and lit a cigarette. No sound but the rain.

Maxim Jakubowski

Notes

This is not a political story.

In fact, as ever with me, it's a story about sex.

Well, isn't that a surprise?

My only fear is that between the time of writing this and the book's publication, some maniac might take it to heart to snuff out our present Prime Minister, and then I'll have a delicate problem on my hands. So, should you be reading this in times unknown, feel free to substitute the name of any damn politician lest you feel mischievous or vindictive. I accept no responsibility whatsoever.

Count Clinton out. Sex and cigars and American politics just lack elegance...

So why do I always appear to write about sex?

It's not an obsession, I swear.

It is mainly because I like to write about people, what they think, what makes them tick, about the deep emotions that motivate them, about the thin line between right and wrong and how easy it is somehow under pressure to cross that line.

My last three novels all follow that pattern, of men and women, creatures of blood and foremost flesh, who take a wrong turning on the road of life. Bad things happen when you're blinded by passion. In *It's You That I Want To Kiss*, you get involved in drug trafficking, in *Because She Thought She Loved Me*, the doomed lovers turn to murder and in *The State Of Montana*, the heroine recognises her submissive nature and throws herself head first into a maelstrom of somewhat unhealthy sex (but then *Montana* wasn't actually a crime novel!). Just like real life.

At any rate, the following story is somewhat tongue in cheek. Or is it?

Under what circumstances would *you* envisage assassinating the Prime Minister?

The Day I Killed Tony Blair

by Maxim Jakubowski

Is the tape recorder on?

OK.

Well, you know I'm guilty, so why do we have to go through all this rigmarole? I confess: I did it. I killed Tony Blair. I killed the Prime Minister.

Come on, you know this isn't like another Sarajevo or another Dallas. Just a crime. A petty crime. Sure, the headlines will loom large but in a few weeks things will fade of their own natural accord. Just another damn politician, after all. Lots of others where he came from. The status quo will soon return. I'm not kidding myself, I know it won't change anything.

Actually, I'm quite ready for jail. At least we don't have the death sentence any longer. I know the food will be no great shakes, but at least I reckon I'll be able to catch up with all my reading. Life sentence, no doubt. That's fine with me. I deserve it. Well, I did kill a man. I'm happy to do my time. After all, that's part of the deal, no? You want to know why? Oh, of course.

Yes, I suppose I owe you some form of explanation.

You? The police, the newspapers, the public.

Do I really have to? It's a rather private matter, after all.

And it's not as if I was denying anything. I'm guilty. One hundred per cent. You have it on camera. You have the weapon, my confession. Can't we leave it at that?

You want it to make some sense. I see. Well, I can assure you I'm not insane, and there's no need for any psychiatric investigation. I've never had much respect for psychiatrists, psychologists and all that ilk. A useless race. A bit like social workers. They invent the sheer causes for their existence. A real con, I tell you.

Political?

Well, not really.

It wasn't Saddam Hussein, Ghadaffi, the Russians or the IRA I did it for. Or even less the Israelis, even though I'm Jewish (well, the only time I've visited a synagogue, I was eleven years old and had to be dragged screaming by my father to make up the male numbers for some religious ceremony). No, no political motives whatsoever. I swear.

Give you a clue: if Labour hadn't been in power, it could well have been William Hague, or Portillo or whoever would have been at 10 Downing Street. See, I'm an equal opportunity assassin.

A thirst for fame or notoriety, then?

No. You're still cold.

Although, ironically, I reckon now that I'll momentarily be in the public eye, my books will probably sell a bit better than they used to. Not that it will do me much good. Criminals can't profit from their crimes, can they? Didn't they devise a law for that? Or was it in the United States only?

You seem puzzled.

You shouldn't. I've an explanation, really. It's a bit convoluted, I admit, but it makes perfect sense.

Must I now?

It's just that I'm rather tired, you see. It's been a long day. Naturally, I've been living on nerves since this morning knowing what I was going to do and some of your colleagues were a bit rough after they seized me. Over-enthusiastic, I'd say. And I wasn't resisting arrest in any way.

No, not tea. I just hate this cup of tea for all occasions thing. So damn English. A can of Coca Cola, yes, that would be much better. And some chocolate. Milk chocolate. Any kind. Brings my sugar levels up and, oh, while you're at it, a couple of Disprin soluble tablets. I'm getting a bit of a headache in here. It is a bit stuffy, wouldn't you say. Water? No, I'll dissolve them in the Coke. It works every time: my miracle cure for all ailments. Have you ever tried it? Maybe the way the caffeine interacts with the Disprin. Gives you an instant boost, clears your mind. Sounds almost druggy, eh? Curiously enough 'I've never been into soft drugs. At all. Tried some of course, but they just had no effect on me. Rather disappointing. For you too, no, would have made good headlines: *'Crime Writer on Drugs Assassinates Prime Minister.'* Sorry.

Ah, that feels better. Thanks.

I suppose I'd better tell you now, then. The sooner the better and I'll be left to get some sleep, I suppose.

But I know you're going to be disappointed.

It's a rather ordinary story, I fear.

A woman.

It was because of a woman.

No. Not her, Cherie. You must be joking. That mortician's smile would deflate a man's hard on instantly!

Mind you, so did his own smile-by-numbers sincere expression of choice. No. No. Don't get excited. I was just being facetious. I'm not gay. The Prime Minister's smile and my past erections have nothing in common. Wouldn't want the country to go on another anti-gay pogrom, would I?

A woman.

A real one.

A beautiful one.

Who knew how to provoke erections and what to do with them with tender loving care .

Yes, I know : sometimes I get a tad too lyrical. It's the way I am, the way I write. What can I do about it? Some reviewer even once said I was a romantic pornographer. Damn right. And proud of it.

A woman.

Her name was Edwina.

Why am I saying 'was'?

Her name *is* Edwina. It's a bit of an old-fashioned name. So she calls herself Eddie. A bit ambiguous, but who cares. Took me ages to find out that Eddie actually concealed Edwina. She'd decided it was her turn to pay the bill when we ate out one evening, and I spied the truth on her credit card. Edwina O'Callaghan. A name like that you'd imagine some old Irish biddy or worse. I'd actually heard of her vaguely some time before we actually met, and the name alone gave me a completely wrong impression somehow. I imagined her middle-aged, dowdy, supercilious, just not my type of person.

It was a shock meeting her the first time, I can tell you.

As you know, my books don't sell in great quantities. I'm strictly second division. I have to supplement the income with a fair bit of arts journalism, reviews, the occasional well-paid travel piece. So, like most jobbing writers I'm always looking out for new markets or publishing opportunities.

An American company specialising in mail-order recipe and gardening cards and part works was making a foray in to the crime and mystery field and was trying to devise some form of whodunit product which people would subscribe to. Their London office was in charge of development. They needed writers to dream up whodunit plots in novella form, longer than a short story but shorter than a novel. A length I, for one, particularly enjoyed but which seldom proved commercial due to a sparsity of outlets. I wasn't into traditional mysteries where the detective hunts down the clues and later by intellect and much eccentric ratiocination assembles the suspects and reveals the guilty party. I'm more into dark streets, femmes fatales, emotions and murky psychology. But the money was good. Three grand for just a third of a book and the rights to the material reverted to the author fairly quickly. In addition, the whole concept of the scheme and the way it was to be sold by mail order only sounded rather dubious to me, and I estimated there was even a good chance it would never get off the ground once the company's marketing boffins had analysed, market-tested, focus grouped it and all and the writers would be three grand to the better and with a story they could sell again.

Edwina O'Callaghan had been recruited to find a dozen or so authors to pen the various booklets and I'd heard through Mark Timlin she was not averse to darker stuff, as long as the whodunit elements were present. I thought to myself the task was not impossible and also a gentle challenge. I could construct the plot in reverse and *hey presto* – easy money.

I was wrong. Like all the women who think writing a Mills and Boon romance is a cinch! It was bloody tough and I was no good at it. We'd spoken over the telephone. She didn't sound as old as I thought. She had sent me the project Bible and I had churned some tongue in cheek opus out. Even as I finished it, I knew already all the elements required were present but it had no heart, was just an exercise in style. Shouldn't even have put it in the post to her. She was a pernickety and fastidious editor and tore my contribution to pieces and suggested we meet up so we could discuss her numerous suggestions for the rewrite.

My initial reaction was to chuck the whole thing, accept the kill fee and move on to better things. There was this publisher in America who was keen on my tale of erotic adventures set in New Orleans, a place I knew well and which always inspired me to much literary excess. I was eager to get started on that story. It was closer to my heart than some damn whodunnit set in the home counties where the butler didn't do it (it was actually the priest – who wasn't really a priest – I'd made into the culprit).

But I agreed to meet her.

Call it gut instinct or fate or whatever you believe in when it comes to matters of the heart, lust and the flesh. I was sort of curious to see the face behind the voice and that decidedly old-fashioned, conservative name. Although nothing could ever have prepared me for what was to happen.

Edwina O'Callaghan.

Fiction Editor.

Just call me Eddie, she had said.

A few days later, we were in bed together. The middle of the day. August sun blazing beyond the lace curtains of a hotel room in a concrete monstrosity of a building near one of the main railway stations.

We had become lovers.

Lust at first sight, you might say.

Oh yes, she was married.

At that stage, blind as we were and slaves to our desires, just a fairly minor consideration .

I suppose I have to provide you with more details. Intimate ones. Personal stuff and all that. Or you just wouldn't understand my reasons. For the assassination.

I suppose so.

Well, Eddie was special.

Very special.

What can I say? That I was consumed by her like no one before. That the initial fire of lust soon changed into mad love, beyond any border I had ever crossed before when it had come to women. That she was different, like a dream literally come true.

No, I haven't a photo of her. She insisted I return all of them after we split.

You wouldn't understand, anyway. These sort of things are so irrational, I realise. Beauty is so much in the eye of the beholder.

You'd tell me she was too slim, didn't really have much in the way of tits. 34A, actually, which for 5'9" isn't that opulent. That the way she wore her hair, in a frizzy perm, was no longer in vogue, even if it ever had been. That her arse was maybe a bit loo large and square. That she walked a touch funny, bent forward. That there was a scar on her left cheek and she should have worn some form of make-up to minimise its presence. That her teeth were crooked.

And if you knew, which you would have eventually, what with all your investigative powers, that she shaved her pubic hair, you would have said, no doubt, that women with smooth crotches have a sluttish nature.

But also, it's all in the details, you see, there are things in a woman that are beyond description. They match your own emotional make-up and when the respective elements line-up together it just goes boom, quietly, boom, forever, boom, boom there goes my heart.

Silly, no?

I fell in love with Eddie and there was no safety net.

I think she fell in love with me too, initially.

It's so difficult to explain.

Eddie's nipples. That shade of pink beyond paleness that moved me so hard, delicate, sad, unique, touching. They never did get very hard, instead as we made love the pinkness spread in concentric orbs outwards until the whole area from breast to throat was flushed in a strong hue of desire.

Eddie's eyes. A brown-eyed blonde. The dark colour like a pool of sorrow in which my eyes would lose themselves attempting to reach the sheer depths of her thoughts.

Eddie's mouth. Her lipsticked lips tightening around my glans with hungry tenderness, taking the sacrament of my vile meat deep inside her with benign acceptance. Tongue caressing my shaft, delineating my cock's corona like a geographer quietly mapping new territory to be explored, invested.

Eddie's words.

The way she would say 'Jesus' when I entered her and again and again on every stage on that road to orgasm, the word a holy or rather so wonderfully blasphemous punctuation of our frenzied sex.

Eddie's sounds.

The moans. The sighs. The deep breaths. The times she would actually stop breathing between thrusts, anticipating the next surge of unadulterated lust or pleasure, in order to magnify its impact, diffuse its terrible, unforgiving waves throughout her whole senses.

Eddie's movements.

The way she would adjust her position so that my hardness would dig even deeper.

The desolating delicacy with which she would twirl some of the curls on my chest in a gesture of tenderness.

The desperate longing in her eyes as we watched the waves of pleasure rise in our bodies as we fucked like animals and the silent way she would acquiesce to my finger invading her even more, crushing the last barrier of her intimacy.

Eddie sleeping. Next to me, her breath shallow, her pale body almost like a corpse, her face at rest, the trace of a contented smile on her still moist lips. The silence, at last. The loneliness of being together. Stirrings again in my stomach and cock. The eternal circle of silence and sex where words were pointless and only bodies spoke the secret language of life.

Head over heels in love, you see.

Captive.

Consumed.

Of course, there were complications. The mechanics of adultery and work make for troubled companions, but then that's no news for you guys. But we managed. We courted disaster on many occasions, took risks, lied a lot, but we were healthy, greedy for more and more sex, and we managed. Breakfast fucks, lunchtime assignments, evening trysts.

Curiously enough, my first indication of future problems in our fevered relationship also had political connotations.

I think we'd been lovers for nearly two months. In rooms, on beds, on floors, wherever we fell on to each other, we never did speak much. It was more motion and deep, significant silences, meaningful looks and all that. But there were also times we acted like normal human beings, went to see a movie together, had a drink in a bar. Eddie suddenly asked me who I usually voted for. She appeared quite concerned. Explained that she'd somehow never gotten round to asking me. My inner radar quickly spotted an obstacle so I fudged my answer. Turned out she was a fervent Labour supporter. Had been since university. But then most intellectuals are. Was actually a volunteer canvasser for her local area. And it had just occurred to her that she might be fucking someone who supported a different political party. All of a sudden, this worried her.

I'd never been a political animal and my voting decisions swayed all over the place, depending on my mood and whichever party had committed the latest political gaffes. More often than not, I had voted for the party which had no chance of winning; a mischievous streak inside me had always felt doing this was both honourable and a way of defying public opinion. Not a man of deep social convictions, you see. What I didn't tell her was that at the previous elections I had actually voted Tory. It's just that the national Labour candidate simply got on my nerves! No way I was going to throw a spanner in he path of our burgeoning affair. I lied. Implied that I shared Eddie's political leanings.

I'm not sure she believed me fully, but the subject was never raised again. Maybe, like me, she had come to the conclusion that the sex was just too good and that principles would have to take a back seat.

By now, I knew the affair with Eddie had quickly reached a point of no return. This was no passing infatuation. It was the real thing.

Just seeing her coming towards me in the street, her flowing skirts billowing gently in the wind, brought a lump to my throat. Her voice on the phone, hesitant, vulnerable was like an arrow aimed straight at my heart. Her lengthy silences when we were together spoke to me more words than a recitation. I knew we had to be together, no longer reliant on stolen, illicit moments of joy. I wanted to travel with her, take her places I'd talked of, praised, loved. But most of all I hankered for whole nights with her. Whole nights. A whole life.

The idea appeared to have some appeal to her, albeit with reservations too, which I could well appreciate.

Which presented us with a problem.

The husband.

A man who took her for granted. Her first big flame, married too early, now too obsessed with his professional career and neglecting her needs it seemed.

They had come together at university. Oxford. He'd done time at the BBC in the News Department, reporting for radio and then, when bi-media was established, for early morning TV, on business in the automotive and nationalised industries. He'd now progressed to Business Correspondent of one of the failing broadsheet newspapers.

Our silences shortened while our talk of the future increased. Hesitancy. Fear. I foolishly insisted, although never quite to the point of giving her the damn ultimatum of him or me. Although I maybe gave that impression in my feverish intensity.

We still fucked like rabbits, and I just couldn't believe how every time it just got better and better as our bodies grew ever more familiar with each other and the fit became so much more intimate, frenzied and tender. Any more of these heart-wrenching heights and I'd be having heart attacks, breaking in two, collapsing in tears of joy, I felt.

I convinced her to spend a whole weekend with me. We knew it would be a test for both of us and that important decisions might be reached by the end of those 48 hours together. I was deliriously happy. Two whole days seemed like an eternity and I was convinced that my fervour would convince her I was her only alternative. All I had to do was just be myself, love her even more tenderly (which was no stretch in the state I was in) and all would fall into place.

Excuses were made, alibis meticulously constructed and we met at Waterloo Station for an early morning Brighton train. Both a bit nervous. Never before had we actually spent so long together. Both of us bursting out in laughter when we discovered we had each packed a book along with our lightweight overnight luggage.

We never did read much. Well, the morning papers on Sunday as we enjoyed breakfast in a bed that stank of sex and sweat and other delightful secretions.

We did all the things you do on a traditional dirty weekend. Enjoyed our bodies. Walked on the sea front. Had fish and ships. Fucked again all afternoon. Found an Italian trattoria full of football supporters for a late snack until we repaired to the hotel room together again for more carnal activities. At some stage, I also remember we went out seeking the local Haagen Dazs ice cream parlour in a back street which she recalled from an earlier visit (with her husband, I assumed). I had chocolate chip and raspberry, Eddie had bilberry cheese cake. We swapped flavours from tongue to tongue like kids.

It was a rainy weekend and there wasn't much else to do but stay in bed, caress, embrace, cuddle, make love until we were both quite raw and wondrous at our renewed vigour and how perfect we were together and how we didn't want these moments to ever end.

But they did.

In Brighton.

Why the hell do political parties have annual conferences, I ask you? It's just an ego trip for politicians. A rubber stamp for redundant policies. And why the hell do they always choose seaside resorts as venues for the damn events? At any rate, neither Eddie or I had realised that the annual Labour political conference was opening in Brighton the Monday following our fated weekend of unbridled lust.

We soon realised, of course, what with television crews setting up all over the place, and gaffer tape and chalk marks dotted across the hotel lobby and the sea front to indicate where the cameras were to be set up.

Innocently, we didn't give it much of a thought.

Lovers live in a private world all of their own, don't they?

How could we know that we (she?) would be recognised in Brighton by a couple of BBC journalists on assignment who had once seen Eddie and her husband at a regional radio Xmas party up in Elstree, and assuredly knew I was not her husband, this scruffy man holding her hand and always touching her rather intimately as we supped our pasta in that damn trattoria. Or, to compound our fate, that we would be observed checking out of the hotel, both carrying incriminating overnight bags, by an activist from her local party.

Of course, neither of us were supposed to be in Brighton that weekend.

And people have big mouths. Bastards!

My final memory of Brighton is the delay at the railway station as we prepared to take the train back to London where we had arranged another assignment four nights later, where we hoped to reach a final decision as to where the affair was going. I had high hopes, of course. Brighton had been good. As we disembarked from the cab, there was an unholy affray outside the station. Tony Blair and his retinue were arriving in town.

Eddie had smiled. 'Our future leader,' she had said.

I can't remember what my mumbled answer was.

We were just a few yards away from him as he trooped past.

We never did meet again in London four days later. I got a tearful phone call from Eddie the day before, telling me that her husband had found out about us.

My heart dropped. So what? I pointed out. Then, how?

She haltingly explained. The Party Conference. Blair.

Shit.

Her husband wanted her to stay. He'd forgiven her. Had sworn he would devote more time to her from now on, things would be different. She had to give him a chance. Just couldn't throw away eight years of marriage that way. I must understand. This was it. It was over. I must promise never to try and contact her again. She was sorry. So sorry. I cried.

Initially felt sorry for myself.

Wrote her crazy letters. Which she never even acknowledged.

That's it. See. What an ordinary story, eh? Man meets woman. Man and woman sleep together. Think they're in love. Labour Party political conference pulls them apart.

So now you know why I did it.

All his bloody fucking fault. Tony Blair, with his insincere smile, his smarmy holier than thou pronouncements.

The bastard.

Why couldn't he have chosen Blackpool or Scarborough or anywhere else than Brighton?

I'll do my time.

He got what he deserved.

Lee Child

Notes

Why crime? Novels are about conflict, and a writer has a wide spread of choices, from internal psychological debate to international terrorism and world wars. Crimes like homicide and theft and fraud sit there dynamically in the middle, not too small, not too big, with a clear good/bad split, driven by clear human passions.

Am I a British crime writer? Well, I'm British, and I'm a crime writer... but I live in New York and I write primarily for America.

Why America? That answer falls into two parts. First, there's a crucial difference between being a reader and a writer. When you read something, clearly it's already been created, otherwise it wouldn't be there on the page at all. But when you write, you try to do something that hasn't been done before. No point in imitating what already exists. And the native British scene is so strong and so diverse I just didn't sense a void anywhere that I could usefully fill. Plus, my instinctive drive was towards plots with a sense of geographic scale and physical loneliness that just couldn't work in Britain.

And second, writing fiction means creating a convincing made-up world, which is not easy, and paradoxically I find it helpful to write about a place I'm familiar with, but not intimate with. It keeps me on my toes, makes me think harder.

So I hope what I've done is bring a British sensibility to American territory. That's the void I sensed I could usefully fill.

James Penney's New Identity

by Lee Childs

The process that turned James Penney into a completely different person began ten years ago, at one in the afternoon on a Monday in the middle of June, in Laney, California. A hot time of day, at a hot time of year, in a hot part of the country. The town sits comfortably on the east shoulder of the road which winds from Mojave to LA, fifty miles south of the one and fifty miles north of the other. Due west, the southern rump of the Coastal Range Mountains is visible. Due east, the Mojave Desert disappears into the haze. Very little happened in Laney. After that Monday in the middle of June ten years ago, even less ever did.

There was one industry in Laney. One factory. A big spread of a place. A long low assembly shed, weathered metal siding, built in the '60s. Office accommodations at the north end, in the shade, two stories of them. The first floor was low grade. Clerical functions took place there. Billing and accounting and telephone calling. The second story was high grade. Managers and designers occupied the space. The corner office at the right hand end used to be the Personnel Manager's place. Now it was the Human Resource Manager's place. Same guy, new title on his door.

Outside that door in the long second floor corridor was a line of chairs. The Human Resource Manager's secretary had rustled them up and placed them there that Monday morning. The line of chairs was occupied by a line of men and women. They were silent. Every five minutes the person at the head of the line would be called into the office. The rest of them would shuffle up one place. They didn't speak. They didn't need to. They knew what happening.

Just before one o'clock, James Penney shuffled up one space to the head of the line. He waited a long five minutes and stood up when he was called. Stepped into the office. Closed the door behind him. Sat down again in front of the desk. The Human Resources Manager was a guy called Odell. Odell hadn't been long out of diapers when James Penney started work at the Laney plant.

'Mr Penney,' Odell said.

Penney said nothing, but he nodded in a guarded way.

'We need to share some information with you,' Odell said.

Then he stopped like he needed a response out of Penney before he could continue. Penney shrugged at him. He knew what was coming. He heard things, same as anybody else.

'Just give me the short version, OK?' he said.

Odell nodded. 'We're laying you off.'

'For the summer?' Penney asked him.

Odell shook his head.

'For good,' he said.

Penney took a second to get over the sound of the words. He'd known they were coming, but they hit him like they were the last words he ever expected Odell to say.

'Why?' he asked.

Odell shrugged. He didn't look like he was enjoying this. But on the other hand he didn't look like it was upsetting him much, either.

'Downsizing,' he said. 'No option. Only way we can go.'

'Why?' Penney said again.

Odell leaned back in his chair and folded his hands behind his head. Started the speech he'd already made many times that day.

'We need to cut costs,' he said. 'This is an expensive operation. Small margin. Shrinking market. You know that.'

Penney stared into space and listened to the silence breaking through from the factory floor. 'So you're closing the plant?'

Odell shook his head again. 'We're downsizing, is all. The plant will stay open. There'll be some maintenance business. Some repairs, overhauls. But not like it used to be.'

'The plant will stay open?' Penney said. 'So how come you're letting me go?'

Odell shifted in his chair. Pulled his hands from behind his head and folded his arms across his chest, defensively. He had reached the tricky part of the interview.

'It's a question of the skills mix,' he said. 'We had to pick a team with the correct blend of skills. We put a lot of work into the decision. And I'm afraid you didn't make the cut.'

'What's wrong with my skills?' Penney asked. 'I got skills. I've worked here seventeen years. What's wrong with my damn skills?'

'Nothing at all,' Odell said. 'But other people are better. We have to look at the broad picture. It's going to be a skeleton crew, so we need the best skills, the fastest learners, good attendance records, you know how it is.'

'Attendance records?' Penney said. 'What's wrong with my attendance records? I've worked here seventeen years. You saying I'm not a reliable worker?'

Odell touched the brown file folder in front of him.

'You've had a lot of time out sick,' he said. 'Absentee rate just above eight per cent.' Penney looked at him incredulously.

'Sick?' he said. 'I wasn't sick. I was post-traumatic. From Vietnam.'

Odell shook his head again. He was too young.

'Whatever,' he said. 'It's still a big absentee rate.'

James Penney just sat there, stunned. He felt like he'd been hit by a train. 'So who stays on?' he asked.

'We looked for the correct blend,' Odell said again. 'Generally, the younger end of the workforce. We put a lot of management time into the process. We're confident we made the right decisions. You're not being singled out. We're losing eighty per cent of our people.'

Penney stared across at him. 'You staying?'

Odell nodded and tried to hide a smile, but couldn't.

'There's still a business to run,' he said. 'We still need management.'

There was silence in the big corner office. Outside, the hot breeze stirred off the desert and blew a listless eddy over the metal building. Odell opened the brown folder and pulled out a blue envelope. Handed it across the desk.

'You're paid up to the end of July,' he said. 'Money went in the bank this morning. Good luck, Mr Penney.'

The five-minute interview was over. Odell's secretary appeared and opened the door to the corridor. Penney walked out. The secretary called the next man in. Penney walked past the long quiet row of people and made it to the parking lot. Slid into his car. It was a red Firebird, a year and a half old, and it wasn't paid for yet. He started it up and drove the mile to his house. Eased to a stop in his driveway and sat there, thinking, in a daze, with the motor running. Then he heard the faint bell of his phone in his house. He made it inside before it stopped. It was a friend from the plant.

'They can you too?' the friend asked him.

Penney mumbled his answer so he didn't have to say the exact words, but the tone of his voice told his friend what he needed to know.

'There's a problem,' the guy said. 'Company informed the

bank. I just got a call asking what I was going to do about the payments I got. The bank holding paper on you?'

Penney went cold. Gripped the phone.

'Paper?' he said. 'You bet they're holding paper on me. Just about every damn thing I got. House, car, furniture. They got paper on everything. What they say to you?'

'What the hell do you think?' the guy said. 'They're a bank, right? I stop making the payments, I'm out on the street. The repo man is coming for the car right now.'

Penney went quiet. He was thinking. He was thinking about his car. He didn't care about the house. Or the furniture. His wife had chosen all that stuff. She'd saddled him up with big payments on all that stuff, just before she walked out. She'd called it the chance for a new start. It hadn't worked. She'd gone and he was still paying for her damn house and furniture. But the car was his. The red Firebird. That automobile was the only thing he'd ever bought that he'd really wanted. He didn't feel like losing it. But he sure as hell couldn't keep on paying for it.

'James?' the guy on the phone said. 'You still there?' Penney was imagining the repo man coming for his car. 'James?' his friend said again. 'You there?' Penney closed his eyes tight.

'Not for long,' he said. 'I'm out of here.'

'Where to?' the guy said. 'Where the hell to?' Penney felt a desperate fury building inside him. He smashed the phone back into the cradle and moved away, and then turned back and tore the wire out of the wall. He stood in the middle of the room and decided he wouldn't take anything with him. And he wouldn't leave anything behind, either. He ran to the garage and grabbed his spare can of gasoline. Ran back to the house. Emptied the can over his ex-wife's sofa. He couldn't find a match, so he lit the gas stove in the kitchen and unwound a roll of paper towels. Put one end on the stove top and ran the rest through to the living room. When his makeshift fuse was well alight, he skipped out to his car and started it up. Turned north towards Mojave and settled in for the drive.

His neighbor noticed the fire when the flames started coming through the roof. She called the Laney fire department. The firemen didn't respond. It was a volunteer department, and all the volunteers were in line inside the factory, upstairs in the narrow corridor.

Then the warm air moving off the Mojave Desert freshened up into a hot breeze, and by the time James Penney was thirty miles away the flames from his house had set fire to the dried scrub that had been his lawn. By the time he was in the town of Mojave itself, cashing his last pay check at the bank, the flames had spread across his lawn and his neighbor's and were licking at the base of her back porch.

Like any California boom town, Laney had grown in a hurry. The factory had been thrown up around the start of Nixon's first term. A hundred acres of orange groves had been bulldozed and five hundred frame houses had quadrupled the population in a year. There was nothing really wrong with the houses, but they'd seen rain less than a dozen times in the thirty-one years they'd been standing, and they were about as dry as houses can get. Their timbers had sat and baked in the sun and been scoured by the dry desert winds. There were no hydrants built into the streets. The houses were close together, and there were no windbreaks. But there had never been a serious fire in Laney. Not until that Monday in June.

James Penney's neighbor called the fire department for the second time after her back porch was well alight. The fire department was in disarray. The dispatcher advised her to get out of her house and just wait for their arrival. By the time the fire truck got there, her house was destroyed. And the next house in line was destroyed, too. The desert breeze had blown the fire on across the second narrow gap and sent the old couple living there scuttling into the street for safety. Then Laney called in the fire departments from Lancaster and Glendale and Bakersfield, and they arrived with proper equipment and saved the day. They hosed the scrub between the houses and the blaze went no farther. Just three houses destroyed, Penney's and his two downwind neighbors. Within two hours the panic was over, and by the time Penney himself was fifty miles north of Mojave, Laney's sheriff was working with the fire investigators to piece together what had happened.

They started with Penney's place, which was the upwind house, and the first to burn, and therefore the coolest. It had just about burned down to the floor slab, but the layout was still clear. And the evidence was there to see. There was tremendous scorching on one side of where the living room had been. The Glendale investigator recognized it as something he'd seen many times before. It was what is left when a foam-filled sofa or armchair is doused with gasoline and set alight. He explained to the sheriff how the flames would have spread up and out, setting fire to the walls and ceiling, and how, once into the roof space, the flames would have consumed the rafters and dropped the whole burning structure downwards into the rest of the building. As clear a case of arson as he had ever seen. The unfortunate wild cards had been the stiffening desert breeze and the close proximity of the other houses. Then the sheriff had gone looking for

James Penney, to tell him somebody had burned his house down, and his neighbors'. He drove his black and white to the factory and walked upstairs and past the long line of people and into Odell's corner office. Odell told him what had happened in the five-minute interview just after one o'clock. Then the sheriff had driven back to the Laney station house, steering with one hand and rubbing his chin with the other.

And by the time James Penney was driving along the towering eastern flank of Mount Whitney, a hundred and fifty miles from home, there was an all-points-bulletin out on him, suspicion of deliberate arson, which in the dry desert heat of southern California was a big, big deal.

The California Highway Patrol is one of the world's great law enforcement agencies. Famous throughout America and the world, romantic, idealized. The image of the West Coast motorcycle cop astride his powerful machine is one of the nation's great icons. Smart tan shirt, white T underneath, white helmet, mirrored aviator glasses, tight jodhpurs, gleaming black boots. Cruising the endless sunny highways, marshaling that great state's huge transient population toward a safe destination.

That's the image. That's why Joey Gunston had lined up to join. But Joey Gunston soon found out the reality is different. Any organization has a glamour side and a dull side. Gunston was stuck on the dull side. He wasn't cruising the sunny coastal highways on a big bike. He was on his own in a standard police spec Dodge, grinding back and forward through the Mojave Desert on US 91. He had no jodhpurs, no boots, his white T was a limp gray rag, and his mirrored shades were cheap RayBan copies he'd paid for himself in LA, which he couldn't wear anyway because he was working the graveyard shift, nine at night until six in the morning.

So Joey Gunston was a disillusioned man. But he wasn't bitter. He wasn't that type of a guy. The way it worked with Joey, hand him a disappointment and he wouldn't fold up. He would work harder. He would work so damn hard that he would escape the dull side and get the transfer over to the glamour side. He figured it was like paying his dues. He figured he'd work US 91 in a factory-beige Dodge with plastic CHP badging stuck on the doors as long as it took to prove himself. So far it had taken thirty-one months. No news about a transfer to US 101 and a motorcycle. Not even a hint. But he wasn't going to let his standards drop.

So he carried on working hard. That involved looking out for the break he knew had to be coming. Problem was, the scope for a break on US 91 was pretty limited. It's the direct route between LA and Vegas, which gives it some decent traffic, and there's some pretty scenery. Gunston's patch stretched a hundred and twenty miles from Barstow in the west over to the state line on the slope of Clark Mountain. His problem was the hours he worked. At night, the traffic slackened and the pretty scenery was invisible. For thirty-one months he'd done nothing much except stop speeders and about twice a week radio in for ambulances when some tanked guy ran off the road and smashed himself up.

But he carried on hoping. That Monday night at nine o'clock he'd read through the bulletins pinned up in the dispatcher's office. He'd copied the details into a leatherette notebook his sister had bought for him. One of those details concerned an APB on a Laney guy, James Penney, arson and criminal damage, believed to be on the loose in a red Firebird. Gunston copied the plate number in large writing so he'd be able to read it in the gloom of his car. Then he'd cruised sixty miles east and holed up on the shoulder near Soda Lake.

A lot of guys would have gone right to sleep. Gunston knew his colleagues were working day jobs, maybe security in LA or gumshoeing in the valleys, and sleeping the night away in their Dodges on the shoulder. But Gunston never did that. He played ball and stayed awake, ready for his break.

It arrived within an hour. Ten o'clock that Monday evening. The red Firebird streaked past him, heading east, maybe eighty-five miles an hour, maybe ninety. Gunston didn't need to check his leatherette notebook. The plate jumped right out of the dark at him. He fired up the Dodge and floored it. Hit the button for the lights and the siren. Jammed his foot down and steered with one hand. Used the other to thumb the mike.

'In pursuit of a red Firebird,' he radioed. 'Plate matches APB.'

There was a crackle on the speaker and the dispatcher's voice came back.

'Position?' he asked.

'Soda Lake,' Gunston said. 'Heading east, fast.'

'OK, Joey,' the dispatcher said. 'Stick with him. Nail him before the line. Don't be letting the Nevada guys get in on this, right?'

'You got it, chief,' Gunston said. He eased the Dodge up to a hundred.and wailed on into the night. He figured the Firebird might be a mile ahead. Conceivable that Penney might slew off and head down into the town of Baker, but if he didn't, then Penney was his. The break had maybe arrived.

He caught up with the red Firebird after three miles. The turn down to Baker was gone. Nothing on the road ahead except fifty-seven more miles of California, and then the state of Nevada. He eased the wailing Dodge up to twenty yards behind the Firebird's rear end and hit the blue strobes. Changed the siren to the deafening electronic pock-pock-pock he loved so much. Grinned at his windshield. But the Firebird didn't slow up. It eased ahead. Gunston's speedo needle was shivering around the hundred-and-ten marker. His knuckles tightened round the grimy vinyl wheel.

'Son of a bitch,' he said.

He jammed his foot down harder and hung on. The red Firebird topped out at maybe a hundred and twelve. It was still there ahead of him, but the acceleration was gone. It was flat out. Gunston smiled. He knew the road ahead. Probably better than a guy from Laney did. The climb up the western slope of Clark Mountain was going to tilt things the good guys' way. The upgrades would slow the Firebird. But the Dodge had plenty of good Detroit V8 torque. New police radials. A trained driver. Fifty miles of opportunity ahead. Maybe US 101 and a big bike were not so far away.

He chased the red Firebird for thirty miles. The grade was slowing both cars. They were averaging about ninety. The Dodge's siren was blaring the whole way, pock-pock-pock for twenty minutes, red and blue lights flashing continuously. Gunston's conclusion was this Penney guy had to be a psycho. Burning things up, then trying to outrun the CHP through the dark. Then he started to worry. They were getting reasonably close to the state line. No way was he going to call in and ask for co-operation from the Nevada boys. Penney was his. So he gripped the wheel and moved up to within feet of the speeding red car. Closer and closer. Trying to force the issue.

Ten miles short of the state line, a spur runs off US 91 down to the small town of Nipton. The road leaves the highway at an oblique angle and falls away down the mountain into the valley. The red Firebird took that turn. With Gunston's police Dodge a foot off its rear fender, it slewed right and just disappeared straight out from in front of him. Gunston overshot and jammed to a stop, all four wheels locked and making smoke. He smashed the selector into reverse and howled backward up the shoulder. Just in time to see the Firebird cartwheeling off the road and straight down the mountainside. The spur had a bad camber. Gunston knew that. Penney hadn't. He'd taken that desperate slew and lost it. The Firebird's rear end had come unglued and swung out over the void. The red car had windmilled like a golf club and hurled itself out into space. Gunston watched it smash and bounce on the rocks. An outcrop tore the underside out and the spilling gasoline hit the hot muffler and the next thing Gunston saw was a belch of flame and a huge explosion rolling slowly a hundred feet down the mountainside.

The California Highway Patrol dispatcher told Joey Gunston to supervise the recovery of the crashed red Firebird himself. Nobody was very upset about the accident. Nobody cared much about Penney. The radio conversations back and forward between the dispatcher's office and Gunston's Dodge about an arsonist dying in his burning car on the slope of Clark Mountain carried a certain amount of suppressed ironic laughter. The only problem was the invoice that would come in next month from the tow-truck company. The protocols about who should pay such an invoice were never very clear. Usually the CHP ended up writing them down to miscellaneous operating costs.

Gunston knew a tow-truck operator out in the wastelands near Soda Lake who usually monitored the police bands, so he put out a call and got a quick reply. Then he parked up on the shoulder near the turn down to Nipton, sitting right on top of the skid marks he'd made overshooting it, and sat waiting for the guy. He was there in an hour, and by midnight Gunston and the trucker were clambering down the mountainside in the dark, pulling the truck's giant metal hook behind them against its ratchet. The red Firebird was about two hundred yards down the slope, right at the end of the cable's reach. It wasn't red any more. It was streaked a fantastic variety of scorched browns and purples. All the glass had melted and the plastic had burned away. The tires were gone. Penney himself was a shrivelled carbonized shape fused to the zigzag metal springs which were all that was left of the seat. Gunston and the wrecker didn't spend too long looking at him. They just ducked near and snapped the giant hook around the offside front suspension member. Then they turned back for the long climb up the slope.

They were panting hard and sweating in the night air when they got back to the tow truck. It was parked sideways on to the road, circled by Gunston's red danger flares. The steel cable snaked off the drum at the rear of the cab and disappeared down into the dark. The driver started up the big diesel to power the hydraulics and the drum started grinding around, reeling in the cable, hauling the wreck upward. Time to time, the remains of the Firebird would snag in the brush or against a rock and the truck's rear suspension would squat and the big diesel would roar until it dragged free.

It took the best part of an hour to haul the wreck the two

hundred yards up to the roadway. It scraped over the concrete shoulder and the driver moved the truck to a better angle and sped the drum to haul the wreck up on to the flatbed. Gunston helped him tie it down with chains. Then he nodded to the driver and the tow-truck took off and lumbered back west. Gunston stepped over to his Dodge and killed the flashing lights and fired up the radio.

'On its way,' he said to the dispatcher. 'Better send an ambulance over to meet it.'

'Why?' the dispatcher asked. 'He's dead, right?'

'Dead as can be,' Gunston said. 'But somebody needs to chisel him out of the seat, and I ain't going to do it.'

The dispatcher laughed over the radio. 'Is he real crispy?'

Gunston laughed back. 'Crispiest guy you ever saw.'

Middle of the night, and the sheriff was still in the station house in Laney. He figured a lot of overtime was called for. It had been a busy day. And tomorrow was going to be a busier day. There was a fair amount of fallout to deal with. The lay-offs at the factory had produced unpredictable results. Evening time had seen a lot of drunkenness. A couple of pickups had been rolled. Minor injuries. A few windows had been broken at the plant. Mr Odell's windows had been the target. A few rocks had fallen short and hit the mailroom. One had smashed the windshield of a car in the lot.

And Penney had burned three houses down. That was the problem. But then it wasn't a problem any more. The silence in the station house was broken by the sound of the telex machine starting up. The sheriff wandered through to the booth and tore off a foot and a half of paper. Read it and folded it and slipped it into the file he'd just started. Then he picked up the phone and called the California Highway Patrol.

'I'll take it from here,' he told them. 'This is Laney County business. Our coroner will see to the guy. I'll go out to Soda Lake with him right away.'

The Laney County coroner was a young medic out of Stanford called Kolek. Polish name, but the guy was from a family which had been in California longer than most. Forty years, maybe. The sheriff rode east with him in his official station wagon. Kolek wasn't upset by the late call. He didn't object to working at night. He was young and he was new and he needed the money. But he was pretty quiet the whole way.

Medical guys in general are not keen on dealing with burned bodies. The sheriff didn't know why. He'd seen a few. A burned body was like something you left on the barbecue too long. Better than the damp maggoty things you find in the woods. A whole lot better.

'We got to bring it back?' Kolek asked.

'The car?' the sheriff said. 'Or the guy?'

'The corpse,' Kolek said.

The sheriff grinned at him and nodded. 'There's an ex-wife somewhere. She might want to bury the guy. Maybe there's a family plot.'

Kolek shrugged and turned the heater up a click. Drove through the night all the way from Mojave to Soda Lake in silence. A hundred and thirty miles without saying a word.

The junkyard was a stadium-sized space hidden behind a high wooden fence in the angle made by the road down to Baker where it left the highway. There were gleaming tow trucks lined up outside the gate. Kolek slowed and passed them and nosed into the compound. Inside the gate, a wooden hut served as the office. The light was on inside. Kolek hit his horn once and waited. A woman came out. She saw who they were and ducked back inside to hit the lights. The compound lit up like day with blue lights on poles. The woman directed them to the burned Firebird. It was draped with a sun-bleached tarp.

Kolek and the sheriff pulled the tarp off the wreck. It wasn't bent very far out of shape. The sheriff could see that the brush growing on the mountainside had slowed its descent, all the way. It hadn't smashed head-on into a boulder or anything. If it hadn't caught on fire, James Penney might have survived.

Kolek pulled flashlights and his tool kit out of the station wagon. He needed the crowbar to get the driver's door open. The hinges were seized and distorted from the heat. The sheriff put his weight on it and screeched it all the way open. Then the two men played their flashlight beams all round the charred interior.

'Seat belt is burned away,' Kolek said. 'But he was wearing it. Buckle's still done up.'

The sheriff nodded and pointed.

'Airbag deployed,' he said.

The plastic parts of the steering wheel had all burned away, but they could see the little metal hinges in the up position, where the bag had exploded outwards.

'OK,' Kolek said. 'Now for the fun part.'

The sheriff held both flashlights and Kolek put on some heavy rubber gloves. He poked around for a while.

'He's fused on pretty tight,' he said. 'Best way would be to cut through the seat springs and take part of the seat with us.'

'Is the bodybag big enough?'

'Probably. This isn't a very big corpse.'

The sheriff glanced in again. Slid the flashlight beam over the body.

'Penney was a big enough guy,' he said. 'Maybe better than five-ten.'

Kolek grimaced. 'Fire shrinks them. The body fluids boil off.'

He walked back to the station wagon and pulled out a pair of wire cutters. Leaned back into the Firebird and started snipping through the zigzag metal springs close to where they were fused to the corpse. It took him a while. He had to lean right in, chest-to-chest with the body, to reach the far side.

'OK, give me a hand here,' he said.

The sheriff shoved his hands in under the charred legs and grabbed the springs where Kolek had cut them away from the frame. He pulled and twisted and hauled the body out, feet-first. Kolek grabbed the shoulders and they carried the rigid assembly a few feet away and laid it carefully on the ground. They stood up together and the body rolled backwards, stiff, with the bent legs pointing grotesquely upwards.

'Shit,' Kolek said. 'I hate this.'

The sheriff was crouched down, playing his flashlight beam over the contorted gap that had been Penney's mouth.

'Teeth are still there,' he said. 'You should be able to make the ID.'

Kolek joined him. There was a distinctive overbite visible.

'No problem,' he agreed. 'You in a hurry for it?'

The sheriff shrugged. 'Can't close the case without it.'

They struggled together to zip the body into the bag and then loaded it into the back of the wagon. They put it on its side, wedged against the bulge of the wheelarch. Then they drove back west, with the morning sun rising behind them.

That same morning sun woke James Penney by coming in through a hole in his motel room blind and playing a bright beam across his face. He stirred and lay in the warmth of the rented bed, watching the dust motes dancing.

He was still in California, up near Yosemite, cabin twelve in a place just far enough from the Park to be cheap. He had six weeks' pay in his billfold, which was hidden under the center of his mattress. Six weeks' pay, less a tank and a half of gas, a cheeseburger and twenty-seven-fifty for the room. Hidden under the mattress, because twenty-seven-fifty doesn't get you a space in a top-notch place. His door was locked, but the desk guy would have a pass key, and he wouldn't be the first desk guy in the world to rent out his pass key by the hour to somebody looking to make a little extra money during the night.

But nothing bad had happened. The mattress was so thin he could feel the billfold right there, under his kidney. Still there, still bulging. A good feeling. He lay watching the sunbeam, struggling with mental arithmetic, spreading six weeks' pay out over the foreseeable future. With nothing to worry about except cheap food, cheap motels and the Firebird's gas, he figured he had no problems at all. The Firebird had a modern motor twenty-four valves, tuned for a blend of power and economy. He could got far away and have enough money left to take his time looking around.

After that, he wasn't so sure. There wasn't going to be much call anywhere for a metalworker, even with seventeen years' experience. But there would be a call for something. He was sure of that. Even if it was menial. He was a worker. He didn't mind what he did. Maybe he'd find something outdoors, might be a refreshing thing. Might have some kind of dignity to it. Some kind of simple work, for simple honest folks, a lot different than slaving for that grinning weasel Odell.

He watched the sunbeam travel across the counterpane for a while. Then he flung the cover aside and swung himself out of bed. Used the john, rinsed his face and mouth at the sink and untangled his clothes from the pile he'd dropped them in. He'd, need more clothes. He only had the things he stood up in. Everything else, he'd burned along with his house. He shrugged and re-ran his calculations to allow for some new pants and workshirts. Maybe some heavy boots, if he was going to be laboring outside. The six weeks' pay was going to have to stretch a little thinner. He decided to drive slow, to save gas, and maybe eat less. Or maybe not less, just cheaper. He'd use truck stops, not tourist diners. More calories, less money. He figured today he'd put in some serious miles before stopping for breakfast. He jingled the car keys in his pocket and opened his cabin door. Then he stopped. His heart thumped. The tarmac rectangle outside his cabin was empty. Just old oilstains staring up at him. He glanced desperately left and right along the row. No red Firebird. He staggered back into the room and sat down heavily on the bed. Just sat there in a daze, thinking about what to do.

He decided he wouldn't bother with the desk guy. He was pretty certain the desk guy was responsible. He could just about see it. The guy had waited an hour and then called some buddies who had come over and hot-wired his car. Eased it out of the motel lot and away down the road. A conspiracy, feeding off unsuspecting motel traffic. Feeding off suckers dumb enough to pay twenty-seven-fifty for the privilege of getting their prize possession stolen. He was numb. Suspended somewhere

between sick and raging. His red Firebird. The only damn thing
in his whole life he'd ever really wanted. Gone. Stolen. He
remembered the exquisite joy of buying it. After his divorce.
Waking up and realizing he could just go to the dealer, sign the
papers, and have it. No discussions. No arguing. No snidey con-
tempt about boys' toys and how they needed this damn thing
and that damn thing first. None of that. He'd gone down to the
dealer and chopped in his old clunker and signed up for that
Firebird and driven it home in a state of total joy. He'd washed
and cleaned it every week. He'd watched the infomercials and
tried every miracle polish on the market. The car had sat every
day outside the Laney factory like a bright red badge of achieve-
ment. Like a shiny consolation for the shit and the drudgery.
Whatever else he didn't have, he had a Firebird. Until today.
Now, along with everything else he used to have, he used to have
a Firebird.

The nearest police were ten miles south. He had seen the place
the previous night, heading north past it. He set off walking,
stamping out in rage and frustration. The sun climbed up and
slowed him. After a couple of miles, he stuck out his thumb. A
computer service engineer in a company Buick stopped for him.

'Car was stolen,' Penney told him. 'Last night, outside the
damn motel.'

The engineer made a kind of all-purpose growling sound, like
an expression of vague sympathy when the person doesn't really
give a shit.

'Too bad,' he said. 'You insured?'

'Sure, Triple A and everything. But I'm kind of hoping they'll
get it back for me.'

The guy shook his head. 'Forget about it. It'll be in Mexico
tomorrow. Some senor down there will have himself a brand
new American motor. You'll never see it again unless you take a
vacation down there and he runs you over with it.'

Then the guy laughed about it and James Penney felt like
getting out right away, but the sun was hot and James Penney
was a practical guy. So he rode on in silence and got out in the
dust next to the police parking lot. The Buick took off and left
him there.

The police station was small, but it was crowded. He stood in
line behind five other people. There was an officer behind the
front counter, taking details, taking complaints, writing slow,
confirming everything twice. Penney felt like every minute was
vital. He felt like his Firebird was racing down to the border.
Maybe this guy could radio ahead and get it stopped. He hopped
from foot to foot in frustration. Gazed wildly around him. There

were notices stuck on a board behind the officer's head. Blurred xeroxes of telexes and faxes. US Marshal notices. A mass of stuff. His eyes flicked absently across it all.

Then they snapped back. His photograph was staring out at him. The photograph from his own driver's license, xeroxed in black-and-white, enlarged, grainy. His name underneath, in big printed letters. James Penney. From Laney, California. A description of his car. Red Firebird. The plate number. James Penney. Wanted for arson and criminal damage. He stared at the bulletin. It grew larger and larger. It grew life-size. His face stared back at him like he was looking in a mirror. James Penney. Arson. Criminal damage. All-Points-Bulletin. The woman in front of him finished her business and he stepped forward to the head of the line. The desk sergeant looked up at him.

'Can I help you, sir?' he said.

Penney shook his head. He peeled off left and walked away. Stepped calmly outside into the bright morning sun and ran back north like a madman. He made about a hundred yards before the heat slowed him to a gasping walk. Then he did the instinctive thing, which was to duck off the blacktop and take cover in a wild birch grove. He pushed through the brush until he was out of sight and collapsed into a sitting position, back against a thin rough trunk, legs splayed out straight, chest heaving, hands clamped against his head like he was trying to stop it from exploding.

Arson and criminal damage. He knew what the words meant. But he couldn't square them with what he had actually done. It was his own damn house to burn. Like he was burning his trash. He was entitled. How could that be arson? A guy chooses to burn his own house down, how is that a crime? This is a free country, right? And he could explain, anyway. He'd been upset. He sat slumped against the birch trunk and breathed easier. But only for a moment. Because then he started thinking about lawyers. He'd had personal experience. His divorce had cost him plenty in lawyer bills. He knew what lawyers were like. Lawyers were the problem. Even if it wasn't even arson, it was going to cost plenty in lawyer bills to start proving it. It was going to cost a steady torrent of dollars, pouring out for years. Dollars he didn't have, and never would have again. He sat there on the hard, dry ground and realized that absolutely everything he had in the whole world was right then in direct contact with his body. One pair of shoes, one pair of socks, one pair of boxers, Levis, cotton shirt, leather jacket. And his billfold. He put his hand down and touched its bulk in his pocket. Six weeks' pay, less yesterday's spending. Six weeks' worth of his pay might buy about six hours of a lawyer's time. Six hours, the guy might get as far as writing down his full name and address, maybe his date of birth. His Social Security number would take another six. The actual nature of his problem, that would be in the third six-hour chunk. Or the fourth. That was James Penney's experience with lawyers.

He got to his feet in the clearing. His legs were weak with the lactic acid from the unaccustomed running. His heart was thumping. He leaned up against a birch trunk and took a deep breath. Swallowed. He pushed back through the brush to the road. Turned north and started walking. He walked for a half-hour, hands in his pockets, maybe a mile and three-quarters, and then his muscles eased off and his breathing calmed down. He began to see things clearly. He began to understand. He began to appreciate the power of labels. He was a realistic guy, and he always told himself the truth. He was an arsonist, because they said he was. The angry phase was over. Now it was about taking sensible decisions, one after the other. Clearing up the confusion was beyond his resources. So he had to stay out of their reach. That was his first decision. That was the starting point. That was the strategy. The other decisions would flow out of that. They were tactical.

He could be traced three ways. By his name, by his face, by his car. He ducked sideways off the road again into the trees. Pushed twenty yards into the woods. Kicked a shallow hole in the leaf-mold and stripped out of his billfold everything with his name on. He buried it all in the hole and stamped the earth flat. Then he took his beloved Firebird keys from his pocket and hurled them far into the trees. He didn't see where they fell.

The car itself was gone. In the circumstances, that was good. But it had left a trail. It might have been seen in Mojave, outside the bank. It might have been seen at the gas stations where he filled it. And its plate number was on the motel form from last night. With his name. A trail, arrowing north through California in neat little increments.

He remembered his training from Vietnam. He remembered the tricks. If you wanted to move east from your foxhole, first you moved west. You moved west for a couple hundred yards, stepping on the occasional twig, brushing the occasional bush, until you had convinced Charlie you were moving west, as quietly as you could, but not quietly enough. Then you turned about and came back east, really quietly, doing it right, past your original starting point, and away. He'd done it a dozen times. His original plan had been to head north for a spell, maybe into Oregon. He'd gotten a few hours into that plan. Therefore the red Firebird had laid a modest trail north. So now he was going to turn south for a while and disappear. He walked back out of the woods, into the dust on the near side of the road, and started walking back the way he'd come.

His face he couldn't change. It was right there on all the posters. He remembered it staring out at him from the bulletin board in the police building. The neat side-parting, the sunken gray cheeks. He ran his hands through his hair, vigorously, back and forward, until it stuck out every which way. No more neat side parting. He ran his palms over twenty-four hours of stubble. Decided to grow a big beard. No option, really. He didn't have a razor, and he wasn't about to spend any money on one. He walked on through the dust, heading south, with Excelsior Mountain towering up on his right. Then he came to the turn dodging west toward San Francisco, through Tioga Pass, before Mount Dana reared up even higher. He stopped in the dust on the side of the road and pondered. Keeping on south would take him nearly all the way back to Mojave. Too close to home. Way too close. He wasn't comfortable about that. Not comfortable at all. So he figured a new move. He'd head west to the coast, then decide. He put himself thirty yards west of the turn and stuck out his thumb. He was a practical guy. He knew he wasn't going to get anywhere by walking. He had to get rides, one after the other, anonymous rides from busy people. He decided as a matter of tactics not to look for rides from solid citizens. Not from anybody who looked like they might notice him or remember him. He had to think like a fugitive. A whole new experience.

After forty minutes, he came up with an ironic grin and realized he didn't have to worry about avoiding the solid citizens. They were avoiding him. He was standing there, thumb out, no baggage, messy hair, unshaven, dusty up to the knees, and one vehicle after another was passing him right by. Glancing at him and accelerating down the road like he wasn't even there. The sun wheeled overhead and dropped away into afternoon, and he started to worry about getting a ride at all. He was hungry and thirsty and vulnerable. Alone and on foot in the exact middle of the hugest and most contemptuous landscape he had ever seen.

Salvation arrived in the form of an open-topped Jeep, dusty and dented, a sandy color that really wasn't any color at all. A guy about forty at the wheel. Long graying hair, dirty tie-dye shirt, some kind of a left-over hippy. The Jeep slowed and plowed into the dust. Stopped right next to Penney and the driver leaned over inside and shouted across over the throb of the worn muffler.

'I'm going to Sacramento, my friend,' he said. 'But if you want the Bay, I can let you off in Stockton.'

Penney shook his head, vigorously.

'Sacramento is great,' he shouted. 'Thank you very much.'

He put his right hand on the windshield frame and his left hand on the seatback and swung himself inside exactly like he'd done with Jeeps in Vietnam. 'You just lay back and look at the scenery, my friend,' the driver shouted over the muffler noise. 'Talking is not an option in this old thing. Too loud, you know what I mean?'

James Penney nodded gratefully at him and the old hippy let in the clutch and roared off down the road.

The Laney County Medical Examiner's office was just that, an office, and a fairly rudimentary one. There were no facilities for post-mortem examination, unless Kolek wanted to clear his own desk and slice the carbonized lump open all over it. So he had taken the bodybag down to the facility the County used over in northern Los Angeles. It was a big modern morgue, well equipped, and busy. It was busy because it sucked in all the business from the ring of small counties surrounding it, as well as handling its own substantial quota of unfortunates. So Kolek had parked the bag in the cold store and signed up for the first free visitor slot of the day, which was mid-afternoon. It was a half-hour slot, but Kolek figured that was going to be more than long enough. Not a hell of a lot of doubt about how Penney had died. All that was left was a routine ID through the dental data.

Laney itself had one dentist, serving the population of two thousand people. He had never seen Penney. But he was reasonably new, and the sheriff said it wasn't unusual for Laney people to forget about their teeth. The Stone factory gave health insurance, of course, but not the best in the world, and dentistry required a contribution. But the surgery nurse was a stout old woman who had been there through three separate tenures. She went through the system and found the Penney file where it had been stored after his last visit, twelve years before. It was a thin packet of notes and film in a buff envelope. Kolek signed for it and threw it into the back seat of his wagon. Checked his watch and headed south for the morgue.

James Penney got out of the old hippy's jeep right on the main drag into the southern edge of Sacramento, windblown, tired, ears ringing from the noise. He stood by the side of the road and waved and watched the guy go, waving back, long gray hair blowing in the slipstream. Then he looked around in the sudden silence and took his bearings. All the way up and down the drag he could see a forest of signs, bright colors, neon, advertising motels, air and pool and cable, burger places, eateries of every description, supermarkets, auto parts. Looked like the kind of place a guy could get lost in, no trouble at all. Big choice of motels, all side-by-side, all competing, all offering the lowest prices in town. He walked down to level with three of them. Figured he'd use the middle one. Hole up and plan ahead.

But then he decided to try something he'd read about once in a travel guide. Check in late, and ask for an even lower price. Late in the day, the motel would be keen to rent another room. They'd figure something is better than nothing, right? That was the theory in the travel guide. It was a theory he'd never tried, but now was the time to start. So he went straight out for a late lunch or an early dinner or whatever it was time for. He chose a burger chain he'd never used before and sat in the window, idly watching the traffic. The waitress came over and he ordered a cheeseburger and two Cokes. He was dry from the dust on the road.

The forty-year-old leftover hippy with the long graying hair drove on downtown and parked the dusty and dented jeep right up against a hydrant outside the Sacramento Police Department's main building. He pulled the keys and stepped out. Stood and stretched in the warmth of the afternoon sun before ducking inside.

The Drug Enforcement Agency's Sacramento office was located in a suite of rooms lent to them by the police department. The only way in was through the precinct hall, past the desk sergeants. Agents had to sign in and out. They had to collect internal ID badges to wear inside the building, and they had to leave them there on their way out. Two reasons for that. They tended to look more like criminals than agents, and the badges kept confusion inside the station house to a minimum. And because they were working undercover, they couldn't afford to slip their IDs into their pockets, absent-mindedly or by mistake, and walk out like that. If they did, and they got searched by whatever new friends they were trying to make, there could be some very bad consequences. So the strict rule was the IDs stayed at the precinct house desk, every moment the agents weren't actually inside and wearing them.

The forty-year-old hippy lined up to sign in and collect his badge. He was behind a couple of uniforms with some guy in handcuffs. One desk sergeant on duty. A wait. He scanned the bulletins on the back wall. High risk of forest fire. Missing children. Then a face stared out at him. An APB teletype. James Penney. Laney, California. Arson and criminal damage.

'Shit,' he said. Loudly.

The desk sergeant and the cops with the cuffed guy all turned to look at him. 'That guy,' he said. 'James Penney. I just drove him all the way over here through the mountains.'

The sheriff in Laney took the call from Sacramento. He was busy closing out the files on the previous day's activity. The DWIs, the broken windows, the smashed windshield, the small stuff. The Penney file was already in the drawer, just waiting for Kolek's formal ID to tie it up.

'Penney?' he said to the Sacramento desk sergeant. 'No, he's dead. Crashed and burned on the road out to Vegas, last night.'

Then he hung up, but he was a conscientious guy, and cautious, so he found the number for the morgue down in LA. He was stretching his hand out for the phone when it rang again. It was Kolek, calling on his mobile, straight from the dissecting table.

'What?' the sheriff asked, although he already knew what from Kolek's voice.

'Two main problems,' Kolek said. 'The teeth are nowhere near. Penney had a bridge across the front. Cheap dentures. These are real teeth.'

'And?' the sheriff asked. 'What else?'

'This is a woman,' Kolek said.

Penney had finished his meal in the Sacramento burger shack when he saw the four police cruisers arrive. He had a dollar on the table for the waitress and was getting up ready to leave. He had actually lifted off the sticky vinyl bench and was sliding out sideways when he caught sight of them. Four cruisers, playing leapfrog along the strip of motels. The cops were going into each office in turn, a sheaf of papers in their hands, coming out, sliding along to the next office. Penney sat back down. Stared out at them through the window. Watched them leapfrog south until they were out of sight. Then he stood up and left. Turned up the collar on his leather jacket and walked north, not quickly, not slowly, holding his breath.

The Laney sheriff was on the phone. He had tracked Penney to his bank. He was aware of the big cash withdrawal yesterday. He had looked at the road on the map, Laney to Mojave, and he'd guessed correctly about the northward dash along the flank of Mount Whitney. He'd called gas stations, one after the other, working north through the phone book, until he found a pump jockey who remembered a red Firebird whose driver had paid from a thick wad of cash.

Then he'd done some mental arithmetic, speed and distance and time, and started calling a thin cluster of motels in the area he figured Penney had reached at the end of the day. Second number, he'd found the right place, the Pine Park Holiday Motel up near Yosemite. Penney had checked in at about nine o'clock, car and all, name and plate number right there on the desk guy's carbon.

Beyond that, there was no further information. The sheriff called the nearest police department, ten miles south of the motel. No report of a stolen Firebird. No other missing automobiles. No knowledge of a woman car thief in the locality. So the sheriff called the Mojave General Motors dealership and asked for the value of an eighteen-month-old Firebird, clean, low-mileage. He added that amount to the bank's figure for the cash withdrawal. Penney had rendezvoused at the motel and sold his car to the dead woman and was on the run with nearly fifteen grand in his pants pocket. A lot of money. It was clear. Obvious. Penney had planned, and prepared.

The sheriff opened his map again. The Sacramento sighting had been just plain luck. So now was the time to capitalize on it. He wouldn't be aiming to stay there. Too small, State capital, too well policed. So he'd be moving on. Probably up to the wilds of Oregon or Washington State. Or Idaho or Montana. But not by plane. Not with cash. Paying cash for an air ticket out of a California city is the same thing as begging to be arrested for narcotics trafficking. So he'd be aiming to get out by road. But Sacramento was a city with an ocean not too far away to the left, and high mountains to the right. Fundamentally six roads out, was all. So six roadblocks would do it, maybe on a ten mile radius so the local commuters wouldn't get snarled up. The sheriff nodded to himself and picked up the phone to call the Highway Patrol.

It started raining in Sacramento at dusk. Steady, wetting rain. Northern California, near the mountains, very different from what Penney was used to. He was hunched in his jacket, head down, walking north, trying to decide if he dared hitch a ride. The police cruisers at the motel strip had unsettled him. He was tired and demoralized and alone. And wet. And conspicuous. Nobody walked anywhere in California. He glanced over his shoulder at the traffic stream and saw a dull olive Chevrolet sedan slowing behind him. It came to a stop and a long arm stretched across and opened the passenger door. The dome light clicked on and shone on the soaked roadway.

'Want a ride?' the driver called. Penney ducked down and

glanced inside. The driver was a very tall man, about thirty, muscular, built like a regular weightlifter. Short fair hair, rugged open face. Dressed in uniform. Army uniform. Penney read the insignia and registered: military police captain. He glanced at the dull olive paint on the car and saw a white serial number stencilled on the flank.

'I don't know,' he said.

'Get in out of the rain,' the driver said. 'A vet like you knows better than to walk in the rain, right?'

Penney slid inside. Closed the door.

'How do you know I'm a vet?' he asked.

'The way you walk,' the driver said. 'And your age, and the way you look. Guy your age looking like you look and walking in the rain didn't beat the draft for college, that's for damn sure.'

Penney nodded.

'No, I didn't,' he said. 'I did a jungle tour, seventeen years ago.'

'So let me give you a ride,' the driver said. 'A favor, one soldier to another. Consider it a veteran's benefit.'

'OK,' Penney said.

'Where you headed?' the driver asked.

'I don't know,' Penney said. 'North, I guess.'

'OK, north it is,' the driver said. 'I'm Jack Reacher. Pleased to make your acquaintance.'

Penney said nothing.

'You got a name?' the guy called Reacher asked.

Penney hesitated. 'I don't know,' he said.

Reacher put the car in drive and glanced over his shoulder. Eased back into the traffic stream. Clicked the switch and locked the doors.

'What did you do?' he asked.

'Do?' Penney repeated.

'You're running,' Reacher said. 'Heading out of town, walking in the rain, head down, no bag, don't know what your name is. I've seen a lot of people running, and you're one of them.'

'You going to turn me in?'

'I'm a military cop,' Reacher said. 'You done anything to hurt the Army?'

'The Army?' Penney said. 'No, I was a good soldier.'

'So why would I turn you in?'

Penney looked blank.

'I don't know,' he said.

'What did you do to the civilians?' Reacher asked.

'You're going to turn me in,' Penney said, helplessly.

Reacher shrugged at the wheel. 'Well, that depends,' he said. 'What did you do?'

Penney said nothing. Reacher turned his head and looked straight at him. A powerful silent stare, hypnotic intensity in his eyes, held for a hundred yards of road.

'What did you do?' he asked again.

Penney couldn't look away. He took a breath.

'I burned my house,' he said. 'Near Mojave. I worked seventeen years and got canned yesterday and I got all upset because they were going to take my car away so I burned my house. They're calling it deliberate arson.'

'Near Mojave?' Reacher said. 'They would. They don't like fires down there.'

Penney nodded. 'I should have thought harder. But I was real mad. Seventeen years, and suddenly I'm shit on their shoe. And my car got stolen anyway, first night I'm away.'

'There are roadblocks all around here,' Reacher said. 'I came through one south of the city.'

'You think they're for me?' Penney asked.

'Could be,' Reacher said. 'They don't like fires down there.'

'You going to turn me in?'

Reacher looked at him again, hard and silent.

'Is that all you did?'

Penney nodded. 'Yes, sir, that's all I did.'

There was silence for a beat. Just the sound of the wet pavement under the tires.

'Well, I don't have a problem with it,' Reacher said. 'A guy does a jungle tour, works seventeen years and gets canned, I guess he's entitled to get a little mad.'

'So what should I do?'

'You got attachments?'

'Divorced, no kids.'

'So start over, someplace else.'

'They'll find me,' Penney said.

'You're already thinking about changing your name,' Reacher said. Penney nodded.

'I junked all my ID,' he said. 'Buried it in the woods.'

'So build a new identity. Get new paper. That's all anybody cares about. Pieces of paper.'

'Like how?'

Reacher was quiet another beat, thinking hard.

'Easy enough,' he said. 'Classic way is find some cemetery, find a kid who died as a child, get a copy of the birth certificate, start from there. Get a social security number, a passport, credit cards, and you're a new person.'

Penney shrugged. 'I can't do all that. Too difficult. And I don't have time. According to you, there's a roadblock up ahead. How am I going to do all of that stuff before we get there?'

'There are other ways,' Reacher said.

'Forgeries?'

Reacher shook his head. 'No good. Sooner or later, forgeries don't work.'

'So how?'

'Find some guy who's already created false ID for himself, and take it away from him.'

Penney shook his head. 'You're crazy. How am I going to do that?'

'Maybe you don't need to do that. Maybe I already did it for you.'

'You got false ID?'

'Not me,' Reacher said. 'Guy I was looking for.'

'What guy?'

Reacher drove one-handed and pulled a sheaf of official paper from his inside jacket pocket.

'Arrest warrant,' he said. 'Army liaison officer at a weapons plant outside of Fresno, looks to be peddling blueprints. Turns out to have three separate sets of bogus ID, all perfect, all completely backed up with everything from elementary school records onward. Which makes it likely they're Soviet, which means they can't be beat. I'm on my way back from talking to him right now. He was running, too, already on his second set of papers. I took them. They're clean. They're in the trunk of this car, in a wallet, in a jacket.'

Traffic was slowing ahead. There was red glare visible through the streaming windshield. Flashing blue lights. Yellow flashlight beams waving, side to side.

'There's the roadblock,' Reacher said.

'So can I use this guy's ID?' Penney asked urgently.

'Sure you can,' Reacher said. 'Hop out and get it. Bring the wallet from the jacket.'

He slowed and stopped on the shoulder. Penney got out. Ducked away to the back of the car and lifted the trunk lid. Came back a long moment later, white in the face.

'Got it?' Reacher asked.

Penney nodded silently. Held up the wallet.

'It's all in there,' Reacher said. 'I checked. Everything anybody needs.'

Penney nodded again.

'So put it in your pocket,' Reacher said.

Penney slipped the wallet into his inside jacket pocket.

Reacher's right hand came up. There was a gun in it. And a pair of handcuffs in his left.

'Now sit still,' he said, quietly.

He leaned over and snapped the cuffs on Penney's wrists, one-handed. Put the car back into drive and crawled forward.

'What's this for?' Penney asked.

'Quiet,' Reacher said. They were two cars away from the checkpoint. Three highway patrolmen in rain capes were directing traffic into a corral formed by parked cruisers. Their light bars were flashing bright in the shiny dark.

'What?' Penney said again.

Reacher said nothing. Just stopped where the cop told him and wound his window down. The night air blew in, cold and wet. The cop bent down. Reacher handed him his military ID. The cop played his flashlight over it and handed it back.

'Who's your passenger?' he asked.

'My prisoner,' Reacher said. He handed over the arrest warrant. 'He got ID?' the cop asked.

Reacher leaned over and slipped the wallet out from inside Penney's jacket, two-fingered like a pickpocket. Flipped it open and passed it through the window. A second cop stood in Reacher's headlight beams and copied the plate number on to a clipboard. Stepped around the hood and joined the first guy.

'Captain Reacher of the military police,' the first cop said. The second cop wrote it down.

'With a prisoner name of Edward Hendricks,' the first cop said. The second cop wrote it down.

'Thank you, sir,' the first cop said. 'You drive safe, now.'

Reacher eased out from between the cruisers. Accelerated away into the rain. A mile later, he stopped again on the shoulder. Leaned over and unlocked Penney's handcuffs. Put them back in his pocket. Penney rubbed his wrists.

'I thought you were going to turn me in,' he said.

Reacher shook his head.

'Looked better for me that way. I've got an arrest warrant, I want a prisoner in the car for everybody to see, right?'

Penney nodded.

'I guess,' he said, quietly.

Reacher handed the wallet back.

'Keep it,' he said.

'Really?'

'Edward Hendricks,' Reacher said. 'That's who you are now, rest of your life. It's clean ID, and it'll work. Think of it like a veteran's benefit. One soldier to another, OK?'

Edward Hendricks looked at him and nodded and opened his

door. Got out into the rain and turned up the collar of his leather jacket and started walking north. Reacher watched him until he was out of sight and then pulled away and took the next turn west. Turned north past a town called Eureka and stopped again where the road was lonely and ran close to the ocean. There was a wide gravel shoulder and a low barrier and a steep cliff with the Pacific high tide boiling and foaming fifty feet below it.

He got out of the car and opened the trunk and grasped the lapels of the jacket he had told his passenger about. Took a deep breath and heaved. The corpse was heavy. He wrestled it up out of the trunk and jacked it on to his shoulder and staggered with it to the barrier. Bent his knees and dropped it over the edge. The rocky cliff caught it and it spun and the arms and the legs flailed limply. Then it hit the surf with a faint splash and it was gone.

About the Authors

Phil Andrews is an award-winning sports journalist who writes for *The Independent* and *The Independent on Sunday*. He lives in Derbyshire and is a film, theatre and opera critic. His first novel, *Own Goals*, is set in the world of Premiership Football and features private eye Steve Strong, who learned his trade watching old movies at the film *noir* Shamus Academy.

Andrea Badenoch lives in Newcastle upon Tyne where she lectures part time and co-edits Writing Women, Virago's annual anthology of new voices. Her first crime novel, *Mortal* was described by Andrew Taylor as 'grim, beautifully written and in many ways profound'. Her second novel, *Driven*, a story of revenge and car crime was published in 1999.

Paul Charles is not only a long-time Beatles fan par excellence but also one of Britain's leading music promoters. He is the creator of Camden Town policeman Christy Kennedy, who has appeared so far in three well-received novels and is already well on his way to the lucrative splendours of your television screen.

Lee Child was born in Coventry and worked for ITV for 18 years following his law degree. His first novel, *Killing Floor*, was a major international hit, translated into 27 languages and won the Anthony Award. It has since been followed by two other adventures featuring ex-US Army investigator Jack Reacher, *Die Trying* and *Tripwire*. Lee moved from England to New York in 1998.

Peter Guttridge is a freelance journalist and broadcaster and currently edits the Crime Writers' Association monthly newsletter. He is a columnist on the BBC's *Bookcase* website, directs the Brighton Literature Festival and, on a less cheerful note, writes obituaries for *The Independent*. He has written four novels featuring the hapless, yoga-obsessed journalist Nick Madrid: *No Laughing Matter*, *A Ghost Of A Chance*, *Two To Tango* and *The Once And Only Future Con*.

Maxim Jakubowski owns London's legendary Murder One book shop, where he prolifically edits anthologies of crime and erotica and reviews for *Time Out* and *The Guardian*. and even twiddles his thumbs on occasions. His novels of crime and lust have proven somewhat controversial and include *It's You That I Want To Kiss, Because She Thought She Loved Me* and *The State Of Montana*. He is a past winner of the Anthony Award for non-fiction and is struggling to complete *On The Tenderness Express* for March 2000 publication.

Paul Johnston was born and brought up in Scotland. His first novel, *Body Politic*, set in 21st century Edinburgh and featuring investigator Quint Dalrymple, won the CWA John Creasey Memorial Dagger in 1997. There have been two sequels, *The Bone Yard* and *Water Of Death*. He divides his time between the UK and a small Greek island.

Adam Lloyd-Baker is the son of a Gloucestershire priest. After studying theology, he travelled extensively in Europe, Asia and the United States. He has worked as a gravedigger, mortuary attendant and Atlantic City croupier. He currently works as a cinema projectionist in Cheltenham. His first novel *New York Graphic* was published to much acclaim in 1998.

HR McGregor was born in Uganda and spent her childhood there and in Zambia. For the past seven years she has lived on a traditional narrowboat on the Oxford Canal. She is a tutor in Screen Arts at the National Film and Television School. Her first novel, *Schrodinger's Baby*, a murder mystery which flirts with the philosophy of physics, was published in 1998.

Denise Mina's first novel *Garnethill* was the 1998 winner of the Crime Writers' John Creasey Memorial Dagger. She was born in Glasgow, where she still lives and was educated in Scotland, London, Paris and Holland. Following law studies, she has taught criminology and criminal law in Glasgow, where her book takes place.

Mike Ripley is the creator of the award-winning series of 'Angel' comedy thrillers, the ninth of which, *Bootlegged Angel*, has just appeared. Throughout the '90s he has been crime fiction reviewer for *The Daily Telegraph* and also has a regular column in the *Sherlock Homes Detective Magazine*. In 1998 he instigated the Sherlock Awards for best detective characters and is currently the judge for the annual crime and punishment short story competition run by the Prison Reform Trust.

Rob Ryan was born in Liverpool in 1951. Following an academic career, he ended up in feature journalism and became Deputy Travel Editor of *The Sunday Times*. His first novel *Underdogs* takes place in the underworld of Seattle. He now lives in London with his wife and three children and has never mastered the legendary scouse accent or wit.

Manda Scott is a veterinary surgeon, writer and climber, though not necessarily in that order. Originally from Scotland, she has spent the best part of the last decade in rural Suffolk with a lurcher and an assortment of wildlife. *Hen's Teeth,* a Kellen Stewart Thriller, was shortlisted for Orange Prize for Fiction 1997. Her second veterinary thriller is *Night Mares.* She has been described by Frances Fyfield as 'The Patricia Cornwell of the animal world'.

Martyn Waites was born and raised in Newcastle upon Tyne. He has lived and worked all over Britain and been variously employed as a market trader, stand-up comic, and teacher of teenage ex-offenders. He has also worked as an actor. He now lives with his wife and daughters in East London. His first two novels featuring tabloid journalist Stephen Larkin are *Mary's Prayer* and *Little Triggers.*

Minette Walters has been winning awards since her ground-breaking début *The Ice House,* for which she was honoured by the CWA's John Creasey Award. She has since also won the Edgar award and the CWA Gold Dagger. In addition, all her novels have been the object of television adaptations. Her five other novels are *The Sculptress, The Scold's Bridle, The Dark Room, The Echo* and *The Breaker.* Her story for *Fresh Blood 3* is also her first ever short story and was obtained by the editors after years of supplication and smiles.

The Do-Not Press
Fiercely Independent Publishing

Keep in touch with what's happening at the cutting edge of independent British publishing.

Join The Do-Not Press Information Service and receive advance information of all our new titles, as well as news of events and launches in your area, and the occasional free gift and special offer.

Simply send your name and address to:
The Do-Not Press (Dept. FB3)
16 The Woodlands
London
SE13 6TY
or email us: thedonotpress@zoo.co.uk

There is no obligation to purchase and no sales-person will call.

Visit our regularly-updated web site:

http://www.thedonotpress.co.uk

Mail Order

All our titles are available from good bookshops, or (in case of difficulty) direct from The Do-Not Press at the address above. There is no charge for post and packing.
(NB: A post-person may call.)